GREEN

GREEN

A Novel

Sam Graham-Felsen

RANDOM HOUSE / NEW YORK

Published in the United States by Random House, an imprint and division of Penguin Random House LLC, New York.

RANDOM HOUSE and the HOUSE colophon are registered trademarks of Penguin Random House LLC.

Library of Congress Cataloging-in-Publication Data
Names: Graham-Felsen, Sam, author.
Title: Green : a novel / Sam Graham-Felsen.
Description: New York : Random House, [2018]
Identifiers: LCCN 2016051028 | ISBN 9780399591143 |
ISBN 9780399591150 (ebook)
Subjects: LCSH: Interracial friendship—Massachusetts—Boston—Fiction. |
Boston (Mass.)—History—20th century—Fiction.
Classification: LCC PS3607.R34765 G74 2018 | DDC 813/.6—dc23
LC record available at https://lccn.loc.gov/2016051028

Printed in the United States of America on acid-free paper

randomhousebooks.com

2 4 6 8 9 7 5 3 1

First Edition

For my parents,
Tolle Graham and Mike Felsen

Why, you could cause us the greatest humiliation
simply by confronting us with something we liked.

—Ralph Ellison, *Invisible Man*

I think everyone should have the kind of life
I've had, going from one extreme to the other.

—Larry Bird, *Drive*

GREEN

CHAPTER 1

Machine

I am the white boy at the Martin Luther King Middle. Well, one of two. Kev, my best friend and the biggest dick I know, is the other. But if you had to pick just one, it'd be me.

There is a public middle school in Boston that white kids actually go to—the Timilty—but me and Kev lost the lotto to get in there. I begged my parents to put me in a private school instead of the King, but they wouldn't budge. They "believe in public schools," even when they're mad ghetto.

The first day of school starts in an hour. If I had a best outfit, I'd be rocking it, but my closet's a disaster of second-hand pants, free tees, and sale-bin sneakers. Kev has an arsenal of stonewashed jeans and silk button-downs. He cops a fresh pair of kicks every couple months and he's debuting some Air Force 1s today. I'll be carrying a toothbrush and a travel shampoo in my pocket so I can scrub spots off my year-old Filas.

Pops is in his pepped-out morning mode. He harmonizes with the folk music blasting from the stereo as he makes me a sandwich consisting of my least favorite cheese (Swiss) and last-ranked veggie (sprouts). He fishes my insulated

L.L.Bean bag out of the cupboard. It's got the initials of my extra-white name, David Alexander Greenfeld, stitched into it.

"I told you I'm done with the DAG bag," I say.

"How else are you gonna keep the ice pack frozen?" he says.

"Forget the ice pack," I say.

"You want warm yogurt? Do it your way."

I repack my lunch in a brown paper shopping bag, throw some extra gel on the dome, and grab my Walkman. Everyone follows me to the porch. Ma kisses me on my head, my little brother, Benno, shoots me a peace sign, Pops squeezes my shoulder and holds up his hand. I five him reluctantly. Then I head down the steps, turn left, and walk slowly, waiting for them to go back inside. When they do, I'll turn around and take the scenic route.

The thing about my house is that it's on top of a hill. At one end of the hill, there's a park—probably the nicest in the city—called the Arboretum. It's huge, manicured, owned and operated by Harvard U. Pops says it has one of the biggest collections of tree species in the world. You can see the Arbs from my attic—endless green, spilling into the horizon. But from the opposite side of my attic, you'll see steam rising off the tops of dark towers. Those are the projects at the other end of my block, the Robert Gould Shaw Homes. Even though it takes me twice as long to get from my crib to Centre Street, where all the stores—and my bus stop—are, I've been looping past the Arbs all summer to avoid the back of the Shaw Homes. I'd take the direct route, but practically every time I walk past the PJs these days, someone stutter-stomps toward me, shouts, "*Fuck* you lookin' at, white boy?" and I end up jetting all the way back home. My first day at the King's gonna be bad enough. I'm not trying to get jacked before I even make it to school.

I wave bye once more and my parents finally close the door. Then I backtrack toward the Arbs. Minutes later I'm strolling under the shade of maples, listening to Geto Boys.

MY BUS STOP is in front of a bodega, right across the street from the main entrance of the Shaw Homes. There's another dude waiting there, a black kid about my size. Thankfully he looks pretty soft: creased khakis, pilled-up flannel, boxy black shoes, and a short, unkempt flattop, more like a clumpy cloud. His chipped leather backpack is way too full for the first day of school. I tilt my head to get a better look at the magazine he's flipping through and see it's the *Boston Celtics 1992–93 Preseason Report,* a newsstand special I've been meaning to buy myself. I'm a little surprised he's reading it in public, because no one openly admits they feel the Celtics anymore. He catches me clocking him and doesn't look happy. I brace myself for a *fuck-you-lookin'-at.*

Instead, he raises his chin and says, "King?"

I nod and he turns back to the C's mag. A few minutes later, the bus comes and he gets on with me.

I head for the most prestigious real estate: the back of the bus. By the end of elementary school, I was rocking the rear pretty regularly, and I want to kick things off proper at the King. There's a seat next to a hulk in a smock-sized X hoodie, who's resting his head on the window. Dude looks voting age. My guess is he's been to the Barron Center—

where they make brawlers go before they get kept back—at least once. Still, it's the only opening near the back, and I've come too far. I start toward the seat. He opens his eyes, stares out the window, and yawns, "Nah."

I smile and start to sit, like I'm in on a joke with him. He stiff-arms me in the chest and repeats, "Nah."

"My b," I say. "You saving it for someone?"

He closes his eyes again and says, all matter-of-fact, "Get your ass to the front of the got-damn bus."

I head back up the aisle toward the bench right behind the driver. Kev's already up there, shaking his head. I read *Nintendo Power* over his shoulder, while the usual bus ruck—pencil fights, seat hurdling, dropkicks—breaks out behind us. At one point our driver, a fat, crinkle-haired white lady with a wack neon windbreaker, pulls over, turns off the gas, and shouts, "Stawp it—all a yuz!"

"Stawwwwp it," someone squawks back.

"'Scuse me?" says the driver.

"Shut up and drive," snaps another voice from the rear.

The driver turns to me and Kev—like all white people are a team or something—and we bury our faces in the *Nintendo Power*. She turns back around, sighs, and starts the engine.

WE WALK THROUGH the front doors and I take a whiff of familiar funk. The King smells just like elementary did: a sour blend of mop juice and soft beans in murky water. A cane-carrying black dude in a brown corduroy blazer shakes everyone's hands as we file past him. He greets the seventh

and eighth graders formally, by last name, and he even pro-
nounces the Spanish ones with decent rolling r's. To the
sixth graders, he says, "Welcome to the King. I'm your principal, Dr. Jackson. And you are?"

"Dave," I say.

"Oh yes. David . . . give me a second . . . Mr. *Greenfeld*?" he says, enunciating the shit out of my last name.
"Had a nice chat with your parents last year at the open
house. You ever need anything—*anything*—you come see
me now, okay?"

I nod, eyeing the student-painted mural on the wall behind him. It's supposed to be Martin Luther King standing
in front of the Lincoln Memorial, but the way they drew
him—wide-open mouth, bugged-out eyes, stiff raised
arms—makes it look like he's trying to step to someone instead of uniting the races. The quote bubble bursting from
his mouth says, "What's *YOUR* dream?"

"LET'S MAKE SURE you're all in the right place," our homeroom teacher, Ms. Ansley, a small black lady with a helmet
of dark, dyed reddish hair, says. She calls attendance, hands
us star-speckled nameplates, and assigns us to our seats. To
my right is Carmen Garcia. She has big pink glasses and
shiny black hair, and she's wearing a flowery dress with ruf-
fled shoulders. The outfit makes her look like a substitute
teacher, but beneath all that she's kind of cute. To my left is
Kaleem Gunderson, a tall, light-skinned kid with faint freckles and a high-top fade. He's got the phattest gear of anyone
in the class: a Chicago Bulls tracksuit, matching red Jor-

dans, and a thick gold chain with a roaring-lion piece. For once I'm happy about my last name; I'm gonna be sitting next to this don all year.

"Why I gotta be next to the white boy?" he grumbles to himself.

The white boy—see? Kev's in our class, too, but he's half-Armenian. He has spiky black hair and lip scruff and sometimes people mistake him for Puerto Rican. I have curly blond hair, pink cheeks, and pale blue eyes. No one mistakes me for shit.

Ms. Ansley walks to the chalkboard and slowly writes the word *why.*

"My favorite word in the world. A three-letter word— a three-letter question! Why. Why? *Why!*"

The class stares, confused. I assume this is some kind of motivational speech. When you come up in the public schools, all you ever get is motivationally spoken to. Our classroom is covered with the same inspiring posters we had in elementary, too. One of them shows a hyped-up white kid ski-jumping off a mountain of books. Another says, AMBI-TION: IT'S CONTAGIOUS!

"Why are we here?" she finally says. "Let's see some hands. No right or wrong answers to this one."

"We got no choice," says Kaleem.

Ms. Ansley smiles and says, "True enough."

"So we can get our diplomas," a girl behind me says.

"All right," says Ms. Ansley. "Anyone else?"

The kid from our bus stop, the one with the C's mag, raises his hand. I glance at his nameplate. MARLON WELLINGS.

"To learn?"

Kaleem snorts into his fist.

"Okay, Marlon, and *why* learn?"

"To get smarter."

"Why?" she says.

"So we can, like, choose better?"

"Why's that important?" she asks, her grin getting bigger.

Marlon pauses. His big eyes roll upward in thought.

"So we don't get tricked as easy?"

"See, now we're onto something. That's a good answer, especially with the election coming up. Took some *why*ing, but we got somewhere. *Why*ing. That means playing your own devil's advocates. Not just thinking, *On the other hand,* but *On the other* other *hand,* too. The good stuff, the worthwhile thinking, usually doesn't come till at least the third round, the third why. My number one goal is to get you to start *why*ing on your own. My number two goal is to get you out of here."

She starts passing out fat test prep books.

"You're my advanced class, and as far as I'm concerned each and every one of you should be aiming for Latin. Don't think I don't love you all, but I prefer not to see your pretty faces in these halls come seventh grade. Unless, of course, you want to come back and *visit* and tell everyone how you're doing at Latin."

Boston Latin is the best public high school in the city—by far. You have to take a three-hour test to get in. I suck at those bubble sheets. I look over at Kev, who's resting his elbows on his test prep book. I know he won't ever bother to crack it. Kev is a standardized test genius. Marlon's already got his book open, running a finger along the text.

"I know you all hate these kinds of tests, but I'm telling you, the more you practice, the more you're gonna learn the tricks—or, rather, how *not* to get tricked. Kids from all over the city—private-school kids, too—are going to be scrambling for spots, and you don't wanna lose out because you were too lazy to take the practice tests. I want you to start studying *tonight,* okay? Because if you get into Latin, you're going to college, guaranteed. And let me tell you something else. You might even get into Harvard."

Marlon grins and I notice he has a gap in his front teeth like I do.

WE BREAK FOR lunch and the sound of new soles hitting fresh wax fills the cafeteria. Hundreds of hundred-dollar-plus pairs, all announcing themselves. *Look at my Pump-infused tongue. Suck on this bright, popping Swoosh,* they say to my sad, scuffed Filas.

I follow Kev to the lunch line. Neither of us qualify for a free lunch card, but Kev gets enough of an allowance to pay cash when he spots something good. There's a sign on the sneeze guard that reads, PROUDLY SEASONING WITH TACO BELL SPICES. The tacos look like they're made with government meat, mystery cheese, and too-sour cream. But still: Taco Bell seasoning. To Kev, this is no big deal. He slams fast food on the reg and his pantry's packed with Gushers and Fluff. I've never been to Taco Bell, barely set foot in a

BK. My crib is world famous for its wack snacks. Pops *grows* most of our food.

"*Awesome.*"

The second I say it, I realize how bad it's gonna be. *Awesome* is a Caucasian catastrophe, a word I haven't uttered in years.

"Awesome!" Kaleem immediately mimics from behind me in line.

My parents—this is on them. *Awesome*'s what happens to a dreamer deprived.

Another kid piles on, giving me two thumbs up. "Awesome," he says in a surfer twang, "duuuuude."

Kev was hoping to sit with Kaleem. Now that he's white-by-association, he has no choice but to follow behind me. The only open seats we can find are next to the one kid who's lower on the pole than us: the Asian. He's reading *Nintendo Power*. At least we have that to discuss.

I GET A-WORDED by a half-dozen kids on my way out of the building. And on the bus home a Puerto Rican dude named Angel, whose skin is even paler than mine, comes up to my seat at the very front of the bus, aka the White Bitch Bench, and says, "Gimme five, gringo!"

I turn the other way. High fives are some hiked-up-shorts *Hoosiers* shit, the physical equivalent of *awesome*. There's no chance I'm getting lured into his trap.

"Fuck's wrong wit' you, gringo?" he says, no longer smiling.

I decide to meet the five as clownishly as possible, hoping

everyone on the bus will laugh with me. I do a sort of rag doll flail and my fingertips graze the bottom of his palm. Angel grips my shoulders, leans right into my face, and shoots hot breath into my glasses. My lenses take a second to defog and he's still inches away.

"You best do it right this time," he says. He has the unreasonable eyes of a maniac, so I meet his five. I mouth along as he screams, "Awesome!" His audience erupts.

When I get to my stop, Kev won't even give me goodbye dap. Marlon and I hop off the bus, and as I'm walking away he calls out to me.

"I've seen you before," he says.

I don't know what he's talking about; I've never seen him before today. He definitely didn't go to the Trotter.

"In that, um, vegetable garden," he says. "A bunch of times, with your family."

"I don't think I've seen you down there," I say.

"Seen you from up there," he says, pointing to one of the PJ towers.

He stands there silently, and I can't tell if he's waiting for me to respond, or if he's gonna start capping on my little brother, or what.

"Aight," he says, swinging his huge bag onto his shoulder. "Peace."

He crosses the street and walks through the blue doors of the Shaw Homes, and I head toward the Arbs.

A FEW YEARS back, Pops helped start a community garden in a lot behind the PJs. It used to be a dried-out field of chip bags and scratchies; now it's packed with worm-filled soil and neat green rows of vegetables. Most of the gardeners are hippies like my parents, but people from the PJs use it, too, like Fernando, this old Dominican guy who's always tending to his tomatoes, and the Xaviers, a Haitian couple who grow huge sunflowers. Once the garden got going, homeless people started coming through at night. They snatched so much food that the garden association voted to put up a fence with a combo lock. Pops felt bad, so he built a wood bin outside the fence, and whenever he goes down there he leaves a load of ripe veggies on his way out.

During harvest season, every night before dinner, Pops makes us roll to the garden as a family. I always try to beg out. It's not because the garden's behind the PJs—I'm not scared of getting jacked while I'm with my fam. I just don't like to be seen with the whitey brigade. Tonight, Pops is in his usual socks and Birkenstocks, and his safari vest pockets are stuffed with garden tools. Ma's wearing these bright Nepali parachute pants she got at the street fair. My rattailed little brother is skidding ahead in his neon-pink Rollerblades. Benno is—how do I put this?—a freak show. He's always been one of those kids who has to be the odd thing out. Like, he decided he wanted to play America's whitest sport, street hockey, when everyone else plays basketball, and then he decided he had to be goalie, the one position that requires tons of extra equipment. A couple weeks after my parents bought him all the pads, he quit sports altogether and decided he wanted to be a street performer, so my parents copped him a unicycle. Now he's into figure blading.

Ma asks how my first day went.

"Fine."

"How'd you like Ms. Ansley?" she says.

"Fine."

"Did you meet Dr. Jackson?" says Pops.

"Yeah," I say. "He remembered you guys."

"He's the reason we went with the King, you know," he says. "We were really impressed with him."

"So, what else?" says Ma. "You meet any nice kids?"

I almost mention Marlon. I look up at the towers, wondering which window is his. I'm still thinking about our strange chat, how he spun around with his giant bag and whispered the only nonwack word I heard all day: *Peace.*

"There's Taco Bell in the cafeteria," I say.

Ma laughs. "So it's not so bad after all?"

"It'd be way better if I could get some new sneakers."

"Your sneakers are perfectly hip," says Pops.

"No one wears Filas anymore. I want some Nikes. Air Force 1s aren't even that expensive."

"They're made in sweatshops," says Pops.

I want to say, "So are Benno's blades!" but I already know how Pops will reply. *Benno's a special case.* My parents pretty much buy him whatever he needs. He even gets to go to private school. I'm the normal one, which means toughing it out at the King—in ancient Filas.

"I'll take Adidas," I say. "Reebok Pumps. I can't make friends with these sneakers."

"Don't worry," Ma says. "You'll make—"

"Look at this baby!" Pops says, passing me an enormous zucchini.

I hold it with one hand, toss a cherry tomato into the air

with the other, swing, and whiff. That's another thing I blame on Pops: my suck status at sports. Normal dads teach you how to hit—or shoot, or dribble. Mine taught me how to hike, load a bird feeder, and sprinkle seeds in cow shit. He snaps off a shining eggplant, hands it to me like a trophy, and says, "You grew this, buddy!" This is the kind of shit that makes him proud. I'd rather have a real trophy, but I grip my dark prize. I'd never admit it to Pops, but I do kind of feel gardening. I hate how veggies taste, but I like the way they grow: from the bottom, from nothing, all that color, flavor, and flair, swirling out of project dirt.

THE NEXT DAY we have our first gym class.

"Whoever taps first gets to be captains," says Kaleem, who casually palms the backboard. "Who's next?"

"Go 'head, Dave," says Kev.

I should've picked dodgeball when our teacher gave us a choice. I walk back to the half-court line, gallop toward the hoop, explode up, and miss by a mile.

"Awesome try," says Kaleem.

"Looked like you just high-fived your invisible friend," says Kev.

Kev double-taps the glass and the picking begins. The short Asian kid—his name is Jimmy—chose dodgeball, so the last two standing are me and Marlon. Marlon's not even wearing gym gear; he's got his thumbs in his khaki pockets. Definitely not a baller. Kev still picks him over me.

After Kev cashes his third jumper in Kaleem's face, the Larry Bird comparisons begin.

"Oh snap, check out thirty-three!"

"Larry Legend! He back, yo!"

Kev hates the Bird talk. It means he's good—for a white boy. But after he strokes three or four more, people start calling him what he wants to be called: a baller. One kid even says, "This nigga's nasty."

After the game Kaleem walks right up to him and gives him dap.

AT LUNCH, I notice Marlon doesn't even get in the lunch line. He just walks straight to an empty table, sits on the edge, and pulls out his test prep book. Eventually, the table fills up with older girls, who ignore him as he fills in bubbles. Most sixth graders have at least one homey from elementary school, but Marlon doesn't seem to know anybody. Maybe he just doesn't like the kids he went to elementary with—or maybe they don't like him. Either way, I don't get a lonely vibe from him. He seems cool with sitting solo, too busy to give a what.

Me and Kev end up at the same table as yesterday, with Jimmy. Kaleem rolls up to us, and Kev looks all excited, like Kaleem's gonna sit down or something.

"Where'd you get that shirt?" Kaleem says to me. "Morgie's?"

I'm wearing a white long-sleeve tee with a bunch of cartoons of famous Boston symbols on it, like the Citgo sign, the Old North Church, and baked beans. The sad truth is that the shirt probably did come from Morgie's, this huge thrift store that everybody shits on. Three kinds of people shop there: the homeless, the very poor, and my mom. I found out after I clowned this traffic-cone-colored coat she was wearing once. "Where'd you get that coat—*Morgie's?*" I said. "Yup," she proudly replied. "Six bucks!"

"My mom got it for me," I say, instead of a simple no.

"She get you them awesome kicks there, too?" says Kaleem.

Kev cackles. Kaleem turns to him and says, "You need to take your boy shopping."

I take one bite of my sandwich and then toss the rest. Kev's icing me, and Jimmy's deep in his *Nintendo Power,* so I examine a recent elbow scab I got from a bike spill in the Arbs. I love scabs—few things are more satisfying than peeling one back. This one's nowhere near ready, but I rip into it anyway.

"Ugh!" shouts a kid sitting at a table across from me. "White boy bleedin' all over!"

Angel, the seventh-grade dickbag from my bus, rushes over to add, "He gay, too. Prolly got AIDS in it."

I get up and head to the can. I generally avoid school bathrooms. I don't drink anything at breakfast or lunch; I'd rather have parched swiss mouth than have to take a piss in one of those hell gutters. At my old school, all of the urinals were always clogged, sometimes with deuces, because the toilet was always clogged, too. The King bathroom's even worse. Not only is it clog city, but someone tore down the walls of both toilet stalls, and all that's left are the metal rods surrounding the thrones like those fancy old beds British people rock on PBS.

There's no TP left—there's never once been any TP left—so I wet the bottom of my tee and use it to mop up the gore. I stand at the sink and take a long, depressing look in the marked-up mirror. The glasses aren't helping. The curly blond hair isn't, either. I try to mat that shit down with LA Looks, but no matter how much I slather on, the curls spring back up by the time I get to school. Add in my soft blue eyes and constantly flushed cheeks and I look like an angel in a church painting. A gay, bleeding angel.

POPS IS AT a block association meeting tonight, so it's just me, Ma, and Benno at dinner. I love it when it's just Ma, because she usually doesn't care when me and Benno go over the thirty-minute TV limit and she lets me take Benno's leftover Tater Tots. Benno's almost nine and he refuses to eat anything other than Tots. My parents still make me grub their health crap, but they let him eat whatever he wants— buy him whatever he wants—because they're desperate to get him to start talking again.

Benno's always been an odd, quiet kid, but last fall he stopped talking altogether. For real: He hasn't said a word, to anyone, for a year. It terrified my parents, especially Pops, because they had no idea why he stopped or how to help him. Then, a few weeks into his silence, Benno cut his arm with a compass. Turned out it wasn't that deep of a slice, but he was in the tub, so it spread quickly. Pops heard him whimpering and ran in, and when he saw the red water he bugged so hard me and Ma ran in, too, thinking Pops was the hurt one. That's the only time I can remember hearing Pops cry in my life, although he didn't actually shed any tears, just kind of barked like a seal while he lifted Benno from the tub and wrapped a towel around his arm.

After that Pops brought Benno to see a psychologist, but Benno wouldn't talk. Then Pops made all of us go to this guy called the Family Coach for a long, wack chat about expressing emotions and communicating better with our teammates (Ma and Pops). Of course, Benno refused to open his mouth, so it was really just me blabbing the whole time about my stress and sleep issues. Ma and Pops were nodding and saying they loved me, but I could tell they were focused on Benno for the entire session, hoping he might finally pipe up. At one point, Coach asked me if I ever felt like cutting myself and I told him the truth. Slice myself? Hell no, I can't even deal with getting poked; my doc has to strap me to a board every time I get a booster. I now realize that was one of the dumbest moves of my life. This year, my parents put Benno in a private school for sensitive kids—something I never thought they'd do, given all the smack they talk about private schools—and I got stuck at the King. If I'd just said yes to Coach, I'd be spending recess kicking a soccer ball on a freshly mowed lawn instead of playing tag on a concrete slab, hopping over half-smashed forties.

When Ma asks about my day, I can't even stomach a *fine*.

"Can't you just transfer me to Benno's school?" I say.

If Pops was here, he'd blow up at me for suggesting it. Ma would never let me leave the King, either, but maybe I can get her to come around on the kicks situation.

"Everyone calls me white boy," I say. "Even the teachers."

"The teachers?"

"Not to my face. But I can tell they're thinking it."

She laughs, slides her hand on top of mine, and says, "Sometimes it just takes a little while to settle in."

"I'm never gonna settle in with these sneakers," I say.

OVER THE WEEKEND, Ma finally takes me to the mall. On our way to Foot Locker, we pass a place that hypes itself as a "streetwear specialist." I spot an outfit in the window. A gigantic pair of jeans—one leg purple, one leg teal—and a matching denim hooded jacket with a ragged patch sewn into the left breast that spells out, in paint-splattered capital letters: MACHINE.

I stand there, stun-gunned with desire. Maybe kicks aren't the answer, after all. Everyone at the King already has fresh kicks. I'm lagging too far behind to catch up with Air Force 1s. I need to come mega-fresh; I need a bold, full-body solution. I need the Machine.

"Could I maybe get an outfit instead of sneaks?" I ask Ma.

"As long as it's in the fifty-buck range," she says.

A young black dude in a backward Kangol greets us at the entrance: "Welcome to the Circus. Can I help you find something?"

"Could I try that suit in the window?" I say. "The one with the Hornets colors?"

"The purple and teal?" he says. "You know what's up."

The Hornets are the hottest team in the NBA right now. Their colors are popping and their star, Larry Johnson, is the league's biggest badass, with his gold teeth and thundering slams. Everyone in the PJs, everyone at the King, everyone on BET, feels the purple and teal these days. I feel a little guilty trying on the Machine, because I'm a Celtics fan and the Hornets are one of our rivals. But, what am I gonna do—buy a green and white suit? I doubt they even carry this thing in green and white, because nobody reps the Celtics anymore. The C's are known for old white dudes like Bird and McHale, and they've got the softest logo in the league— a smiling Irish midget with a cane.

I walk into the dressing room and slide on the enormous suit. I assume various hardcore poses in the mirror: arms folded, lips pursed, chin cocked upward; both arms raised, eyes bulging, head hanging left. *Come step to this,* I mouth in the mirror, *see what happens.* I emerge from the dressing room feeling immortal in the Machine.

"You lookin' *aight,*" the salesman says.

Ma looks concerned.

"You pullin' it off!" he says.

I shoot Ma a *See?*

"How much?" Ma says.

"Matter of fact, there's a promo on that. Ninety-nine ninety-nine."

"Let's go to Filene's Basement," Ma says.

"Ma," I say, "I need this one."

"It's a Circus exclusive," says the clerk.

I turn to Ma and plead with my eyes so hard they hurt. From the way she looks back at me—small shifts in her lids that make her seem annoyed at first, then curious, then softened—it's like she can see the desperation's legit.

"This is between us," she finally says. "Don't tell Dad how much it cost."

. . .

"MACHINE?" KEV SAYS at the bus stop on Monday. "What kind of off-brand shit is that?"

"Cross Colours suits cost, like, two hundred dollars," I say.

"Purple and teal, though?" he says, sucking in air through his teeth. "I don't know, yo."

"What are you talking about?" I say. "These are Hornets colors."

"You shouldn't be rocking those colors," Marlon butts in.

"How come?" I say, and he just shakes his head like I should know the answer. Who does this khaki-wearing choirboy think he is, shitting on the Machine? He's the worst-dressed fool in school.

On the bus, the first person to comment is this eighth grader named Vicki, who sits across from us in the first row. There is actually one other white kid in the school—her—and she keeps trying to give me and Kev advice, even though we never ask for it.

"Oh my Gawd," she giggles. "What size is that thing? You look like a friggin' mascot."

I can't even pass the white girl test. I turn to Kev for support. He pivots away. This is my purple suit problem, not his.

"*Mira,*" says Hector, one of Angel's boys. "Gringo's tryin' a get down."

"He look like that gay-ass dinosaur!" crows Angel. "Barney!"

. . .

KALEEM POUNCES THE second he spots me in the hall.

"Fuck you wearing, white boy?"

I'm gonna head for the nurse's office, fake a stomach-ache, call Ma to come pick me up, and light this damn suit on fire.

"For real, where'd you cop that?" says this girl Tasha, who I've seen Kaleem trying to mack on.

"The, um, Circus," I say, steeling myself for another diss.

"Word. Got them Hornets colors, huh?" Tasha says. "That shit is *phat*."

And then a couple seventh-grade girls come up to me and spin me around. One of them says, "Look at this little white boy, coming fly."

The other takes my glasses off and says, "He cute, right?"

"THE CIRCUS?" KALEEM says in homeroom. "The one in Downtown Crossing?"

"Cambridge," I say. "Better selection over there."

Confidence skying, I turn to my other deskmate, Carmen, the cute Dominican girl with the big pink glasses.

"You feel it?" I say.

She nods and says, "Stylish." The first word she's ever said to me: not phat, dope, ill, or banging, but *stylish*. An old-school compliment, the kind of thing a mom might say. I could actually have a chance with this shorty.

I look over at Kev, grinning greedily, trying to get his attention. He doesn't look up, but his deskmate does. I meet Marlon's eyes, and once again, he shakes his head at me.

. . .

I'M TRYING MY hardest not to play out the Machine, but I want to come correct heading into the weekend, so I rock it again on Friday. Kaleem caps on me for the instant replay; otherwise my day slides by without drama. After two weeks at the King, I still don't have any boys, but thanks to the Machine I'm getting way fewer *awesome*s. Even Angel's laying off.

When school gets out, I do what I do every Friday: get my third wheel on with Kev and Simon. Since Simon started coming around, things have gotten way worse, but I've always been Kev's peon. As far back as I can remember, Kev's been taller, stronger, sicker at every sport. Everything comes easily to him, even random shit like archery. He gets straight A's with zero effort. He skyrocketed through puberty. He has an older sister, who's off in college, so he even knows how to act normal around shorties. The only reason we're friends is because our parents are friends; they forced us to play when we were infants. And the only reason he still lets me hang is because his mom is still forcing him.

Simon keeps trying to get Kev to dead me. He's two years older than us, an eighth grader at Latin. He brags about jacking off, saves the labels from every forty he drinks, and steals shit from stores. He claims he even mugged an old lady once. None of his evil ever catches up with him. Like Kev, he's smart as hell—genius level. Both of his parents are doctors at Mass General. He aced the Latin test in half the allotted time. He smokes blunts before school and still makes honor roll. Nothing touches him; he just sins his way to the top. He'll probably end up at Harvard. This is why he's down for whatever, whenever—why Kev feels him, and why I don't. Anytime I'm with them, I'm the automatic bitch. I'd stop chilling with Kev, but I'm not exactly flush with friends. Besides, his house has everything mine doesn't: cable, consoles, snacks.

We listen to Geto Boys on Kev's stereo while we wait for Simon to get out of school. I bite into a Ring Ding and nod along to my number one track, "Mind Playing Tricks on Me." I remember the first time I heard it. It wasn't the beat that got me—though the beat is one of the best of all time—or even the rhymes. It's what's *in* the rhymes. You listen close to the lyrics and you realize there's something very different about this song. Sure, they're still bragging about the usual shit—cash, cars, killing fools—but that's not the point. The point is that these dudes are *scared*, not just of rival gangs but of their own strange brains. Scarface is so shook he can't even sleep; he tosses and turns all night, agonizing like I do. *Every time my eyes close / I start sweatin', / and blood starts comin' out my nose.* This G drenches his pillow, just like me. This hard-ass killer gets nosebleeds out of nowhere. This dude, secretly, is *soft*—and he's actually admitting it.

Kev grabs his Casio and starts up a beat. The only thing I'm better at than Kev is freestyling. He knows it, too. I've smoked him in so many battles that he's resigned himself to being my beat man. He presses the Samba preset and starts messing with some chords till he lands a proper hook. I lift the Machine hoodie over my head, bob and grunt to the beat while a rhyme coalesces: "Green is on the mic / Bringin' light to the dark / I may be white / But I'm a great white shark."

"Oh *shit*," says Kev, "Green still got it!"

Just as I'm getting into the zone, Simon rolls in. He's rocking a tee with a weed leaf embossed on it and brown jeans so large they look like two potato sacks sewn together. Simon takes one look at the Machine and convulses. Kev stops the beat and laughs along.

"Nothing *ever* looks right on you," Simon says. Saliva's dripping from the rubber bands in his braces.

"Keep the beat going," I say. I'm planning a rhyme about the galaxy of acne on his extra-large forehead. But Simon's never down to flow, because he can't, so we're out the door, on our way to the courts behind English High. They're not the best courts—the asphalt's cracked all over and chamomile shoots out of it—but they're the closest to Kev's.

The courts are empty, so we start off with some H-O-R-S-E. I'm on fire and I figure it must be the Machine. A black dude in a Larry Johnson jersey rolls up and asks if we want to play twos. I've never seen him on these courts before. He's got short dreads and green eyes, and he looks around Simon's age. We shoot for teams and the new kid's on my squad. He's nasty, and we're vibing. We smoke Kev and Simon eleven to four and they bounce to the bodega to cop some Gatorades. I decide to keep playing. I take the Machine jacket off and hang it on the fence.

I ask the dude if he's from around here, and he says he's just visiting a cousin. So I ask where he's visiting from and he says, "Down south." Beyond that, we don't get real deep, but things are easy between us, we're cool with each other, and maybe it's just because my shots have been falling, but I get the sense he doesn't give a what about the fact that I'm white. We're talking about the new Ice Cube track and last week's *In Living Color,* just shooting the shit, shooting around, as the sun sets and sprays gold across the court. Kev and Simon are taking forever and I'm hoping they don't come back. It's been almost two hours and I'm spent, but I don't want to stop playing. We're still going when it starts getting dark.

Then I take a shot, and it clangs off the rim, and the kid doesn't even bother to rebound it. He just lets it bounce off to the other side of the court and glares at me with his green eyes. He takes a look behind his back, walks over to the fence, grabs my jacket, slowly slides his arms through, and walks back toward me. His face is like a mask. A second ago, those same lips were laughing at my jokes, those same eyes were opening and closing and following the arc of an orange ball across a gray sky. Now everything is flat, still, hard.

"Dope jacket, right?" I say, pretending I sense nothing.

"It's a real dope jacket," he says. "I'ma take it with me."

I laugh softly, trying to crack the mask.

"Run your pants, too," dude says.

I stand there for a few seconds, trying to think of something to say, when I hear Kev and Simon approaching. They walk back to the court, holding a pizza box, but keep their distance like they sense something's up.

"Tell your boy to run his pants," the kid says to Kev and Simon.

Kev chews his slice slowly. Simon's jaw just hangs.

I turn to Kev. I can't figure this out alone. Do we fight him? I mean, there's *three* of us. But Kev's eyes are locked on the concrete.

So I try the whitest move in the book.

"You're playing, right?" I say to the dude, fighting to maintain my smile. "I mean, I thought . . ."

I try to make eye contact.

"I thought we were boys."

"Run your fuckin' pants," he says, reaching into his backpack. "Now."

Dammit, Kev! Come on, Simon! The food co-op's right around the corner. I've hid out from jackers there in the past. Just give me the sign and we'll book it. I just want to make sure we're on the same motherfucking page!

"I'ma count to ten," he says. "Then you gonna find out what's in my bag."

We're a half block away from a world of health food whiteys. But it's a dark and empty half block. The court's penned in by four stories of brick. Yelling *help*'s not an option.

"Ten.

"Nine.

"Eight."

"Kev," I say, and he finally looks at me. The second I meet his eyes, the shame wrings me like a sponge. Bitchwater trickling, trembling, I mouth the words *Should I?*

"Four.

"Three. Don't make me take it out."

Kev turns to Simon and Simon turns away. Kev gives me a little nod.

As I'm undoing my belt, I notice a pile of dog shit. It's the orange kind, looks fresh. Two flies are fighting over it. One dive-bombs the other, and for a second the shit is his. Then the other returns and dive-bombs him back. As I watch the flies, a thought occurs to me. What if I dive-bombed that dog shit myself? What if I sat down, right on that nasty pile, rolled in it? Would he still want the pants? Without the pants, would he still want the matching jacket? Smearing myself might make him more likely to shoot me. But maybe he'd leave me alone.

"Fuck you lookin' at, white boy?" he says. "You think I'm playin'? Leave 'em on the ground and walk the fuck away."

"Y'all too," he says to Kev and Simon. "Best not turn around, neither."

Simon and Kev start walking out of the court. I unzip my pants and slide them down my legs. The openings at the bottom are so wide I don't even have to take my shoes off. I shake my way out of the purple leg, then out of the teal, and walk away slowly, hunched and cupping my crotch. Once I'm sure the kid's long gone, I run toward Kev and Simon. They're way ahead, speed-walking, rounding the corner to Centre Street, not even waiting for me.

"Hold up," I say, but they keep walking.

"He's gone," I whisper.

Kev finally slows down, then Simon does, too. They're both still looking straight ahead. I want to scream at them.

I didn't get jacked—*we* got jacked. *Kev's* the one who nodded. But I'm standing there in my Hanes and Filas, glowing
white under the streetlights, and I just want to get home
before my parents do. If they find out, they'll call the police,
make me file a report. Even though the kid's just visiting,
he'll tell his cousin, and his cousin's crew will be on the
lookout for a snitching little white boy.

"Keep this on the low?" I say.

Simon just pulls his hoodie over his head, but Kev nods.
I peel onto a side street and walk home the Arbs way, taking
cover in the long-limbed shadows.

CHAPTER 2

Shook

Benno hears me breathing hard in the middle of the night, climbs down from the top bunk, and returns with tissues from the bathroom. I whisper, "Thanks," and he climbs back up. Even if I could talk to him about what went down on the courts, I wouldn't want to. It's not because I'm afraid he'd squeal to my parents. It's because I'm afraid if I started telling him about the jacking, I'd end up telling him the darker truth, something way more terrifying, something I hope he doesn't know about yet: the force. This isn't some Jedi bullshit; the force I'm talking about is real, and its energies are everywhere, working on everyone. I don't even blame that kid for what he did to me, I blame the force, for what it did to him.

In my elementary school, the Trotter, I barely felt the force. Got called white boy occasionally, but always in jest, and never got called white bitch. The Trotter was the most diverse school in the city—even though by the time I graduated there were only a couple dozen white kids left—and it was proud of that rep. Our motto was "Together in Friendship," and our logo was a stick-figure drawing of a white kid and a black kid holding hands. Me and most of the other white kids were in the famous school choir. We performed "We Wish You a Merry Christmas/Hanukkah/Kwanzaa" in fancy law firm lobbies and did the national anthem at Fenway. When Nelson Mandela got freed and came to Boston on his world tour, *our* chorus was chosen to put on a private show for him. We did "This Little Light of Mine" and "Thank You, Miss Rosa Parks," and everyone got to shake his hand. Anytime anyone comes to our house, my parents bust out the picture.

That was the force-free world I lived in, till a few months ago. My parents talk about how they'll always remember where they were when they heard Martin Luther King got shot. I'll always remember where I was on April 29, 1992, the day the L.A. riots started. It was a Wednesday and I was at Kev's; Simon was there, too, and we were glued to cable news all afternoon. Coming up at the Trotter, singing those Civil Rights songs in my TOGETHER IN FRIENDSHIP tee, I thought it was all progress from here on out, a steady march to harmony. Then that Wednesday happened. The cops who stomped Rodney King on a video everyone saw over and over, the guiltiest four dudes who ever lived, got off. I couldn't believe it, and when I watched those rioters smashing up strip malls, I understood, even rooted for them. What I didn't understand was what they did to Reginald Denny, that white trucker with long blond hair, who happened to be at the wrong intersection at the wrong time—how they pulled him out of his cab and whooped him to near death on live TV, the way he wobbled on all fours, trying to get back up, how every time he raised his head, another guy would come back and knock it down, one with a bottle, another with a brick. But what I really won't forget was the way that, after each blow, those dudes did *victory dances* for the helicopter cameras. Simon and Kev cheered them along, went "Oh!" the same way they did watching WWF. But I stayed quiet, ashamed that I was secretly rooting for this white guy with long, headbanging hair to get out alive, sickened at myself because I found those victory dances sickening. That was when I started seeing the force in others, and when I felt it in myself, too. I didn't just hate those dances, I hated those *dancers,* and I couldn't help, in the heat of that hating moment, but hate them even more for being black. I couldn't believe I was feeling this—me, the same kid who sang for Mandela—but I was. The verdict, the victory dances, the *oh*s, the secret, seething hate inside me—it was the force come full circle, the first time I felt its cyclonic strength.

   I tried my best to bury the force, but I felt it shaking inside me, cracking its way out, a couple days later when I passed the PJs on my route home from the bus stop, a path I'd taken a thousand times without an ounce of caution or concern, and heard, for the first time in my life, "*Fuck* you lookin' at, white boy?" I turned around and saw a couple of kids, one of them my age, the other no older than eight, each of them glaring at me through the stiff mask of the force. It seemed like the smoke of those riots spread all across the continent, all the way to Boston, like they were looking for their own Reginald Denny, because as far as I could tell they stepped for no other reason than the fact that I was white. But as I ran away, up my hill, I began to wonder if maybe I *was* looking at them the wrong way, the same way I must have stared at the TV screen when those dudes bundled Denny—a shook and boggled look that said, *You are predators*—and maybe that made them want to treat me like prey.

All summer, I tried to deny the force, but I felt it every time I got checked on my way past the Shaw Homes. And for a while I walked past the PJs anyway, because it didn't happen every time, and I wasn't gonna let the force play me like that, but eventually I started taking the Arbs route and never stopped. And I felt ashamed of that, and felt ashamed that I was so scared about going to the King in the fall, and yeah, I've been feeling ashamed that the force has been with me, pretty much nonstop, since I got to the King. And now, just as I was hitting a semi-stride, just as I was getting propped instead of clowned, just as the force was fading, I got jacked. And jacked like this: on my favorite basketball court, by someone who seemed to feel me, by someone I stupidly dreamed, for an hour or so, was my boy.

"I HEARD DAVE got jacked for his purple suit," Kaleem says on Monday, loud enough for everyone at lunch to hear. "I heard he had to walk home in his drawers, yo!"

I see Kev grinning and pretending to inspect his tacos. I want to knock his nose into his brain.

"I heard of people getting their wallet took, or even their kicks," Kaleem says. "What kind of bitch lets a nigga take his pants?"

"Dude had a gun in his bag," I say.

"No he didn't," Kev says under his breath.

"*What?*" I say.

"He didn't," Kev says louder.

"What are you talking about?" I whisper-shout. "He said he was strapped."

"He didn't say shit. He just put his hand in a bag."

I want to spork him in the eye.

"Coulda been a sandwich."

A sandwich? I want to *fillet* this motherfucker.

But I just sit there while Kaleem howls.

BY THE END of the day, it seems like half the school's heard about what "happened"—how I got spooked by a tuna sub, how I had to scamper home naked, cupping my shrunken jewels. I've made up my mind. I'm not gonna be known as the kid who got stripped, the soft little white boy who once had the Machine. No. I'm going back to the Circus. I'm buying a new suit, the exact same one—same size, same colors. I don't care what anyone says. Fuck Kev, fuck Kaleem. Angel can suck my purple-suited cock.

The only problem is my cash flow. I barely get an allowance; I have zero savings. Whatever money I make from hustles, I immediately spend on bodega grub. I only own one thing of real value: the Bird-Magic. It's my prized possession—not just a basketball card but the greatest ever minted, straight from the 1981 set, the year I was born and the year Topps weirdly decided to create perforated, three-in-one cards. One third of the card is a Larry Bird rookie. Another third is a Magic Johnson rookie. The final third? Julius Erving. That's right: a Bird rookie, a Magic rookie, and a Dr. J. *on the same card*. I traded it off some Bird-hating clown at the Trotter, who wanted nothing more than a Jordan All-Star and a couple silver dollars.

The Bird-Magic's now worth three hundred bones, but I've never wanted to sell it, because I actually like Larry Bird. When he called it quits this year, I even cried. No one else I know—my age, at least—cared. Kev and Simon were *happy*. Despite twelve All-Star nods, back-to-back-to-back MVP titles, and three championship rings, they could never admit they felt him. Granted, Bird's not just white—he's blond mustache white, Indiana white, rickety-ass-peach-basket-on-the-side-of-his-barn white. It's true that he could barely dunk at six nine, that he clopped around the court like an old Maine moose, but he was nasty, soaking wet from anywhere on the floor, even *on* the floor. For real, he once made a shot while lying on the ground. And he was hard, too, had no deez at all but was always down to brawl, no matter who was stepping. Once, he talked smack to Dr. J after a hard foul. Doc talked back and Bird *choked* his ass.

It's obvious that Kev and Simon feel Bird, too. And the fact that they'll never confess it, can't ever confess it—claim to hate not only Bird but the whole storied Celtics franchise—that's the force. The force is a match *and* a muzzle. It doesn't just spark the hate, it smothers the love, holds us back from the most natural shit of all—rooting for the home team. I'm not saying I'm exempt. I only cheer for the C's behind closed doors, in my own crib, but I can at least admit it to myself: I love the green and white. And even though Reggie Lewis is by far my all-time favorite Celtic, I love Larry Bird, always will. I really wish I didn't have to sell the card, but I don't see another option. I have a whole year ahead of me at the King. I need a new Machine, now.

IN SCHOOL THE next day, Ms. Ansley shows us another installment of this long, made-for-TV movie we've been watching called *Roots*. When she introduced it, she said we needed to know our history, especially after what happened in L.A. The main character is a slave named Kunta Kinte, who gets whipped constantly for trying to run away. It isn't easy watching *Roots*, especially as one of only two white boys in the room. Every time Kunta gets whipped, I feel the eyes of the whole class on me. In today's episode, the wicked white master tries to make Kunta accept his new name, and Kunta isn't having it. So the whitey forces another slave to whip Kunta, over and over and over again.

"I want to hear you say your name," the redneck growls. "Your name is *Toby*. What's your name?"

Kunta keeps refusing and getting rewhipped, but he finally gives in and says, "Toby, my name is Toby."

Then the master replies, "That's a good nigger."

I hear people shifting in their chairs. The violence is one thing: We all know the wounds are just makeup, the whip's just a prop, the loud crack's only a sound effect. But the n-word is different. Even if it's just acting, it's still the real n-word. I've heard it ten thousand times—from the Trotter to the King to *In Living Color*—but always with the soft ending. Hearing it with the hard *er* is like biting into a crab apple. It makes my face muscles clench up even thinking about it. All that evil, all that power, packed into two tiny syllables.

At lunch I'm still thinking about it, repeating it in my head, chewing on its vile, addictive rind. I'm afraid if I don't stop I'll end up blurting the word out loud. Kev's deep in the latest *Source,* so I turn to Jimmy.

"You like basketball cards?" I say.

"Hell yeah," he says.

"If I show you something, promise you'll keep quiet about it?"

Jimmy nods, but the second he sees the Bird-Magic he lets out an "Oh!" and anytime someone goes, "Oh!" in a cafeteria, kids start swarming. I slip the card into my lunch bag and wrap my body around it.

"What you hidin', white boy?" says Kaleem.

"My lunch," I say.

"For real. I'm just curious," he says. "Yo, Kevin, tell your boy I ain't gonna do nothin'."

"He's just curious," Kev says.

Jimmy shakes his head, but I undo the Velcro and give Kaleem a peek.

"Oh *snap.* Lemme see that real quick?" Kaleem says, grabbing the card. He slides it out of its protective plastic and threatens to tear it right along the perforation line.

"Say I won't," he says.

"C'mon, yo," I say.

"Say I won't rip Bird *right* out this bitch."

"Yo, give it back."

"*Say* I won't, white boy," says Kaleem.

"You won't," a voice in the crowd calls out calmly.

It's Marlon. Bodies clear around him. I look over at Jimmy. *This dude?*

"What?" says Kaleem.

"You *won't*," says Marlon. He's a couple inches shorter than Kaleem, but he's got fury in his eyes like a turtle ready to snap.

"Nigga, mind your own business," says Kaleem.

"Put the fuckin' card down," says Marlon. Why's he doing this for me?

"All I'm tryin' a do," says Kaleem, "is take this white faggot off a perfectly good card."

"Don't be callin' Larry a faggot," says Marlon.

"I ain't even talking to you," Kaleem responds, eyes still turned on me.

"Now you are," says Marlon, getting right in Kaleem's face.

"Best get your Buckwheat-lookin' head out my face," Kaleem says. "Nappy-ass crack baby."

This sets Marlon off. "Fuck you just call me?"

Marlon shoves Kaleem and the crowd goes bonk. Someone shouts, "You gonna let him do you like that? You need to whip that li'l nigga!" Kaleem hesitates, then arches his back and digs his shoulder into Marlon's. They stare past each other, rocking slightly as their bodies press together. It almost looks like they're slow-dancing.

"Best step off," Kaleem says into Marlon's ear.

"Best put that motherfuckin' card down," says Marlon.

His eyes are bulging out of their sockets and I can't help feeling like he's acting—that his mask doesn't fit right. Still, it's working on Kaleem.

"Hell's goin' on over here?" shouts Rawlins. Kaleem and Marlon spring off each other.

Rawlins is our janitor–slash–lunch monitor. Everybody loves him, because he's always singing to slow jams and swaying in his bright orange snow hat while he gets his mop on. But everyone's shook of him, too—dude's six and a half feet tall, tatted, and built like a blocking back.

"This ain't no *arena*," says Rawlins. "Siddown before I drag all your behinds to Dr. Jackson's office. That's a warning."

Kaleem flings the card at me, and when I pick it up I notice there's a dent in the corner.

On the bus home, I'm doing my best to smooth out the card when Marlon pops his head over our seatback and whispers, "Put it *away*, dummy."

Angel's coming. He swings up the aisle, launching himself from seat to seat like an evil gymnast. I slip the card in my armpit.

"Let's do this," Angel says. He's not after the card; he just wants to deliver the daily Indian burn.

"Why don't you do him today?" I say, offering up Kev.

"Nah, it's more fun wit' you, gringo," says Angel. Not only is he paler than me, he's an absolute pretty boy, too: big glossy curls that boing when he walks, gold hoops in both ears, almondlike eyes with trim little brows. He smiles with his perfect teeth as he wrings my wrist flesh. I last about five seconds before letting out a whimper, and Angel moves on.

"What'd you even bring it in for?" Marlon says through the crack between the seat and the window.

I turn around and whisper, "I'm selling it."

"You crazy? How come?"

Kev, who's sitting by the aisle, cranes his neck to the crack and butts in: "He wants to cop another purple suit."

"Hold up," Marlon says to me. "You *are* a C's fan, right?"

I pause before nodding.

"Then you can't be going around rocking rival colors. That's why the C's can't get out of this jinx. At least part of it. Way too many sellouts repping Hornets colors. No offense, but your Machine probably got took for a reason. And now you're trying to sell a Bird rookie? For real? You wanna keep this curse going forever? Never sell a Bird rookie."

I've never heard of a Celtics curse. I know about the Curse of the Bambino—everyone in Boston believes in that one, because it's been seventy-five years since the Sox won the Series—but a Celtics curse? The C's were champions six years ago.

He sees I'm confused and says, "You know about Len Bias, right?"

"Of course," I say. I was only five when it happened, but every real fan knows the basics of the tragedy. In '86, the year of their last championship, the Celtics made Bias their number one pick. The hype was unbelievable. He was supposed to be the next Jordan, the future of the franchise. Nobody could wait to see him play alongside Larry, McHale, and Parish. Then, two days after the draft, Bias OD'd at a party and died. The whole city went into shock. At Bias's funeral, Red Auerbach said Boston hadn't been hit so hard since JFK got killed.

"If he hadn't done that coke, Celtics would've won at least three more rings," says Marlon. "Since Bias died, Larry got mad injuries. McHale too. C's never been the same. That shit ain't a coincidence. That's a curse."

I glance over to Kev, expecting some kind of skeptical smile. I'm pretty superstitious, too, especially about the Celtics, and Kev's constantly trying to debunk my shit. But he just nods and listens while Marlon talks. Kev still doesn't have any real homeys at the King, either. It's obvious that he wants to get down with Marlon, now that he knows Marlon's hard. When our stop comes, Kev gets off with us.

"Man, even the Red Sox got cursed by it," Marlon continues as we step onto the curb. "You remember when the dude let the ball roll through his legs in the World Series? What's his name?"

"Buckner," I say. "Curse of the Bambino." We're standing in front of the PJs and I'm ready to get moving.

"That shit had nothing to do with Babe Ruth," says Marlon.

"I'ma head this way," I say, walking toward Buck's, our shitty local card shop. Marlon's so wrapped up in his theory he ends up following me down Centre Street. Kev comes, too.

"That Buckner shit happened *right* after Bias OD'd, like, just a few months later. That's not the Bambino, that's the Curse of the Coke. Messed up everything—the Celtics, the Sox, the whole damn city."

We walk past Arborway Farms, the pink-and-yellow-painted health food co-op; O'Casey's, the dim, reeking Irish pub; and Vines, the new, bourgie wine bar. Marlon looks around like a lost tourist.

"You ever been here?" I say, as we pass the Slice, me and Kev's pizza spot. "Two-slice special's my shit."

"I don't really come down this way," says Mar. "But yo, you seriously trying to sling that Bird rookie? That's like the dopest card ever. My pops used to have one of those."

"What'd he do with it?" I ask.

"You really gonna sell out the last dude who brought home a banner for the C's, so you can buy a stupid-ass suit?" Mar says, ignoring my question. "That's just gonna jinx us worse. Especially with those Hornets colors. I'm telling you: Curse of the Coke."

Marlon walks right into Buck's with me and Kev. It's obvious he's never been here. Buck's is the dirtiest, darkest establishment on Centre Street. It's really a motorcycle parts store, but in the back of the shop, there's a glass case full of cards for sale. You wouldn't even know Buck's was open unless you pushed on the door, because the blinds are always down. Marlon suspiciously eyes the piles of used helmets, the racks stacked with rusty pedals and grips and stickers of bald eagles clutching bloody hatchets. There's so much dust swimming in the light beams, you feel like you could grab a handful, make a ball, and play catch with it.

We walk to the back, where Buck is sitting on a stool, polishing a muffler. He's wearing his usual skintight leather jacket, which he's too fat to zip up, ripped black jeans, and steel-toed boots. He doesn't look our way until I do a couple throat clears.

"Yah?" he says, bored. As far as I know, me and Kev are the only business he gets, but he still looks pissed every time he sees us.

"Came here to sell something," I say.

Buck keeps his eyes on Marlon as I slide the Bird-Magic onto his counter. He takes it out of the plastic and inspects it for about two seconds.

"Thirty dollahs."

"He's playing, right?" Marlon says to me.

"There's a dent in the cornah," says Buck. "Thing's not even close to mint."

"I was thinking more like a hundred?" I say.

Buck laughs. "You want that kind of money? Bring me a Shaq holofoil. In mint."

"Ninety?"

"Thirty-five. Final offah."

It's nowhere near enough for a new Machine, but it's enough for a dozen fresh packs. Maybe I'd land a Shaq holofoil.

Marlon pulls me aside.

"You out of your mind? You might as well be giving that shit away. If you're dying to get rid of it, I'll take it."

I consider Buck's offer for a few more seconds but then put the Bird-Magic away. I'm ready to bounce, but Marlon asks Buck if he can check out one of the cards under the glass—an '89 Bird that's priced at six bones.

"Not for sale," Buck says, looking down at the case.

"Says six right there," says Marlon.

"Old stickah. Not for sale."

"How 'bout this one," says Marlon, pointing to an '88 Dennis Johnson.

"Let's see ya money first."

"Why I gotta show you money to look at the card?"

"You know what?" says Buck. "You guys've been in here long enough."

I want to call Buck a fat racist fuck and jab my finger in his face, but I'm too busy chewing on it. I always bite my nails in stressful situations.

"You let Dave look at that card last week," Kev says.

"You see the sign on the door?" says Buck.

"How come I can't look at the card?" says Marlon.

"You can't hang out here all day," he says, pointing to the NO LOITERING sign.

Then, out of the corner of his mouth, he adds, "This ain't the projects."

I've been waiting for years for a moment like this—to catch a blatant bigot in the act and put him in check—and here I am, silent, ripping cuticle. I know I owe it to Marlon after he caught my back at lunch. But bonk as this may sound, I feel like Buck *knows* about me, like there's some kind of fellowship of the force and Buck's an old master who can detect it in others. *I know what word's been in your head all day,* I hear him thinking. *Who the fuck are you to tell me off?*

"What'd you just say?" says Kev.

"Beat it," says Buck, lifting the phone. "Or I'm calling the BPD."

At this point, I'm halfway out the door. Kev—and it kills

me to see this—is standing tall. Marlon takes his time walking out, staring back at Buck. Kev follows, shouts, "Fat racist fuck!" and we bolt down the block.

THE NEXT DAY at the bus stop, I'm expecting Marlon to bring up my bitch moves at Buck's, but he doesn't. The only thing he says is "You bring it in today?"

"Nah," I say. "Decided not to sell."

"Good."

And a few hours later, he does something even more surprising: asks if he can sit at our lunch table.

Kev seems excited and embarrassed at the same time—amped to have Mar, ashamed that the other two dudes at the table are me and Jimmy. I have to say, though, I think Jimmy's all right. Sure, he's elf-short, comes into school with constant bedhead, and rocks those knockoff Nikes with the too-skinny Swoosh—but once you get to know him, he's hilarious, and pretty hard, too. He hates the King even more than I do, especially because everyone calls him Chinese. He's Vietnamese and he despises the Chinese for what they did to his people, and no matter how many times he says he's not Chinese, heads are like, "Whatever, Ching-Chong," and make slit eyes at him. He'll calmly talk back to them in Vietnamese and they'll laugh and do even more of the singsong ching-chong stuff, and when I ask what he's saying to them, he tells me, "Just some shit like *May your whole family starve.*"

Marlon takes a bag of chips and a bottle of Fresca out of his backpack and starts talking about how wack it is that they're gonna tear down the Garden—yet another Curse of the Coke casualty.

"Yeah, but the new stadium's gonna be sick," says Kev. "You heard about the Jumbotron?"

"Shit's gonna be tight," Jimmy says.

I'm excited about the Jumbotron, too—they're saying it'll be the biggest stadium screen ever. And I don't have that much love for the Garden anyway. It's basically the Morgie's of stadiums, the oldest in the NBA, a sweaty, stinking mold-cave with a leaky roof. Every other seat is obstructed-view and the court's made of ancient parquet squares. One of the squares is so loose that if you dribble on it at the wrong angle, you'll bounce the ball right off your knee and out-of-bounds. (Larry loved to lure opponents to the loose square.)

"Man, fuck the Jumbotron," says Marlon. "C's won sixteen championships in the Garden. Why's everybody always gotta mess with shit that's working?"

"Yeah," I say. "Fuck the Jumbotron."

Kev scowls at me and gets up for more tacos.

We eat in silence for a sec, and then Marlon asks, "Yo, you got a VCR?"

"Uh-huh," I say.

"I got the illest collection of C's tapes," says Marlon. "All the dope playoff games from the eighties—all that classic Big Three shit."

"Word? Where'd you get 'em?"

"My pops. Haven't watched 'em in a minute, though. My VCR's broke."

"You could come peep 'em at my crib."

There's a long pause and I'm worried I said something that sounded soft.

"I'm down," he finally says.

"Word. Today?" I say. "I mean—"

"Today's cool," says Marlon. I mentally fist-pump.

I know Kev's gonna wanna chill with Marlon, too. For once he'll be the tagalong.

"Yo, could I roll?" Jimmy says.

I tell him my mom only lets me have two friends over at a time, max, on school days. I know Jimmy detects the bull, and I feel like a Clinton-level sham, but I'm trying not to mess up a chance to be boys with Marlon.

WE GET OFF the bus and Marlon asks us to wait outside, by Pops's garden, while he runs into the Shaw Homes. He comes back a few minutes later with a backpack full of tapes.

"Ain't even half what I got," he brags. "Ain't even *close* to half."

"Y'all wanna watch at my crib instead?" Kev asks. He's got one of those TVs that sits on the floor and takes up half the room. I've got a thirteen-incher with wood casing, knobs, and tinfoil wrapped around the bent-ass antenna.

"Nah," says Marlon. "Let's stick with Dave's."

Maybe he thinks my house has good luck because of the Bird-Magic? Either way I'm not about to protest. Kev eyes a gourd poking through the garden fence and kicks it. We head up my hill.

My house, like almost every other house on the block, is a crumbling Victorian that needs a paint job. And like most of our hippie neighbors, we've got political signs all over our front yard: a bunch that say VOTE NO ON #2, an old one that says PEACE IN THE MIDDLE EAST, and an enormous RE-ELECT SKIP sign my parents jammed into our hedge.

"Who's Skip?" Marlon asks.

"Skip Taylor," I say. "City councilor. My parents are friends with him."

"No Clinton sign?" Marlon says.

"Nah," I say. My parents are voting for Clinton, but they won't put up a sign for him, because he's too corporate. I also can't stand Clinton's ass. One minute he's fronting on *Arsenio* with his sax, next minute he's shitting on Sister Souljah.

"You feel Clinton?" I ask.

"Nah, I like that independent, Perot," Marlon says. "Dude makes me laugh."

"For real? He's my favorite, too."

If my parents heard me say that, they'd disown me, but it's true. I love that Elmer Fudd–looking fool with his crazy charts and extra-long infomercials, especially the one with his family chilling by the pond next to his mansion, with all those ducks swimming by in the background. He doesn't need to plan it all out and pose like Clinton. He's rich—duck-pond rich—he can say whatever the hell he feels. He doesn't hate on gangster rap like all the other politicians; he *is* a gangster.

We head inside my house and I try to get them upstairs as quickly as possible. I don't want Marlon to see all the hippie shit my parents put in our living room: the ratty couches covered with ethnic throws, the dusty kachina dolls, the antique medicine bottles stuffed with dried flowers. I especially don't want him looking at all the old photos of Pops's ancestors: giant-bearded Jews with their smocked wives and way too serious children. I stand out enough at the King. I don't need anyone knowing I belong to that weird, wimpy tribe.

Marlon walks through the living room without comment, but he lingers by the books in the hallway next to my bedroom. He scans the shelves and runs his fingers across the spines, the way I do every time I see a piano.

"These are yours?" he says.

"Some of 'em," I say, doing my best to move him along to the back stairway.

"Which ones?"

"Kinda lost track."

Pops has given me hundreds of books, and each one comes with a mini-lecture about why it's so great. I haven't read any of them.

"That's your bedroom?" Marlon asks. On my door, there's a sign I never got around to ripping down that reads, DAVE ZONE: ENTER AT YOUR OWN RISK.

"Yeah, but it's all messy," I say.

"I don't care," Marlon says.

"Show him, D," Kev says, grinning.

There's lots of other stuff I need to shitcan in there—the old posters of dump trucks, dinosaurs, and whales, the Day-Glo stars on the ceiling, and worst of all, my trophies. You know the kind they give out for good effort, team spirit, and third place—those columnless chumpstumps where the golden guy is standing right on the platform? Every single one of my trophies is like that. I can't bring myself to throw them out, but I don't want Marlon seeing them, either.

Kev yanks my door open and Marlon walks right up to Benno's easel. This is the other reason I didn't want Marlon in there. Benno's hockey pads, the unicycle, and all the other shit my parents bought him are piled up in a corner of our room, gathering dust, because now he's into the softest thing of all—art.

"You drew that?" Marlon says, pointing to the charcoal sketch on the easel. It's some kind of abstract daffodil.

"The little sapien drew it," Kev says.

Marlon looks puzzled. Kev got in trouble for calling Benno a faggot last spring, so now he calls him a sapien.

"My little brother," I say.

"He can draw," Marlon says.

As we're walking out of my room, Marlon spots the Bird-Magic, nestled between my chumpstumps. He picks it up and says, "You need to get a better case for this, one of those screw-on joints. That way Kaleem never could've bent it."

"Like this?" I say, pulling out my other prized card, a Reggie Lewis holofoil. It's in a case the size of a small brick. Reggie's my hero, the Celtics' captain and leading scorer. He's known more for his soft touch than his dunks, which is why he doesn't get his due from dudes like Kev and Simon. Still, he can throw it down hard when he wants to.

"You go maximum security on a *Reggie* and put a Bird-Magic rookie in that flimsy-ass sleeve?" Marlon says. "What's wrong with you?"

"Reggie's gonna be even better than Bird," I say.

"I mean, I like Reggie, too," he says. "But that's crazy."

I finally get them upstairs and Marlon takes out his tapes. We pop in the epic Jordan-Bird showdown. It's from the '86 playoffs, right before Bias died, the one where Jordan drops a postseason-record sixty-three points and Bird *still* manages to carry the C's to a double-overtime win. Every real C's fan knows about this game, but to watch the whole thing, play by play, with those old-school Hood milk commercials, to see every sick Jordan drive and Bird miracle, with Johnny Most's cig-scorched voice calling the plays, is some next-level shit. Marlon's got almost all of Most's calls memorized, but every time Bird cashes one, he wails and flails around the couch, like he's seeing it for the first time. At one point, he drops to the floor, yelling, "He didn't! He didn't!"

When the tape ends, I'm hyped.

"I think it's time for some nasketball," I say.

"Fuck that," Kev says. "Let's roll to my spot and play *Street Fighter II*."

"What's up with nasketball?" Marlon asks.

Nasketball is a game I invented to make up for my pathetic rise. Once Kev started tapping the backboard this summer, I decided I had to at least get net. I worked at it every day for weeks. I'm talking calf raises in the shower, wraparound ankle weights, fifty leaps a day, minimum. Nothing helped. All I ever got was air. I couldn't take it anymore, so one day I lowered my adjustable-height hoop to its five-foot minimum, dragged Benno's trampoline beneath the basket, took off for a tomahawk jam. Nasketball was born. It's basically one-on-one, but there's no traveling, the only way to score is to dunk in someone's face, and every time you dunk in someone's face, you yell, "Nasty!"

"I'll show you," I say to Marlon.

He grabs his backpack and we go outside.

I kick things off with a three-sixty and scream, "I'm nasty!"

"Green getting big!" yells Marlon.

He just said my emcee name, and I didn't even push it on him. *Green.* It's what they called me at camp a couple summers back. It took a while to grow on me, because I saw green as a semisoft color. But it was better than my last name, it was way better than *white boy,* and the more I thought about it, the more I realized it was a solid rap name, too. Green: the ultimate emcee aspiration, the tint of the dream.

"Assty," says Kev. "You barely did a one-eighty."

He grabs the ball and looks down at it, disgusted.

"Wish I'd known we were gonna ball. Would've brought my shit."

He has a leather Spalding, the official kind they use in the NBA. I have a cracked rubber Voit with a cancer hump. The cancer came after I left it outside last winter. On the plus side, it makes the ball grippable with one hand—perfect for Lady Liberty dunks.

Kev rips his shirt off, moves the trampoline back several feet, gets a running start, springs up, and soars to the hoop, arms extended like wings, tongue wagging in the wind. He hangs on the rim with one hand and beats his chest with the other, screaming, "Who's the nastiest?"

Marlon's about to take his turn when Ma pops her head

out the door. She's wearing her United Steelworkers Union hoodie and she gets all smiley when she sees Marlon's here.

"Hi, Davey. Hi, Kev," Ma says. "And you must be Marlon?"

Marlon nods shyly.

"Very nice to meet you," she says. "Can I get you guys some snacks?"

"We're straight," I say.

She keeps watching us. "I said we're *good*, Ma."

She goes back inside and Marlon warms up for a dunk. He's still got his backpack on; I guess he's extra-protective of those C's tapes. He looks up at the hoop, and before he takes off he nods toward my bedroom window and says, "Who's that?"

It's Benno. He's filming us through the window with Pops's Handycam.

"What the hell, Benno?" I yell.

"That's your brother?" asks Marlon.

"Yeah."

"Ben?"

"Benno," I say.

He *was* Ben, but in second grade he decided that name was too boring because two other kids in school had it. So he made my parents take him to City Hall and legally change his shit from Benjamin to Benno, a name he got from Pops's great-uncle, one of the old Jews in the photos. Kids started clowning him immediately, and Ma said if he wanted to he could go back to Benjamin, but he refused. Same thing happened when he grew his hair long last year. Kids shit on him, pantsed him in the schoolyard, asked if they could see his pussy. He'd come home and cry for hours, but when Ma offered to give him a trim he shook his head. That's the thing about Benno. Most kids make an attempt to act *more* normal after their steez gets shit on. Benno digs in. Not only did he keep growing it out, a couple months later, in the spring, he dyed it—*bleached* it. He got on the bus the next morning and the first kid who spotted him shouted, "Yo, look at this faggot gay!" Later that day in the schoolyard, Kev, Jason, Rich, and Robby—the other white boys I was semi-friends with at the Trotter—surrounded him and chanted, "Fag-got gay, fag-got gay," and Benno said nothing back, because he was already deep in his silence by then. I was standing a few feet away, watching this all go down, feeling terrible that I was doing nothing to protect my brother but also feeling ashamed of my blood, pissed at him for bringing it on himself. Benno started crying, which just made the chants louder, and then one of them pointed out that he looked like Reginald Denny. Kev started a new chant—"*Den*-no, *Den*-no"—and they started mock-beating him with their rolled-up jackets, doing victory dances and everything. Finally, a teacher came over, screamed at them, told all of them to go to the office, and asked me, "What were they calling him?" I said I didn't know and then she threatened to send me to the office, too, so I replied, "Faggot," because, for some reason, it seemed like it would get them in less trouble than "Denno." The principal ended up calling all of their parents and I became known, forever more, as the snitch with the sapien little brother.

"Stop filming, sapien!" Kev shouts.

"Nah, keep rolling," Marlon says. "I want a highlight reel."

Benno usually stays inside, but he comes out now, I guess so he can get a better angle on Marlon. He looks a little less embarrassing these days because he finally cut his hair, but only a little—he kept his rattail. Marlon moves all the way back to the end of my driveway and tells Benno to do a close-up. I keep waiting for Marlon to comment on Benno's black nail polish—or at least his rattail—but I guess he's in the zone.

"It's Game Seven of the NBA Finals," says Marlon in a Johnny Most rasp. "Celtics are down two, with three seconds left on the clock. DJ inbounds to Bird. Three. Two. One!"

Marlon hoists the ball in the air, yells, "Cut!" and directs Benno to move right underneath the hoop and zoom in on the rim.

"Roll!" says Marlon, who walks right up to the hoop and lightly tosses in the ball.

"Larry Bird!" he screams into the camera's mic. "Ladies and gentlemen, Larry Bird has done it again!" Marlon breathes static into the mic and Benno laughs, something I haven't heard him do in a minute.

Benno rewinds the tape and plays it back for Marlon.

"That looks crazy real!" Marlon says. "You killed it!"

He extends his fist. Benno softly meets Marlon's pound.

Kev raises the hoop a couple notches, kicks aside the trampoline, grabs the ball, and double-pumps it as hard as he can through my ragged rim. He's screaming, "No trampoline, son! Watch me do it again. Watch!" but I'm watching something else: Marlon, who's watching Benno. Just standing there, thumbs in his pants pockets, shoulders sloped under the weight of that huge backpack, watching Benno fiddle with the Handycam.

Marlon turns to me and says, "He don't talk?"

"Nah," I say.

Marlon makes a gesture so tiny Kev doesn't even notice. He just nods, like it's no thing, like he understands.

THAT SATURDAY, KEV has his annual sleepover birthday jam. The usual crew shows up—Simon plus the other white boys we went to the Trotter with. The second I arrive, Simon whimpers, "I thought—I thought we were *boys,*" and the other dudes start rolling. I try to explain how Kev and Simon just stood there, like the world's biggest bitch twins, but nobody listens. The only reason I'm here at all is because Marlon was invited, too. A couple hours later, he still hasn't shown up, and Kev kicks off the Freddy Krueger marathon without him. There's no way I'm sticking around for this.

The truth is I'm shook of sleepovers. That might have been normal when I was seven, but I kept being shook of them at eight, and I've gotten even shooker since. I'm not exactly sure how the fear began, but most of the sleepovers I've ever been to have been at Kev's, and it doesn't help that Kev's always watching horror movies. It's not just the movies, though—it's, like, scariness itself that scares me. Like, once I start getting into shook mode, everything spooks: the way Kev's porch light shoots through his blinds and slices up the wall, the swirls on the carpet, the blinking red colon on the clock radio. But what's scariest of all is the hugeness of Kev's house, how long it takes to walk to the bathroom, the horrible feeling that I'm the only awake person not just there but on the whole planet.

I don't like my house, but I feel safe there. With its shitty snacks and worn couches, it feels too wack to attract evil. Still, ever since the Machine thing, I can barely even sleep there. Right after I got jacked, I spent a couple days sleeping on the floor next to my parents' bed. Eventually my parents booted me, and I started sleeping in the hallway outside their door, but I decided that was too sapien, even for me, and I went back to my own bed. Now I have a trick where I tune into Celtics talk radio and twist the volume to the lowest point before it clicks off. Lonely losers from all over New England complain about the Celtics preseason and how bad they're gonna be without Bird, and I can't even hear half of what they're saying. As I try to make out the whispery whined words—"rebound . . . effort . . . disgrace . . ."— I fade away.

I'm getting ready to jab my fingers down my throat and make myself yack. Then I can call Ma and she'll come pick me up in the Whale (Kev's name for our white Plymouth Voyager with all the dings, scratches, and shredded bumper stickers on it) and I'll go home, as I've done so many other times, in total, humiliating relief. But then Kev's mom knocks on the door.

"Kevin!" she calls. "Your friend is here."

It's Marlon. He didn't know the deal—to knock on the back window instead of ringing the bell.

"Oh snap, what up, Marlon?" Kev says, giving him extra-showy dap in front of the white boys.

"You going to introduce me?" Kev's mom says.

"This is my moms," Kev mutters.

"I'm Ann," she says, extending a hand. "It's nice to meet you. Listen, Marlon, I don't want to be nosy, but does your mother know you're out so late?"

Kev's face flares up. People like to clown me about my parents, but Kev's mom is just as corny. She's got long, frizzy red hair and she's rocking the wackest mom gear ever: maroon clogs, loose jeans, long sweater, purple pashmina, and silver earrings that look like wind chimes.

"She, um—" Marlon starts.

"Ma," Kev says. "Can you bounce already?"

"Okay, boys. Have fun. And try to get a *tiny* bit of sleep?"

"Yo, this is Simon," Kev says to Marlon, refusing to introduce the other dudes. "We were just about to rock a Freddy marathon—start with *Nightmare on Elm* and go all the way through the latest joint."

Marlon's eyes are on the candy bowls in the kitchenette.

"You ready to watch some bitches get *laced* up?" Kev says.

Marlon heads for the candy and I follow him. Kev puts on his Freddy glove and beckons us with the claw on his middle finger. Marlon ignores him, downing a bag of Skittles.

"You ready to fuck with Freddy?" Kev says in the raspy voice.

My chest pounds like microwave popcorn.

"Y'all could start watching without me," Marlon says. "I seen them too many times already. That shit's kinda played."

Kev walks into the TV room, deflated, and turns back to me.

"Dave, you coming or what?"

"I'll be in there in a sec," I say. *"Damn."*

"You're so fuckin' *soft,*" says Kev, slamming the door.

"Wanna play Nintendo?" I ask Marlon. "There's another TV in the guest room."

Kev's mom is one of those parents who buys her kids every tape available, even the ones they don't ask for, so there's about a hundred to choose from. Marlon picks out *Final Fantasy* and I spend a half hour watching his dwarf wander around, picking up hatchets and rations, bonking the occasional orc, before he asks if I want a turn. I'm not about to tell him I don't know how to play *Final Fantasy*—that I've never played *Final Fantasy*—because Kev only likes the fast-paced fighting games and never lets me pick. A lot of people can't stand *Final Fantasy* for the same reasons Kev can't—it's too slow and wordy and numbery; there's too much roaming and too little murder. But this is exactly what I want to be doing right now, with the screams of Freddy's victims piercing the walls: watching someone else scuttle through forests and peek into huts, listening to the same sixteen-bit tune on repeat.

"You guys coming or what?" Kev shouts. Marlon pauses the game.

"You wanna?" he asks.

Maybe Marlon just wants to be selfish and play video-games all night at someone else's birthday, but it seems like he senses how badly I don't want to watch Freddy. Maybe he's secretly shook, too. Either way, without even waiting for my reply, he yells, "We're cool!"

"What?" yells Kev.

"We're *cool*!" Marlon yells, even louder.

Kev turns the volume up to fuck with us. A couple hours later, I can tell that they've all fallen asleep because the sounds stop and no one bothers to put in a new tape. I'm still watching Marlon play when Kev's mom knocks on our door.

"It's after three, guys," she says. "It's time you got some sleep."

Marlon didn't bring a sleeping bag, so I take the couch and let him take the bed. Kev's mom turns the lights off and closes the door.

"Night, Green," Marlon says.

"Night, Mar," I say.

"That's what my pops calls me," he says.

"Oh."

"It's cool."

About ten minutes pass and I can tell he's still awake from the way the springs are squeaking.

"You still up?" I whisper.

"Yeah," he says.

"I can't sleep," I say.

There's a long pause and I'm scared I went way over the softness line.

"Me either," he says.

"I bet if we turn the volume off, we could keep playing," I say.

Mar lets me pick the game this time, and I go with *Excitebike*. But I still prefer to watch, not play. It's the most repetitive and relaxing game of all time. There's no bad guys or anything. All you do is ride up ramps, do flip-jumps, and land. It's like watching leaves fall off trees. In minutes, I'm out.

CHAPTER 3

Paper

On Monday, Ms. Ansley tells us to put away everything except our pencils.

"The Latin test is coming up in two months and change."

She passes out a pop practice test and everybody groans.

"Save your moaning. I'm doing this for your own good. I'm not expecting you to ace this thing. I just want to diagnose your strengths and weaknesses."

I already know my weakness: the reading section. I'm probably the slowest reader in America, and the stuff on the tests is always some snooze-fest about ballet or the French Revolution, which makes me even slower. So I always jump straight to the questions and then go back and scan the passage for the answers. Of course, the tests are designed to make it impossible to find the answers like that, so I end up scrambling to reread it before the buzzer and can never finish. I want to guillotine myself just thinking about it.

A couple days later, Ms. Ansley hands me back my test. There's a note stapled to it that says: *David— You are currently in the 81st percentile overall and the 73rd percentile for reading. To get into Latin, your overall percentile needs to be in the 90s. Please return this to me, signed by a parent.*

"I don't want to put pressure on you," Pops says that night. "But what's going on here?"

"It's just one test."

"I think it's time for us to start studying together."

"I've been studying plenty on my own. I'll be fine. It's only October."

"*Have* you been studying on your own?"

"I keep telling you. Like every afternoon."

"Let me see your prep book."

"Why? You don't believe me?"

"Let me see it."

I bring it to him. He inspects the wrinkle-free spine and frowns as he fans through the untouched pages. I bite my lip and smile when he looks up at me, which makes him even angrier.

"This isn't funny, Dave. You need to start taking this a little more seriously. No more videogames at Kevin's house. On school days, you're coming straight home or going to the library."

"Fine." He doesn't know I've already decided to ice Kev anyway.

I start walking off, and he says, "No allowance for the next two weeks, either."

"What the *hell*? Since when are you so into Latin? I thought you didn't care about brand names."

"What I care about is effort. You're not even trying."

"How 'bout one week of allowance?"

"How 'bout three?"

. . .

I'VE NEVER BEEN more desperate for loot. I've been Machine-free for weeks and I'm fiending for a replacement. Even though I still like the purple and teal most, I'll probably go with a green and white one next time around, to appease Mar. I'm more motivated than ever because I've started feeling Carmen Garcia, the shorty who propped me for the Machine.

I've been trying to spit some game, but it's hard to mack in Morgie's gear. Here's our entire history since *stylish:*

Me: Can I get a piece of paper?

Her: [Tears a sheet and passes it without making eye contact.]

Kev clowns me about Carmen. I don't know why I still tell him shit. I guess I feel obligated because back in the day, we made a pact: First, if either of us ever felt a shorty, we'd tell each other, and second, neither of us would ever, ever get with a white girl. He feels this big-bootied eighth grader named Aisha, who's so out of reach, I don't know why he even bothers. He says Carmen has a mustache. It's true she has a little bit of lip hair, but it's barely visible—a couple faint pencil shades, not the whole way across, just on the sides. And I don't know why she rocks those giant plastic granny glasses, but honestly I think they're cute. They're pink. That's cute as hell. And if Kev's dumb ass looked a little bit closer, he'd see she's got dope light brown eyes with crazy long lashes under there. I'm kinda glad she rocks that steez anyway. I bet she's never even kissed a dude and that makes me feel her even harder, because if I ever did get with her, she'd have no idea how bad I am at it, and neither would

I. Sometimes, when I can't sleep and even the low-volume C's talk doesn't help, I'll start thinking of Carmen sitting at her desk, her long black hair pinned up with those yellow barrettes, scribbling away with her fat rainbow pen. Instead of picturing fence-hopping sheep—an image that's always stressed the shit out of me—I'll imagine Carmen moving her pen across a page, writing in that adorable-ass cursive, the swooping, loopy kind, with a circle instead of a dot on the *i*.

If I'm gonna make another attempt to kick it to her, I'm gonna need a new Machine, and for that I'm gonna need to fatten my muenster stack, fast. Leaf-raking season won't start for another week or so, and I can't think of any other hustle, so I resort to my old standby: canning. If you can get over the whole looking-homeless thing, it's pretty decent money.

In my years of canning across Beantown, I've found that the top gold mines are sporting events and street fairs. First of all, there's always a lot of people drinking stuff, and most of them'll be happy to throw an empty your way if you hover around until they're done. Second, there's usually police around to scare off the actual bums, which means way less competition. In the off-season, the big payday is Thursday, recycling day. That's assuming you get to the blue bins before the truck does—or before Jerry does. He's the homeless guy with duct tape wrapped around his feet who kicks it in front of Woolworth's on Centre Street. Everybody knows him. He has this disease that makes him yell, "Suck my dick!" if you say hello. Ma still says hi every time.

It's a Sunday, and I'm not trying to wait till the next recycling day, so I drag my old Radio Flyer down to my bus
stop and hit up the dumpster behind the bodega. Jackpot:
twelve cans, one two-liter bottle, and a couple St. Ides forties. I'm about to go cash in at the machine next to the liquor store when I see Mar, who's all suited up, walking out
of the PJs with a lady in a long red coat. She's rocking a huge
white hat topped by a bouquet of bright fake flowers.

"Mar!" I shout across the street.

He doesn't seem to hear me, but the lady turns my way.

"Marlon—over here!"

I cross the street with my clanky load.

"What's up?" I say to Mar. "Where you heading?"

"Church," he says, looking ashamed. Not of church,
of me.

I turn to the lady with the hat. She has Mar's big friendly
eyes, and when she smiles at me her cheeks pop out like
plums.

"You're Marlon's mom?" I say.

"His grandmother."

"I'm Dave." I hold out a grubby hand. She's wearing
white gloves and gives a little wave back. "I'm in Marlon's
class. At the King?"

I was hoping for something like "Oh yes, I've heard so
much about you." But all I get is a look that says, *Who's this
weird, dirty white boy, holding us up?*

Then another woman walks out of the PJs and yells,
"Hold up!"

She's wearing these purple socks pulled halfway up her

legs, over her jeans, and her feet are pressing down the heels of her sneakers, slippers-style. She's mad skinny and her hair is staticking out in every direction, like a Fraggle. I've seen her before, walking down Centre Street, with the socks pulled up like that. Not too long ago I saw her chilling in front of Woolworth's, talking to Jerry. I assumed she was his homeless homey.

"Who y'all talking to?" Fraggle says to Mar and his grandma.

"This is Marlon's classmate, Dave," his grandmother says.

The woman tilts her head slightly and grills me with a spooky, emptied-out stare. I turn to Mar for some kind of explanation, but he's looking at his shined-up shoes.

"We've got to be going," Mar's grandmother says to me. "It's nice to meet you, Dave."

She takes Fraggle by the arm and they walk off. Mar doesn't even give me goodbye dap.

ON THE BUS the next day, I sit next to Mar. I ask him about the lady with the socks and his face goes tight. Instead of answering, he says, "Hell you digging in the trash for?"

"It's your fault," I say. "If you'da let me sell the Bird-Magic I wouldn't have to."

"Well, it's nasty," he says. "You showered after?"

"Nah. Still got bin grease all over me," I say, wiping my hands on his hoodie sleeve.

"Ugh!" he says, punching my arm back.

"'Course I showered," I say. "I'm a businessman."

"How much you make?"

"Dollar thirty. In like twenty minutes, though."

"Ain't worth it."

"I'll take loot any way I can get it."

"Well, I'm not trying to dig around for nickels," he says. "I'm trying to go to Harvard, come up for real."

We've got a field trip today. One of Ms. Ansley's old students is giving us a tour of Harvard.

"Do your thing," I say. "My parents went there and they definitely didn't come up."

He thinks I'm kidding. I don't push it, because Ma told me not to brag about them when she signed my permission slip.

A couple hours later, me and Mar are back on the bus together, on our way across the river to Cambridge. To kill time, I suggest some rock-paper-scissors. I have this trick that almost always works, where I throw paper on the first draw. Pretty much everybody I've ever played with throws rock, because it seems like the hardest play. But Mar throws paper. We shoot again and I decide to double down on paper. He throws paper again, too. This time, I lose patience and decide to throw rock. Mar sticks to paper and wins.

"You know about the paper trick?" I say.

"What trick?"

"Throwing paper right away. Because most people assume rock is the move. They *might* pick scissors. The last thing they're gonna pick is paper."

He's not buying the theory.

"Cuz, like, it's the only one that's not a weapon," I say.

"That's the dumbest shit I ever heard."

"You know what I'm saying. People think of paper as soft."

"What they think money's made out of?" he says.

We pull up to a big gate and our guide greets us as we file off the bus. We follow her into the courtyard and everybody looks around, all quiet and uncomfortable. This is the first time I've ever been on campus. I don't know why my parents hate Harvard so much. This place is proper: buildings made out of dark red bricks instead of the yack yellow I'm used to, windows without grates, vines crawling up chimneys, no trash or glass-chunked dirt, oak trees everywhere.

Our guide brings us to this statue of a mean seated Puritan and introduces herself. "My name is Jabrina Wilkins. Hel-*lo*, y'all. I can't *hear* you."

A couple kids drone hellos. Whoever invented the *I can't hear you* method of public speaking needs to get got.

"What's *up*, King School? That's a little better. *The dreamers united can never be defeated!* They still say that over there?"

They do if you're Principal Jackson or a giant worm. Jabrina's one of those Potato Head types who walks around all day with a snap-on smile. She's got beaded braids and she's trying to talk like she's down, but you can tell right away she's corn to the bone. Then she snaps off the smile.

"If you take a look around, you'll notice there aren't too many people like me around here. Not too many people who came from schools like the King. And the God's honest truth is that I'm only standing here"—she pauses to clear her throat—"I'm standing here for one reason—Ms. Ansley.

She didn't want me to be a sta*tis*tic, which is what too many kids at the King end up as. Believe me: Y'all gonna *know* kids who'll end up upstate or underground."

I look over at Mar. He's staring straight at Jabrina, still as the Puritan.

"I didn't get A's my whole life. It took me a while to start believing in myself. I used to think there was *one* way— I used to think places like Latin and Harvard were for *other* people, not me. But Ms. Ansley didn't buy the one-way talk for a second. She told me *nothing*'s for *other* people if you apply yourself. You put the work in, you could be standing *right* where I am today. You hear me?"

Everyone nods, so I nod, too.

"You may only be in middle school, but Ms. Ansley brought you here for a good reason. And that's because if you stay out of trouble and study for that test, you got a real shot of getting into Latin. And *no* school, not even the fanciest private schools in the whole country—not your Andovers or your Exeters or your Miltons—sends more students here than Latin."

"That's right," Ms. Ansley says quietly.

"You get into Harvard, you're taking the *reins,* you understand? More presidents come from Harvard than any other school—more senators and congressmen and governors, too. More millionaires—more *billionaires*—from here than any other school."

Now she has my attention.

"You wanna be president?"

Kaleem snickers.

"You wanna stack a *bill*?"

Everyone nods.

"Then get serious and get off your Game Boys. Don't wait. Start studying for that test."

We continue on the tour and Jabrina brings us through the cafeteria. It's a huge hall with stained glass, giant chandeliers, and long, medieval-looking tables. I salivate as I watch a student fill up two Cokes from the soda fountain. Another swirls a huge helping of vanilla soft-serve onto his plate. I don't see a menu anywhere, so I ask Jabrina, "How much does that ice cream cost?"

Mar scowls at me.

"It's all-you-can-eat," Jabrina says.

"You mean it's free?" I say. "All of it?"

"It's included in tuition," she says.

On our way out, I spot an untouched grilled cheese, abandoned on a plate at the end of a table. I swipe it and tuck it in my hoodie pouch. As we're walking back through Harvard Yard, I tear off half for Mar.

"You bonked?" he whispers.

"It was free," I say. "I wasn't gonna just leave it there."

"You act like a straight-up hobo sometimes," he says.

He refuses his half, so I house the whole thing. It's soggy but incredible. None of that wheat bunk, no tomato slices. Just Wonder and American.

"This is the hustle," I say.

"Nah, dummy," he says. "*Harvard*'s the hustle."

"My moms really went here," I say with fresh-minted pride. "My pops, too. They met here and shit. Probably in one of these dorms."

"I've seen your crib," he says. "Your parents definitely didn't go to Harvard."

"Swear to— swear on my grandma's grave. Kev, tell him how I don't play when I swear on that shit."

"There goes your exaggerating ass as usual," Kev says. "You never said shit about your pops going to Harv."

"My pops went here—ask him!" I say.

"You serious?" Mar says.

Kaleem turns around and says, "No one gives a fuck about your faggot-ass father."

A few kids in the line turn around, too, waiting for my reaction. I just keep walking and pretend like I didn't hear anything. Sticks, stones, and all that Gandhi bunk Pops is always preaching.

"Don't let him do you like that," Mar says to me.

"Forget it," I whisper back. A second ago Mar was worried about me swiping free sandwiches. Now he wants me to beef, right in the middle of Harvard Yard? What's he care about my father for, anyway?

"You hear me, white boy?" says Kaleem.

"Nobody's talking to you," says Mar.

"Nobody's talkin' to your nappy-headed ass, either," says Kaleem.

One kid "Oh!"s and Ms. Ansley rushes over from the front of the line.

"We're *guests* here," she whisper-yells.

She walks back to the front of the line, and a few seconds later Kaleem turns around, stutter-steps toward me, and whispers, "Fuck Harvard and fuck your faggot-ass father."

"You best step off," says Mar.

"Fuck you, too," says Kaleem. *"Oreo."*

"The *fuck* you say to me?" Mar says.

Ms. Ansley's too far ahead to have heard, but a couple Harvard students have stopped walking and started staring.

"Oreo," Kaleem says. He sniffs in a big wad and spits it onto the raised roots of a tree. "Goes real good with milk."

Mar's face starts trembling. He looks over at the Harvard students for a second, seems ashamed to be making a show for them, and turns away. A second later, he turns back to them and they're still staring—and now the look on his face says, *Fuck you looking at?*

He pivots to Kaleem and walks right up to him. "Say it again."

Kaleem digs his shoulder into Mar's and they waltz around. Then Mar lowers his head and shoves Kaleem with both arms. Kaleem staggers back a few steps, and Ms. Ansley dives between them.

"What's *wrong* with you?" Ms. Ansley whispers furiously. "You lost your minds?"

"Next time he calls me a . . . next time I'ma kill his ass!" Mar shouts in Kaleem's direction.

"You're embarrassing the King," she says, gripping Mar's coat. "You're embarrassing *yourself*."

A Harvard rent-a-cop rolls up.

"Everything okay here?" he says to Ms. Ansley.

"Thank you, Officer," she says. She closes her eyes and runs her palm down her face, flattening her nose. "I'm handling it."

"You guys here with a tour guide?"

"We were," she says.

"So tour's over?"

"Yes," she says, blinking hard. "We're on our way out."

THE NEXT MORNING, Ms. Ansley has a meeting with Mar, Mar's grandma, Kaleem, and Kaleem's parents. Mar fills me in at lunch.

"Ms. Ansley made *me* apologize," he says. "I would've been like, *Hell no*, if my grandma hadn't been there."

"He didn't have to say sorry for the Oreo thing?" I say.

"Nah. Ms. Ansley never heard him say it," he says. "I wasn't about to snitch, so . . ."

"That's some bullshit," I say.

"Only reason he's always talking smack is because he knows he ain't real. I went to elementary with him. He used to call me Urkel all the time, even though his ass got straight A's, too. You know he lives in *Brighton*?"

"For real? That's basically Brookline."

"I'm saying! You know that spot Zanzibar? That, like, bookstore downtown?"

"The one that sells all that stuff from Africa?"

"Yeah, yo, his parents *own* that spot!"

"*What?* Kev's mom has like five masks from there. Those things are mad expensive. Kaleem must be looted."

The good news is that Mar's not in trouble. He's been acing his assignments and tests all year, so Ms. Ansley cuts him a deal. She keeps his conduct record clean, but she says if he has another incident he's going straight to the Barron Center, which means an automatic F in conduct, which means goodbye, Latin, and peace out, Harvard. In return

Mar promises to pass in a practice test and memorize twenty new vocabs a week.

I SIT NEXT to Mar on the bus—second row—every day now. I don't know if it's because I'm out of the White Bitch Bench or what, but at least for the time being Angel's stopped fucking with me. When we get off the bus, I ask Mar if he wants to come over. He says he's heading to the library on Centre Street to study, so I roll with him. Mar and the librarian must go back, because she greets him by name when we walk in. On our way to the desks at the back of the room, Mar keeps stopping and pointing to the shelves, saying, "This one's dope. You read this one?" and I keep nodding, even though I've only read one real book in my life: *Drive,* the autobiography of Larry Bird.

Eventually he takes a seat and pulls his Trapper Keeper, his test prep book, a wood pencil case, a neon sharpener, and four rubber-banded stacks of three-by-five cards out of his bag.

"You carry way too much shit around," I say. He's already going through his vocabs, so absorbed he doesn't even respond.

"Lemme see one of those stacks?" I say.

"You don't have your own?"

"I didn't know we were supposed to make cards."

"How else you gonna learn 'em?" He passes me one of the stacks, and the word on top is *jettison.* I flip the card and read the definition: to throw something out of an airplane.

"When would I ever say this shit in real life?"

"You know that ain't the point. Just memorize it," he

says. "Ms. Ansley says it's easier if you come up with tricks for each word. Like that one—*jettison*—it kinda sounds like Jetson, right? So you just gotta remember one of those Jetsons getting tossed out a spaceship."

My next card is *grotto*. It means small cave.

"Kinda sounds like ghetto," I say.

"Yeah. The ghetto's kinda like a small cave, too," says Mar.

"How?"

"You know what I mean," he says.

"Put it in a sentence."

He thinks for a second, grins, and says, "If I pass this test, I can climb out of the grotto."

AFTER STUDYING, MAR comes over to my crib. It's too cold for nasketball, so I suggest wrestling. I figure it'll be a good way to prep for real-world beef, in case Angel or Kaleem decides to start stepping again. The way I wrestle with Kev, there's only two real rules: no dick jabs, and you have to stop when the losing guy, usually me, says, "You're the master!" But it turns out Mar's not down to wrestle. He even admits he's never been in a real fight. I don't believe him.

"Then how come you stepped so hard to Kaleem?"

"That's the whole trick with dudes like Kaleem," he says. "Step like a maniac and get 'em shook. Then you don't even need to fight."

"What happens if someone, like, actually steals on you?"

"Hasn't happened yet," he says. "Most dudes are bitches."

"But, like, why risk it?" I say. I've punched myself in the face before to see what it felt like.

"You gotta step sometimes. Like, down at Shaw? You don't step at least some of the time? You're *done*."

So instead of fighting, we practice stepping. Really, we just do WWF intros. First we get our costumes together. Benno has this treasure chest full of crap Ma hauled home from Morgie's over the years: rubber biceps and abs, a Pippi Longstocking wig, a Viking helmet with a broken horn, a limp lightsaber, a Santa coat with a sewn-in stomach, gold pirate pants, a sequined juggler vest, and tons of other stuff Kev clowns on.

I throw on a gray mechanic's onesie that once belonged to a dude named Chet, cut the brim off a NEW YEAR'S EVE 1989 visor and tape it to the back of my neck, face-paint some gills on my cheeks, pop in plastic vampire teeth, and call myself the Great White Green. I've always sweated great white sharks, not just because they can conquer any animal in the kingdom but because they're the only thing I know how to draw. Mar finds a glow-in-the-dark alien mask and a ninja hood and calls himself the Ninjalien. We wait in the hallway behind the closed front door. Benno sets up the camera outside, holds a cymbal from a string, and smacks it with a hammer so we know he's rolling. I press play on my boom box—my intro song is Geto Boys' "Mind of a Lunatic"—bound out of the door, jump up and down, make muscles, do a swim-circle dance around the porch, and move toward the camera, chomp-motioning with my arms. In a hyped-up announcer voice, I shout, "At five four, one hundred and eight pounds, from Boston, Massachusetts, representing the King School, the undefeated, undisputed, undiluted . . . *Great White Green!*" I do a jump-kick off the bottom two stairs of my stoop, right into the camera.

Then Mar comes out and does a strange swirling ninja dance to Guns N' Roses' "Sweet Child O' Mine," which he found in Benno's cassette collection. He spin-jumps off the stoop, and in a Texas accent (for some reason, Mar always does a cowboy voice when he mimics white dudes) he announces, "At fahv two, one hundred 'n one pounds a pure muscle, hailin' from the home of the sixtain-tahm champyun Bawston Celtics, the inconceivable, unbuhlievable, unbeatable *Ninnnjaaalien!*"

Benno hooks the camera up to our thirteen-incher so we can watch the recordings. He presses play and I scramble to block the screen with my body. Benno reused an old tape and rewound too far.

"Fast-forward it!" I say.

"Hold up," Mar says. "I wanna see that."

"It's nothing," I say. It's footage Benno took from my community theater group's performance of *Annie Get Your Gun*. The sound blares from the shitty little speaker and Mar sings along to it: "Anything you can do, I can do better."

"You actually know this song?" I say.

"Move your ass," Mar says, shoving me aside. "Who's that singing?"

It's this rich white blondie named Meghan, who gets the main part in every single show.

"You know her?" Mar asks.

"Not really."

"She's mad cute."

I'm a little surprised to hear Mar say this. I'd never go with a white girl, let alone admit one was cute. It's not just because of the pact with Kev, either. At this point, I really only like Latinas and black shorties. Maybe it's the force talking, but I can't help it. White girls are way too corny.

"You in this play or what?" Mar says.

"I'm just in the chorus."

"Anybody can try out?"

"I mean, it's a musical theater group. You gotta join first."

"It costs money?"

"Think so. My moms signed me up."

"How old is she?"

"Meghan? Like a year older than us."

"She go to Latin or something?"

I nod, and I can tell from the jump in his eyelids that this makes him want to go to Latin even more.

We move on to the wrestling footage. The feed gets blurry and Benno whacks the side of the box.

"If your parents really went to Harvard, how come they got this budget-ass TV?" Mar says.

"You want me to prove it?" I say. I run to the recycling bin and pull out this thick red booklet that came in the mail the other day. I show Mar the cover, which says *Harvard-Radcliffe Class of 1972 Twentieth Anniversary Report,* and flip to Ma's page. She never sent in her update pic, so it just shows her college yearbook photo.

"Elizabeth Smith?" Mar says.

"She kept her last name," I say. I'd way rather my parents had given me Smith instead of Greenfeld, but Ma said she didn't want us to have a boring WASP name.

"She looked way different back then," Mar says. She has long brown hair in the picture; now it's short, grayish, and spiky, like every other mom in Jamaica Plain.

"Let's see your pops's page," Mar says.

"Actually, my pops didn't graduate," I say.

"I thought you said both of 'em went to Harvard."

"They did. He just didn't graduate."

"How you gonna drop out of Harvard?"

"I think because of Vietnam," I say.

I can never get the full story, because there's nothing Pops hates talking about more than Harvard. All I know, I know from my grandfather. He lives nearby and comes over for dinner all the time. He's constantly shitting on Pops for dropping out—and on Ma, too. Ma's a year older than Pops, and after she graduated she bounced to Vermont to live with all these hippies on a farm. When Pops left Harvard during his senior year, he hitchhiked out there to join her. My grandfather says she brainwashed him.

Mar leaves and I sit with the red booklet for a while. Daniel Showalter, CMO. William Washington, Jr., CFO. Miles Strand, COO. Archibald Mather III, CEO. Melissa Farnsworth, Executive VP. Ma's the only community organizer listed. There are a decent number of doctors and lawyers, some college professors (no *community* college professors, like Pops), a couple scientists, but mostly I see C-dash-Os. And according to the survey at the back of the book, a lot of them work for Fortune 500 companies, too. I don't even know what the Fortune 500 is, but it sounds prestigious as fuck, and I want in.

At dinner, I ask my parents to point out who they know in the booklet. I figure I may try to purr at one of these fat cats for a job hookup someday. As Ms. Ansley says, "You want to make it in this world? I got four words for you: It's the contacts, stupid." Pops flips through and makes a bunch of weird sounds with his throat.

"*Stan Rivers* works for Goldman Sachs?"

Ma grabs the book and says, "No way."

"Guy was the goddamned VP of SDS!"

"Is Goldman Sachs in the Fortune 500?" I ask.

"Who cares?" says Pops.

"I care. The study in the back says the median salary of the class of '72 is four hundred K. How much you think Stan Rivers makes?"

Pops looks at the study and starts making choking noises. "This is sick. Four hundred *thousand* dollars? Who *needs* that kind of money?"

"It's not that much," I say. "I'm trying to make at least a mil."

"Where's he getting this stuff?" Pops says to Ma. Most dads would be happy to hear their son wants to go to Harvard and get rich. Most dads would say, *Where's he getting this stuff?* about Benno, who brought a wad of gray clay to dinner. He's making a sculpture of an oversized nose.

"Recognize this guy?" Ma says to me. She's pointing to the only black face on the page, a guy named Ronald Taylor.

"One of the few who stuck to his guns," Pops says.

Like Ma, Ronald Taylor doesn't have an updated pic or a job description.

"Is he some kind of celebrity?" I ask.

Ma laughs.

"You don't recognize him?" she says. "That's your city councilor."

"That's *Skip* Taylor?" I ask. My parents sweat Skip Taylor. He's the one whose sign has been on our lawn for months. We've been to a thousand rallies he's spoken at, and my parents go door-to-door for him every time he runs for reelection. Skip's bald and has a long gray beard, but in his picture he's got short wavy hair combed off to the side. I had no idea he went to Harvard.

"That's how you know him?" I say.

"Actually, we barely knew him in college. We became friends later, through organizing work," says Ma. "He kept to himself back then. The movement wasn't really his thing."

"He might be the only guy we know who got *more* radical after Harvard," adds Pops.

A COUPLE DAYS later, more Harvard mail comes. Checking the mail is my shit. It's like cracking packs or bashing geodes: almost all duds, but if you're lucky, you might pull a life-changer. My dream mail is a giant check from Ed McMahon or a love letter from a fly admirer, but I'll happily settle for a cash-stuffed card from distant relations. Today there's only two items of interest: an L.L.Bean catalog, because of the sports bra section, and an invite to a Harvard '72 tailgate buffet brunch.

My first thought: unlimited grub, made by Harv. This is

gonna be way better than grilled cheese. I'm thinking iced shrimp, caviar, and giant juicy steaks. My second thought: loads of millionaires, maybe even a few billionaires. Even if I don't get to press flesh with a CEO, I'm bound to catch some kingpin vibes just hanging around.

When my parents get home, I beg for a family trip to the tailgate. Pops, predictably, says no.

"Please?" I say. "It's all-you-can-eat."

"I only go to one sporting event a year."

He means the Latin-English game. English High—the school down the block from me, right where I got jacked—is the second-oldest school in Boston. Their football rivalry with Latin is a billion years old—the oldest in the country (just like everything else in crusty-ass Boston). Pops roots for English because he was a guidance counselor there for ten years, before he moved on to work at the community college. Even though English is now one of the worst high schools in the city, Pops still rocks his beat-up Bulldogs hoodie.

"You don't have to come," I say. "How 'bout I go with Ma?"

Ma seems open to it.

"I already told Marlon about it," I lie. "He's really into Harvard. He was all excited."

Ma tilts her head at Pops.

"You guys want to spend your Saturday standing around in the mud?" he says. "Go right ahead."

I'VE NEVER BEEN around so many rich people in my life. Actually, I've never been around any rich people before

today, unless you count Kev's mom. And it's not like she's a
CEO; she's a not-for-profit sucker like all my parents'
friends. Only reason she's semi-looted is because Kev's grand-
parents hooked her up when they died. Kev got some cash
from them, too. I'm not inheriting squat from my cheap-ass
grandfather. I'm gonna have to hustle for every dollar on my
own.

Ma starts yapping with the only other semi-hippie-
looking lady there, and me and Mar march over to the buffet. It's pretty disappointing. No shrimp or steaks, just cold,
cratered burgers, wrinkled dogs, and mac salad. Basically
classed-up King grub. Still, anytime I see a smorgasbord, I
load up like it's the last chance I'll ever get. I eat as quickly
as possible, refill, and repeat, till I'm well past the point of
pain.

Mar grabs two Frescas and fills his plate with chips and
cookies.

"Can't believe you like Fresca," I say.

"Fresca's my shit," he says. "Mad crisp."

There's a parking lot next to our tent, so me and Mar
play My Car No Copy. It's an old bus game, where you
point to a phat whip and say "My car, no copy" as fast as
you can. Whoever says it first wins lifetime exclusive rights
to the car.

"Mycanocopy!" I shout, pointing to a glossy Porsche.

"Mycanocopy!" Mar yells, spotting an old-school
Caddy.

"*What* are they saying?" a woman near us whispers, too
loud.

Her husband shrugs.

"Are they *with* anyone?" she says.

We walk back to the food and I can't help scoping the can situation. It's pretty bleak because there's a servant dude who keeps zipping around the room with a big trash bag, clearing the tables.

"You're not separating?" I ask him.

"Huh?"

"The cans from the trash?" I say, and he tells me to buzz off with his eyes.

"You better not be getting ideas," Mar says.

I can't get Ma to stop yapping with her homey, so me and Mar bounce from the tent and start wandering around the rest of the tailgate. The field where the students are partying is a whole different world from the geezer alum area. Naughty by Nature is blasting from speakers, shirtless dudes in snow hats are grinding on shorties, and everybody's slamming back beers and tossing empties in the mud. It's an aluminum mother lode. The only issue is transport. It's not like I brought Benno's wagon with me, and I can't find any bags around that aren't already full of trash and yack. I tell Mar I'll be right back and run over to the '72 tent. I spot a Harvard flag lying in the mud next to one of the tables and drag it back over to the student section.

"Oh *hell* no," says Mar when I start kicking cans onto the flag.

"There's gotta be like five hundred cans here," I say.

"Don't play. There's mad po around," says Mar.

"Canning's not a crime."

"What you doing with that flag?"

"We're not gonna, like, *take* it," I say. "We'll grab the

cans, load 'em in the van, and then bring it back here where we found it."

"We're gonna look shady," says Mar.

"Just wait here while I collect, and make sure no one takes our shit."

Nearby, a big crowd circles around a pigtailed redhead with an *H* painted on her forehead. She's barely taller than I am and looks like a freshman in high school.

"Down in one! Down in one!" two stubbly cave-dudes shout at her. One of them takes a beer, shakes it up, stabs a key into it, and shoves the spraying can into the redhead's mouth. She takes a short gulp and spews the rest out into the mud.

"Boo!" Flintstone shouts. "Do-*over*. Do-*over*!"

"I can't," she says, snot, spit, and beer mixing on her face. I grab the discarded can and bring it back to the pile.

"Chug-a-lug! Chug-a-lug!" cry the apes.

Once I've got a decent pile, I try to tie up the flag's corners and turn it into a satchel. Half the cans fall out. We're gonna need to make more than one run to the Whale. I head back to the alum tent to get the keys from Ma, but she's not there. So I ask Mar to hold the hobo sack while I look for her.

"You're starting to piss me off," he says.

"I'll split the coin with you," I say. "Fifty-fifty."

Mar sighs, looks over his shoulders, and grabs the load.

I scan the grounds twice over but still can't find Ma. I decide to go back and check on Mar. When I return to the alum tent, there's a cop talking to him. The whisperer from before is standing nearby, watching with her arms crossed.

I jog over to the cop and tell him Mar's with me. If he was a real cop, I'd be way too shook to say something, but I'll step to a rent-a-cop any day.

"Oh yeah?" he says. "And who're *you*?"

"Alumni. I mean, my parents. My mom."

"Point 'er out to me," he says.

"She was here a second ago," I say. "I don't know where she went."

"Sure ya don't," he says. "Where you kids from?"

"Jamaica Plain," I say.

"Oh yah? I was born in J.P. Anyway, whattaya guys doin' heah? This is a *private* pahty."

"Officer," I say, "I'm not lying. My mom's here somewhere."

"Ya just makin' it harder on yahself. I don't like liahs. I was a kid once, ya know. I did plenty a stupid things when I was your age and I can let stupid go. Lyin's another story."

"Officer, I swear," I say. "She'll be back in a minute."

"Open the flag," demands Renty.

Mar lets go of the corners and the cans cascade out. The whole tent gets quiet, and then I see Ma walking toward us.

"What's going on here?" she says to the cop, who turns to the whisperer.

"These . . . kids . . . have been acting strangely all afternoon," the whisperer says. Her husband looks down and visors his face with his hand.

"These are *my* kids," Ma says.

Ma's never shook. When she was a kid, she put a bar of soap behind her ear and pierced herself with a sewing needle. She'll check the shit out of drivers if they don't respect the crosswalk. She even shouted off a mugger once. Pops was pissed, told her she was crazy and that she should give them everything next time. I must've gotten his genes.

"Well, your *kids* have been digging through our garbage," the woman says.

"Well, Harvard should be recycling on its own. As far as I can tell, they're doing a service to Harvard—and our planet," says Ma.

"I don't think taking other people's property counts as 'service,'" says the whisperer, eyeing the flag.

Mar hangs his head and stares into the mud. I dragged him into this stupid situation.

"Honey," says the whisperer's husband, "why don't you let it go?"

"That's my flag," Ma freestyles, "and they can do whatever they damn please with it."

"Well," says the woman. "It's pretty clear where your son gets his manners from."

"It's people like you," says Ma, "who remind me how much I fucking hate this place."

Mar turns to me, giant-eyed. Even he can't help but crack a smile now. I scoop up our haul and swing the sack over my shoulder, and we walk back to the Whale, triumphant, clattering, rich.

CHAPTER 4

Penned

Not only does Mar still want to go to Harvard, he's more determined than ever, like he wants to prove everyone under that tent wrong. He's been acting mad serious—superstitious, too. He stopped swearing and stepping on cracks, and he has this whole routine every time we go to the library. He doesn't even browse the shelves anymore, just goes right to the table in the back, sharpens three pencils, lines up his homework, card stacks, and prep book in a neat row, and starts in on the studying. Even if he finishes early, he won't leave and keeps going through his stacks until the clock strikes four. Anytime I suggest doing anything other than going directly to my house after the library, he refuses, and once we're there he always wants to do the exact same thing. First we play best-of-three H-O-R-S-E on the nasketball-level hoop. The winner gets to "own" the Bird-Magic card for the day. After H-O-R-S-E, we watch C's tapes with Benno till six, and then Mar bounces.

The routine seems to be working for Mar, because his practice scores keep going up. Mine are barely budging, and I'm starting to get shook about what might happen to me if

I don't get into Latin. I keep thinking about what Jabrina said on our Harvard tour—the way she made it seem like it was either Latin, upstate, or underground. And these little things keep happening that make the stress even worse. The other day Ms. Ansley was absent and our sour old sub, Mr. Timkins, showed us a documentary called *Scared Straight!* about a bunch of delinquents who take a field trip to jail. I guess he didn't realize we were the advanced class, because when he introduced it, he said, "For all you wise alecks who think it's all fun and games, I hope this serves as a wake-up bell." At one point in the video, a giant, tank-topped inmate barked like a pit bull as the juveniles passed his cell, and two of them got startled and clutched each other like *Scooby-Doo* characters. Some of the kids in our class laughed. Mar didn't and neither did I.

Today our janitor Rawlins stops by our lunch table to chat Celtics. We're peeping *Sports Illustrated*—there's a big article about Reggie Lewis—and Rawlins asks if he can check it out. When I pass him the magazine, I notice one of his fingernails is all wrinkly and mangled.

"You bite your nails?"

I ask because I've been biting mine since second grade. At this point all of my nails are ragged stumps, but one is way worse than the others: my right pointer. I've gone at that thing so hard, it's not even a nail anymore. Some other semisoft mutant flesh grew back where the nail was supposed to be. It hurts whenever it gets pressed, so basically, anytime someone gives me some love, I writhe inside.

"Nah," says Rawlins, chuckling. "You don't wanna know how I got this."

"Biting's how mine got like this," I say, showing him my pointer.

"Dag, Dave," he says. "You did that to yo'*self*?"

"Most people think I jammed it in a car door," I say. "That's what happened to yours?"

"Nah," he says, smiling. "To be honest with you, I got this in the pen."

"You mean, like . . ."

"The penitentiary," he says without glancing up from the magazine.

After a few long seconds, he says, "Some people mind talkin' 'bout it, but I don't. I did my time and that's all behind me now."

I want to ask him how his finger got like that. Did someone shiv it off in a brawl? Did he try to scratch his way out of his cell? I know that's not a move, so instead I ask, "What'd you go in for?"

Mar's nose curls, like I just ripped record-book wind.

"You know you shouldn't be askin' people that, right?" Rawlins says.

"My bad," I say.

"It's aight. You didn't know. Anyway, like I said, I did my time. So I don't even mind tellin' y'all. Same thing pretty much everybody else in for: slingin'."

He flips the page, pauses on a Drakkar ad, and sniffs the fold-out sample.

"You wanna know somethin' funny? I used to buy these off other dudes in the pen. Not the magazine—just the ripped-out ad. Sounds funny, right, but when you inside, you got nothin' to do all day but sit on your butt and think, and it'd drive you crazy if you didn't find somethin' to distract you. So I'd save up just to buy one of these sample cologne strips. And I'd rub it on my upper lip and just sit there for hours, smelling my lip, you know what I'm saying?"

We nod uneasily.

After Rawlins moves on, Kev takes a thick wad of ones and fives out of his pocket and says, "Who wants tacos? Shit's on me."

"You get a raise from your mom?" I ask.

"Nah," he says. "Been hustling."

"Babysitting?" I ask.

"Nope."

"Cat-feeding?"

"Fuck no," he says. He looks over his shoulder, slowly turns back to me, and grins. "Slingin'."

Chronic? I'm pretty sure he's started doing it with Simon.

"Come over after school," he says. "I'll show y'all."

"I DON'T EVEN wanna know what he's up to," Mar whispers to me on the bus ride home.

"You're not, like, curious?" I say.

"I'm not trying to accessorize," he says. "I thought you were done with Kevin anyway."

"I am," I say. "We'll see what's up, grab some snacks, and bounce."

"Eff that," he says. "I'm not trying to sniff magazines. I'm going to the library."

"We'll go right after," I say. "Kev's mom usually has Fresca in the fridge."

Mar sucks his teeth and says, "Five minutes."

On our way to Kev's, me and Mar get back into this debate we've been having.

"Whales don't even have teeth," I say.

"Oh my *goodness*," he says. "They got mad teeth!"

"Not the ones I saw. Just had long liney bones under their lips."

Kev gets bored right away, puts on his headphones, and walks ahead of us.

"I'd be down to go on a whale watch," Mar says. "Sounds mad fun."

"Nah, it got old quick. Just whale, ocean, whale, ocean. I kept hoping some sharks would come and feast on one of 'em."

"You sick sometimes, Green. Besides, sharks can't mess with whales."

"What's a whale gonna do? Head-butt a shark? Swallow it? The shark would just bite its way out the belly."

"Whales don't even need to head-butt. They can just do their thing. They're too big to mess with. Nothing steps to whales."

When we get to Kev's, Simon's waiting on his porch, smoking a Newport.

"I thought Latin didn't get out for another hour," I say.

"I *cut*, Corky," says Simon.

Simon passes the cig to Kev. He takes a drag and tries to blow a smoke ring. It comes out like a limp lasso.

"What'd you bring Dave for?" Simon says. "You know he's gonna snitch."

"I don't snitch," I say.

We head up the stairs toward Kev's bedroom. This is the first time Mar's seen the rest of Kev's crib. I can tell Kev's trying to rush us through the living room, just like I did when Mar came to my house for the first time. There's stuff from Kaleem's family's store, Zanzibar, all over the place, including a five-foot ebony statue of a pregnant woman. She has a huge belly button and two long pointy tits aimed out of her like Scud missiles.

Kev boots up his computer. His dad does high-tech shit for work, so Kev always gets the latest, hottest PC compatibles.

"You heard of bulletin boards?" Kev asks Mar, not waiting for an answer. "Peep this."

The computer screeches and gurgles like a dying eagle.

"We're on," Kev says.

He clicks on "pamela anderson." The screen loads from the top, line by line, and after an eternal minute, we get a glimpse of gold: wisps of blond hair. A thousand trickling pixels later, some bronze: a sliver of forehead.

Mar asks where the bathroom is and I point over my shoulder, eyes locked to the screen. The slowness is agony, like watching honey drip down the bear bottle. Finally, I see shoulder. There's no strap.

"Is she gonna be, like, actually . . . ," I say.

"Butt-fuckin' naked," says Kev. "Titties, pussy hair. Todo."

I cross my legs as casually as I can.

"You're getting wood already?" says Simon. "We haven't seen shit."

"I'm the only one allowed to nut in this house," says Kev.

Two breast tops slowly emerge, like rising suns.

"So you can just . . . all of this is, like, *free*?" I say.

"It's the Internet, stupid," says Simon. "There's a billion more titties. Stuff way better than titties—open pussies, dicks in pussies . . ."

"I'm good with titties for now," I say.

It wasn't a joke, but they both roll.

"Here comes the nipple," says Simon. "Watch out, yo. Dave's about to shoot some sap."

I've never seen a real nipple, unless you count those two-second flashes in R-rated comedies. Or the time I accidentally walked in on Ma getting out of the shower, but I quickly Control-Alt-Deleted that from my memory. The screen loads all the way to the hay strip between Pam's legs, but I'm still focused on the top half.

Breasts. Not freakish wood spear tits but soft, squeezable roundies—*real* ones. I can already tell I'm addicted for life. I want to smear my face across the screen.

"Click on the bubble-bath one real quick?" I ask.

"Chill out, Hornelius," says Simon. "We got business to do."

Kev prints five copies. They're black and white and the ink's running low, which makes it look like you're seeing her through blinds.

"I told you to re-up the fuckin' bubble jet," Simon says.

This is their hustle: slinging printouts to Latin kids for a dollar a pop. Kev's the one with the Internet hookup, so he gets half of the haul. Simon claims they each made fifty last week. That's a new Machine in two weeks.

"Let's load some harder shit," says Simon.

"I gotta be out," Mar says from the hall.

I'm actually relieved. I'm not down for the triple X.

"Yo, *Green*," Mar says. "I gotta do that practice test. You comin' or what?"

"Before you bounce, you wanna cop?" Simon asks me. "Since they came out chopped, I could go two-for-one on these Pam pics."

"I'm straight," I say. "I don't feel white shorties."

"I could pull up some white dudes for you," Simon says.

"Nah, Dave likes girls," Kev says. "Just ones with mustaches."

"Carmen doesn't have a 'stache," I say.

"You know she has a 'stache," says Kev. "Dresses like a librarian, too."

"I'm out," Mar calls from the hallway.

I follow him outside and say, "Never seen a porno before. That was kinda . . ."

"You shouldn't be peeping that stuff."

I was about to say *kinda dope*.

"I didn't know that's what they were up to," I say.

"You knew they weren't selling carnations," he says. "You're Christian, right?"

I was afraid he'd eventually ask. Technically, I'm half atheist, half secular Jew. Ma was raised Christian, but she can't stand her parents because they're crazies who kicked her brother out of the house when they found out he liked dudes. Ma never talks to them, and I've only seen them like twice in my life. The only thing we really do that's Christian is Christmas, because me and Benno forced it on my parents. We don't do much on the Jew side, either. Pops hates religion even more than Ma.

Anyway, I'd definitely *rather* be Christian than Jew. I mean, pretty much everyone at the King rocks a cross—everyone at the Trotter did, too. Whenever people asked me if I was Christian, I just nodded and left it at that. Being white was enough drama already.

"Yup," I say to Mar.

"My youth pastor says porno's the devil's bait. He said once you bite, you could get reeled right in, and before you know it something happens to you—like, before you get a chance to repent and stuff—and you wake up in *hell*. And you know the worst thing about hell, right? You can't get out—*ever*—and the devil pokes you with a hot rod, in your ears, your eyes, up your nose, and down *there*, too."

"Damn."

"What church you go to?"

"St. Thomas?" I say. It's the name of Kev's church, the only one I can think of off the top of the dome. Once, I tagged along with him on Easter.

"They got food there?" asks Mar.

"Just those wafers," I say. At Kev's church, the priest was popping snacks in people's mouths and I wanted to see what they tasted like, so I got up in line and stuck my tongue out like everyone else. The wafer was pretty wack—like a saltine minus the salt—and I didn't think anything of it. But once church got out, Kev told me it was the body of Jesus, that only confirmed Christians were allowed to eat it and I'd probably end up in hell unless I converted. So I asked my parents if I could convert and they didn't let me go back to Kev's church. I eventually stopped stressing about hell, at least until now. I'm not trying to get dick-pokered for eternity.

"At my church, after services, we do this big lunch in the basement," Mar says. "My grandma usually cooks up her bomb mac and cheese. From scratch, too—none of that powdered bull."

"Word?"

"You wanna come through sometime?"

"To your church?"

"You could come this Sunday if you want."

"I'm down."

"You gotta wear a suit, though," he says. "Not, like, a Machine suit either. Like, a actual suit."

PROBLEM IS, I don't own a suit. I've never rocked one in my life. Even at Morgie's, a suit would set me back at least a twenty, and that's a lot of empties to snag. Pops owns a raggedy brown suit that he wears a couple times a year, when he's forced to, for conferences. I try it on and it's even baggier on me than the Machine was. I'm kind of feeling the look. When Pops gets home, I ask if I can borrow it.

"What could you possibly need a suit for?"

"Church," I say. I figure I may as well be straight up. He'll be down when I tell him Mar invited me.

Pops laughs. "This again?"

"Not Kev's—Marlon's. I already told Marlon I could go."

"Well, tell him you can't make it."

"How come?"

"Because you're Jewish—that's how come."

"I thought we were atheists."

"We're secular."

"So what does it matter if I go to church?"

"Because Jews don't go to church."

"Even secular ones?"

"Especially secular ones!"

"Well, what if I don't want to be secular—*or* Jewish?"

"You don't want to be secular? No one's stopping you. But the Jewish thing? You're stuck with it."

"Can't I just go and watch?"

"Look," he says. "Why don't you ask him if you can go another time? Cramps is coming over for dinner Sunday. He'd flip if he found out you were coming from church."

CRAMPS IS MY grumpy-ass grandfather. When I was little, I called him Cramps instead of Gramps by accident and he thought it was hilarious, so the name stuck. Cramps has two modes: joking or not at all joking. One second we're trading puns or doing our favorite comedy scenes (he's obsessed with comedies, everything from the Marx Brothers to *Bill and Ted*). The next he's screaming in my face about the Holocaust and how I need to study harder. He's been sweating me nonstop about test prep, especially since I made the mistake of telling him how Latin's a feeder school for Harvard. Now he wants me to go there to make up for Pops dropping out.

Cramps shows up to dinner on Sunday in his usual outfit: tight blue sweatpants and a T-shirt with one of his own catchphrases printed on it. He has about a dozen of them, which he gets from those carts at the mall. Today's says, HOW DOES IT LOOK LIKE I'M DOING? Cramps has muscular dystrophy, so he weighs about a hundred pounds and has the posture of a chimp. He grimaces as Pops lowers him into his chair, takes his hat off, mats his three remaining strands of hair over his liver-spotted head, and steadies his blood-shot blue eyes on me.

"So?" he says.

"Can we talk about something else?" I say.

"What else is there to talk about?"

"Dad, why don't you eat something?" says Pops.

"Not hungry," Cramps says. "I'll take a doggie bag."

He's always asking for doggie bags, always saving things *for later*. He flies all over the world for math conferences and has two trash bags full of plane snacks in his closet. We got him a cheesecake for his birthday once. He put it in the freezer and chipped away at it for a whole year.

Pretty much every wack thing that can happen to a human has hit Cramps, and he loves to remind us of it all: how he got his ass regularly whooped by his Nazi teachers, how he got booted from school even though he was the valedictorian, how he had to get on a boat by himself at fifteen while the rest of his family got left behind and holo-caused, how he had to work in a sweatshop to afford a single lousy kraut dog each night before he went back to the rat-slum apartment he shared with a zillion other sweaty Jews, how he had to fight in some mud pit in the Philippines and got deuced on by the Jew-haters in his battalion, even after he took a chunk of shrap in his shoulder, and how—

after all that—he came back, got his hustle on, got married, saw his son off to Harv, and just when it seemed like everything had finally panned out for him, my grandma suddenly died in an accident and Pops dropped out. By the time the MD diagnosis came, it was just the sour cherry on top of his suck sundae.

"So?" Cramps says. "How'd you do on the last practice test?"

"I haven't taken one since that last time you asked," I say.

"You don't have a lot of time left," he says. "This is serious stuff."

"I know."

"No, you *don't know*. This is serious stuff. If I hadn't studied my tuches off and aced my exams—"

"Dad," Pops interrupts. "He knows. He's heard it a thousand times."

"Let him hear it a thousand and one times. If I hadn't aced my exams, there wasn't a hot chance in hell I'd have gotten my visa. My parents—they applied for my sister, too, and only mine got approved, and you want to know why?"

"All right, Dad."

"Because she *didn't* ace her exams. Because she was out dancing and doing who knows what with her boyfriends while I was in my room, studying under a damned candle. And you know where she ended up? Not on a boat. On a train—to the *ghetto*."

"For Christ's sake," says Ma. "He's in sixth grade."

. . .

GROTTO. A SMALL CAVE. *If I pass this test, I can climb out of the grotto.*

I'm used to Cramps, but still: I'm starting to feel like everything *is* riding on this test. Pass and I'm on the golden road to Harvard. Choke and I'm on the rusty track to the grotto. Not only will I have two more years at the King, I'll have to go to a regular public high school, someplace like English, where they *really* don't like white boys.

After choking on another practice test, I finally go to Pops for help. He got a 1600 on his SATs, so I ask him to teach me the tricks. Instead, he goes over every single answer I got wrong and even some I got right, and gives me long-ass lectures about the concepts behind each question.

"This is why I didn't want to study with you," I say.

"You're gonna learn it better if you let me explain what it means."

"I just want the tricks."

"This isn't magic. It's math. There are *strategies*. You can memorize the formulas. You can eliminate the red herrings. But there aren't tricks. There are only tactics."

"Herring sucks," I say. You can always find a cloudy, onion-clogged jar in my fridge.

"Are you cracked? Herring's delicious."

"WHAT ARE THE tactics for reading faster?" I ask at our most recent session. After a couple weeks of studying with Pops, I've gotten better at math and vocab, but I'm still swiss at the reading section.

"Actually reading. Like, something other than the sports page. What are you reading in Ms. Ansley's class?"

"We just started *Tom Sawyer*."

"Nice! You liking it?"

"Can't get into it. Boring as hell."

"You're out of your mind. *Tom Sawyer*'s genius. We'll read some together tonight."

After dinner, Pops props a pillow up against me and Benno's bunk bed and starts reading it to us from the beginning. He gets all excited during the fence scene, where Tom fronts like he's having fun whitewashing his aunt's fence when really it's this swiss chore. Then all the other boys try to get down and he's like, nah, I got this, and that makes them fiend even harder. So he makes them *pay* to paint and he ends up with a stash of marbles, firecrackers, and other loot.

"What a great line," says Pops. He starts rereading the passage, slower. " 'He had discovered a great law of human action, without knowing it—namely, that in order to make a man or a boy covet a thing, it is only necessary to make the thing difficult to attain.' What do you make of that?"

"Just keep going," I say.

"No, this is good practice for the test."

"I don't know. I guess it's like my Bird card?" I say. "It's worth so much because there's so few of them floating around?"

"Mmm . . . I'd say it's more like Nikes," says Pops. "There's plenty of them, they're made for nothing, but Nike decides to charge an arm and two legs and all of a sudden everyone wants a pair."

I'm pretty sure I'd still want a new Machine even if it wasn't a hundred bills, but I see Pops's point. There's stuff people fiend for naturally—pornos, tacos, crack—and things people fiend for because they're actually rare. Pretty much everything else is worthless whitewash. But if you *sell* it right, you can *create* fiends. At first the idea thrills me. I see multiple paths to moat-lined mansions. But after Pops stops reading and Benno starts snoring, when still I'm up hours later and alone on the planet again, this *selling* stuff starts to mess with me. I'm dying for loot, but I don't want to sling the Bird, I don't want to hawk printouts, and I'm not really down to hustle fools. The more I think about it, those are the only real options: Sell what you love, sell poison, or con. You need to be kind of hard to sell. *Sell.* Say it in a whisper. It's got that snake sound. Something like the hiss of the force.

THE ONLY TIME I'm not stressed is when I'm peeping C's tapes with Mar after the library. We like watching the crowd shots almost as much as the actual games, and we have names for the old-school fans we see over and over, like Arlo, the drunk jumbo whose beer belly pops out while he's doing the Y on the YMCA dance; or Superfan, a pale, middle-aged guy with neatly parted black hair, who sits alone and wears his shiny green button-up C's jacket to every game. Superfan never gets emotional. He just stays in his seat, logging stats into his scorecard—even if we're up thirty with two minutes to go and everyone else has already filed out of the Garden—until the final buzzer blares.

When commercials come on, instead of fast-forwarding, we'll press mute and do voice-overs. The Rogaine ads are our shit. When the sad baldy looks in the mirror, we'll flail our arms and shout, in British accents, "Where oh where did my lovely hair go?" and then when the hair grows back mad fast, we'll explode in celebration, run around the room, and scream, "It's back! Yes! It's baaaaaaack! YESSSSS!!!!!! ROOO-GAAAAAAINE!" Benno films us doing it, and when we see our faces we roll mad hard, and just when I think we're finished rolling, Mar will let out a loud squawk and that'll make me roll even harder, and we'll roll together for minutes straight—just making eye contact will keep things going for another round—and we'll keep rolling till our abs hurt and the only way we can stop is turn our backs to each other. It's starting to hit me: Mar isn't just my best friend, he's my first. Up until now I had no idea just how lonely I'd been.

The second Mar bounces, the stress sets back in. Pops makes me go over my practice tests, Cramps calls to check in on my progress, and after lights-out I lie in bed for hours, staring at the fading comets on my ceiling. It's not just the test that's keeping me awake. Since seeing those Pam pics, I've been plagued by unrelenting wood. I lie there with a tent in my sweats, trying to think of Carmen, but Pam keeps edging her way back in. I swear, I don't dig white girls, but it's impossible to get Pam off the dome. It's not just the tits, either. There's something about the whole package—the bleach-blond hair, the blue eyes, the little bumpless nose—that's almost, I don't know, exotic.

Sometimes the wood lasts so long, it hurts. When I can't take it anymore, I start trying to bend it back down. I should've learned my lesson on that move the first time. When I ask Kev about how he deals with this kind of thing, he starts laughing and says, "Jerk it, jackass!" But to be honest, I don't even know how. I mean, I have my hand down there on the reg, but I assume that doesn't count. I don't even really want to know how. That stuff Mar said about the devil's bait is still bopping around in my brain. I'm worried enough about the grotto; I don't need to be stressing about hell, too.

And now I've got a new problem where the stress has started *causing* the wood—at least that's what it seems like. It'll happen out of nowhere, when I'm in class or in the halls. Something will remind me of the test—like the motivational posters in homeroom—and the wood will start up and I'll have to duck into a corner and do this tuck move where I strap it down with my undie elastic. Even after the tuck move there's usually a trace of tent, so I'll stretch my tee as far as I can for maximal overhang.

Kev doesn't have these problems. He can beat off whenever he wants, and besides, he's not stressed about the test at all. On the off chance that he somehow chokes, he knows he'll be straight at the King if he has to stay for a couple more years, because he made the basketball team. He dropped fifteen points in his first game, and now he gets fist bumps from seventh and eighth graders in the halls. He has a rally girl assigned to him, and she tapes candy and balloons to his locker. He even gets to sit at his teammate Kaleem's lunch table.

I'm watching Kev yuck it up with his new homey when

Rawlins rolls up to our table—just me, Mar, and Jimmy now—and says, "You still feedin' on that finger? Stressed, huh?"

"It's all good," I say. Of course, Rawlins makes me even more stressed. Every time I see him, I think about the pen.

Lying in bed that night, I'm still thinking about the inescapable. The test is a pen: There's no way I can scratch my way out of it. Getting older—that's a pen, too. When you're little, you play whatever sapien games you please; you don't give a fuck and no one else does, either. Then you turn my age and you can never be soft again. Your dick gets hard and you start fiending for ripe, round tits. You start acting hard, too, beefing to survive. You start jacking, conning, selling whitewash, even to your boys. You walk around with a hard look on your face and a hard dick in your Hanes, scowling and horny for the rest of your life.

CHAPTER 5

Tactics

It's a Saturday, three weeks till the test. Ma sees how anxious I am and suggests hitting the Aquarium to destress. I invite Mar to come with us. He's never been before and he's especially amped about the tank in the middle. I've gotten tired of that tank—usually, when I go to the Aquarium, I speed ahead to the gift shop to cop shark teeth—but Mar gets me hyped about it again. It's a gigantic, three-story tube, with a spiral concrete ramp that runs around it. The best thing about the ramp is that there are these dividers that chop up the tank glass into private window booths, and because it's mad dark in the Aquarium it feels like you have your own little movie theater.

There's a massive coral reef at the center of the tank, and a billion different fish, from tiny neon guppies to long, swooping sand sharks, circle around it endlessly. We find an empty booth and Mar bugs when a moray eel snakes out of a hole in the coral. He says, "Oh snap," when a geezer sea turtle glides by. He cracks up when a fish that looks like a pancake, with a skinny protruding beak and wide googly eyes on each side of its body, stalls in front of our glass. Then we walk up a flight and find a booth on the opposite end of the tube. A shark swims by and glares at us with its big black and white eye.

"How come nothing ever eats anything in there?" I say, even though this is the kind of question Ma never seems to have the answer to. "You'd think those sharks would get their grub on."

"Those are nurse sharks," says Mar. "They just eat algae and stuff. They're more like whales."

"How do you know?"

"Used to wanna be a marine biologist."

"Doubt marine biologists make much loot."

"I'm saying. I *used* to."

"You think that dude's a marine biologist?" I say, eyeing a diver who's hand-feeding a ray.

"Nah, he's like a rent-a-cop version. Real marine biologists don't mess around with tanks. They're out in the ocean, with *whales* and stuff. I saw this show on PBS about these French dudes who dive with blue whales. You know how big a blue whale is? Like a *hundred* feet—like a NBA court."

We watch the fish circle for a minute or so.

"You ever think about how bonk the ocean is?" Mar says, staring through the glass. "I don't know . . . like, a lot of the time I forget about it even being there, but then I'll be on the bus or doing groceries with my grandma or whatever, and outta nowhere I'll start thinking about it—how, if you look at a map, it's mostly blue. And then I'll start thinking about it more and I'll be like, this is *bonk*, there's this huge pile of water splashing all over the planet, and a lot of it's deeper than the biggest mountains go tall, and there's, like, blue whales swimming around in there, like, bodies big as towers just *swimming around* in there. That's bonk, right?"

"Sounds like maybe you still wanna be a marine biologist," says Ma, smiling.

"Maybe a little," Mar says.

"That's bonk, though, right?" he says a couple seconds later.

Benno nods. I'm tempted to bulge my eyes and say, *RO-gaine.*

Instead I say, "I feel you."

THAT NIGHT IN my room, I stare at the blue whale poster on my wall. Pops bought it for me a few years ago, at the Natural History Museum in New York. When he was a kid, he went to that museum all the time with Cramps, and his favorite part was the life-sized whale hanging from the ceiling. I'd heard so much about that whale, and when I saw it in real life I was a little disappointed. The way Pops hyped it, I assumed it was alive and in a tank. Still, I loved that poster because Pops loved that whale. Eventually I stopped feeling it and I almost tore it down. But now, with all the stress in my life, I'm glad I didn't. It's calming to have that chill-ass whale up there. I wouldn't mind being a whale— preying on nothing, letting the seaweed and plankton slip through my lips, a soft, untouchable king.

Hours later I'm hard as a harpoon, fending off midnight thoughts of breasts and tests, and I realize I'm conning myself with this whale talk. Pops gives mad loot to Greenpeace; I've seen enough of their mailings to know better. Whales aren't above shit. They're getting smoked to extinction. I start imagining my puny white ass at English. I see Rawlins wave his hideous fingernail at me and I feel my pulse going past the speed limit. I try to think of Carmen and her sweet loopy letters to calm down. Then Pam creeps back into the picture, but now she's in the bubble bath, behind prison bars. I try to force Carmen back in and now I'm trying with Jesus, too. Carmen and Jesus at their desks, practicing cursive. But the vile shit keeps worming its way back in, and I guess my hand has been moving down there this whole time without me even realizing it, because, all of a sudden, my whole body tenses up and my legs go straight as a mummy and my heart beats so hard I think it's an attack, but then a bolt flashes through me and flashes again and mini-flashes a couple more times and then I feel more relaxed than I can remember in my whole life. My pajamas are wet, but I'm too chill to care. I'm floating. For a few seconds, I don't need anything, fear anything, *think* anything. This is the best part, even better than the explosion—the paradise of no thought.

Now THAT I'VE discovered the tactic, I can't stop. I'm back at it that night, and the next morning. I'm at it all week. Some people cope with cologne on the upper lip; I escape with a palmful of Jergens. The problem is what happens a minute or so later, after the thought-free feeling wears off. That's when the guilt sets in. Covered in my crime, I start thinking about where I'm headed if I don't stop. Hell—the permanent pen.

I didn't use to stress that much about hell—didn't need

to. I barely dabbled in evil, and when I did, it was usually small stuff, like dismembering daddy longlegs. When I messed up, I'd pray out an apology to G-dash, not knowing if he was Jewish or Christian, just knowing he was up there, heated. I always felt like he eventually forgave me and moved on. But this is different—the tactics are a big-league sin—and I'm not sure if my homemade G-dash is legit enough to get me out of hell. I've tried asking Jesus to pardon me, but this just makes me feel worse. A fake Christian can go to hell just for eating a wafer. So I assume a fake Christian, especially a masturbating Jewish one, isn't supposed to ask Jesus for favors. I wish I could just convert, clear up all this confusion, and roll to Mar's church.

MAR COMES OVER after the library as usual. Even though it's a Friday, we're both stressed because the test is a week away. Mar wants to relax with his C's tapes, but before he pops one in, I turn to this local access show I've been watching lately. It makes me feel a little cleaner after tactics, and I figure Mar might like it, too. It's hosted by this guy Reverend McGee and a younger dude named Bobby, who just amens everything the Reverend says. The Reverend always wears a red suit with a black tie, and Bobby always wears a black suit with a red tie. I'm not sure if they're doing it on purpose, or if, like Pops, they each only own one suit. They sit behind this slim wood table, and the background is just a white wall, which is totally empty except for a small cross hanging in the corner, sort of crookedly. The only prop on the desk is a Bible, which the Reverend constantly picks up and waves around.

"The other night I was up late," the Reverend says. "And sometimes, when I'm up late, against my better judgment, I end up watching one of those late-night trash talk shows. Now, normally I try not to spend a lot of time watching television. And that may seem funny, given my role as a television personality. But the truth is, the Bible keeps me busy most days—the Good Book keeps me *plenty* entertained!"

"Amen," says Bobby.

"Give me John 3:16 *any day* over Johnny Carson."

"Preach it!" says Bobby.

"Yo, put on the C's," says Mar.

"I like these dudes," I say. "They're inspiring."

"Man, why don't you just come to my church?"

"I told you, my pops said I had to study. I definitely would if I could. Let's just watch for a couple more minutes."

"I'm up the other night," says the Reverend, "thinking about . . . what we been going through as a community. And I turn to one of those programs, seeking some kind of mental relief. The host brings on a man with all kinds of exotic and dangerous animals: snakes, big reptilian monstrosities, and other things you'd be crazy to go near. The zookeeper stays onstage, and the next guest, a *supposed* stand-up comedian, comes out, too. And once I hear that sorry excuse for a comedian open his mouth, I start to wonder whether *he* isn't the most dangerous animal on the stage. This man—and I suppose it doesn't matter, but he's a white man—opens his act by asking the crowd . . ."

Reverend McGee closes his eyes and takes a deep breath.

"Tell it, Reverend," says Bobby.

"All right, I'll tell it. 'What,' the comedian asked, 'is the most *confusing* holiday in the ghetto?' And the crowd went silent and he said—and it pains me to repeat this—'Father's Day.' "

Bobby shakes his head in disbelief.

"I seen enough of this," Mar says.

"You're not feeling this?" I say.

"I already got a pastor. I don't need no TV preachers."

"Two more minutes."

"I turned off the program and lay there in the dark, next to my wife," the Reverend continues. "What bothered me more than anything—even though this so-called comedian had no right to stand up there and denigrate the so-called ghetto—is that his words rang true."

Bobby looks a little surprised.

"But I'll tell you what. I haven't given up hope. I'm not despairing!"

"Okay."

"I'm not gonna let that funnyman have the last laugh!"

"Amen!"

"I know in my heart that the next generation of young men from this community"—he looks over at Bobby—"is gonna be the *greatest* generation of young black men this city's ever seen."

"Man, I'm trying to relax," says Mar. "Throw on a C's tape already!"

We settle on Game Six of the 1986 finals, one of Larry's greatest playoff performances. We watch for a while, rooting along as Larry inches toward his triple-double, and then the phone rings. Ma picks up in the kitchen, talks to someone for a few minutes, and walks over to us.

"That was your grandmother," Ma says to Mar.

"Something going on?" Mar asks, looking anxious.

"How would you like to sleep over tonight?" Ma says.

"She said I could?"

I've asked Mar to sleep over a few times. He always said he couldn't and I figured it was because his grandma thought I was some kind of cracked can-bum.

"She did," says Ma.

"Okay," says Mar.

I'm amped to have Mar stay over, but the timing's not ideal. Cramps is coming for dinner, which means there's at least a fifty percent chance we're gonna hear about the Holocaust.

An hour or so later, we're at the dinner table and Pops walks in with Cramps, who's hunched at a hundred-degree angle. His MD has gotten so bad he can barely walk or sit up, and he refuses to rock a wheelchair like a sensible geezer. He cranks himself upward to greet Mar, and his T-shirt reads, MY GOLDEN YEARS ARE PYRITE.

"That's funny," says Mar. "Fool's gold."

"Smart kid," says Cramps.

"I know what pyrite is," I say.

I used to be obsessed with pyrite. The Museum of Science was my *spot*, even more than the Aquarium, because its gift shop had the dopest souvenirs: 3-D dino puzzles, trilobite fossils, astronaut ice cream, and a massive bin of rocks and gems. Pyrite was the most expensive-looking rock in that pile, and at fifty cents per, it felt like a sick bargain. I stacked over thirty pieces. My goal was to get enough to fill a tank and then dive like Scrooge McDuck into my giant, glittering pool. But, one day, Cramps quizzed me about what I was learning from the exhibits and ruined everything. I told him the truth—that I didn't really care about the exhibits, that what I really cared about was copping pyrite. He laughed and said, *You have any idea what pyrite actually is? It's fool's gold. You know why it's called fool's gold? Because crooks used it to con morons during the gold rush. It's worthless. It's an unbelievably abundant and technologically useless resource. But it sure is shiny. You feel like a fool now? Good.*

"I'm well aware of your knowledge of pyrite," Cramps says, smiling. "How'd your latest practice test go?"

"So, Marlon," Ma interjects. "How are you liking the King?"

"Pretty good," Mar says shyly. "I like Ms. Ansley."

"Got a favorite subject?" Pops says.

"Reading, I guess," says Mar.

"That was mine, too," says Pops.

Mar nods, looks down at his asparagus, lifts his fork, and reconsiders.

"Could I ask you something?" Mar says.

"Sure," Pops says.

"What was Harvard like?"

"That's a great question," Cramps says. "What *was* Harvard like?"

"We didn't spend a lot of time in the classroom," Ma says to Mar, ignoring Cramps. "There was a lot of other stuff happening on campus back then."

"Why don't you tell him about your favorite subject," says Cramps. "Vietnam!"

Pops breathes out a little laugh, takes a sip of his beer, and turns back to Marlon. "What have you been reading, Marlon?" he says.

"For school or for fun?" Mar says.

"See that?" Cramps says to me. "He reads for *fun*."

"I'm too busy studying to do anything for fun," I say.

"Studying? Or fussing over your outfits and arcade tapes?"

"Lou," Ma says to Pops. "Please get him to cool it."

"That's *all* life is to you, grooming and games," Cramps says.

"We've been doing plenty of test prep together," Pops says.

"You've been going over your vocabulary cards?" Cramps says.

"Constantly," I say.

"Good. What does *charlatan* mean?"

"All right, Dad," says Pops, still trying to be patient. "Enough about the test."

"You don't know, because you are one," says Cramps. "Long on glitz, short on substance. Look it up! C-H-A—"

"He gets it!" Pops says, finally losing it.

"You mean *char*latan?" says Mar, pronouncing the *ch* like *chard* instead of *shark*. Cramps slowly turns to Mar. "That's like somebody who, um, pretends like he knows stuff. Like a phony or a fakester."

"Excellent," says Cramps. "For that, you get a Quick Nickel." Quick Nickels are for when you get one of his questions right. He pulls his ancient, cracked leather change purse out of his sweatpants pocket and passes the nickel to Benno, who passes it on to Mar.

Cramps gets off my case and we eat peacefully for a while. Ma tells Mar about her organizing work, Pops talks about teaching at the community college, and Mar does his best to seem interested. Cramps keeps glaring at Benno.

"What's with you?" Cramps eventually says to Benno. "When are you going to start eating like a human being again?"

"At least he eats," I mutter. As usual, Cramps piles food on his plate, takes two tiny bird bites, and leaves the rest for his doggie bag.

"Benno can speak for himself," Cramps says. "Oh right. I forgot—"

"Dad," Pops says, trying his best to be calm again. "We're trying to have a relaxed dinner. Why don't you lay off?"

"I'll lay off when I'm finished. You never let anyone finish, you know that? Benno just decides one day he's going to forgo language—the top trait that distinguishes us from hogs at the trough—and *every*body's fine with it. If I pulled a stunt like that when I was your age, back *there*"—he's holding his fork like a weapon, underhanded, jabbing at the air—"I'd be sausage meat. But in this house, anything goes. You want freedom of speech, I'll give you freedom of speech: *Grow up!*"

Benno runs to the living room and scrambles under this fort he made out of blankets and chairs.

"Go ahead, hide under your towels! Why don't you join

him, David? You two can make grunts and hand signals while I have an intelligent conversation with your friend Marvin."

"I think everybody's had enough by now!" Ma says.

"Dad," says Pops. "Why don't we get going?"

Pops hoists Cramps by the armpits and delicately drags him toward the front door. This is the second time in three meals that Pops has had to drive him home early.

"What about my doggie bag?" shouts Cramps.

"Liz," Pops says. "Make him a doggie bag?"

"The future of the Greenfeld line!" Cramps yells back at me.

"Come on, Dad," says Pops.

"Charlatans!" Cramps screams as the front door closes.

Mar looks stunned. I tell him it's normal.

"At least we didn't have to hear about Iraq," Ma says.

Or the Holocaust.

"He's always like that?" asks Mar.

"Usually he's a little more down to joke around," I say.

"He gets very anxious about exams," Ma says. "You wouldn't believe how much pressure he put on your dad about the SATs."

Ma scoops some salmon and asparagus onto my plate.

"I think we forgot to do grace before?" says Mar.

I turn to Ma and she eye-smiles me.

"Would you like to lead us, Marlon?"

Mar closes his eyes and puts his hands in the prayer position. I clasp my hands together and close my eyes, too, but then open them and look over to Ma again. She shoots me a quick, teasing eye roll.

When Mar finishes his prayer, I ask Ma if we can go watch the Celtics pregame show.

"You guys need to eat a little. I don't think Alma would be too happy if I let Marlon go to bed without dinner."

I look down at the puke pile, hold my nose, and cram a mammoth forkful into my mouth. Mar stabs at some asparagus, takes a cautious nibble, swallows painfully, and chugs his entire glass of water.

"Miss?" Mar asks, all polite.

"You can just call me Liz," Ma says.

"Okay," he says. "Um . . . Could I possibly get some of those Tater Tots?"

"Sure," she says, passing over Benno's plate.

I jump on the chance. "Can I get some, too?"

She sighs. "If Marlon feels like sharing with you, it's fine with me."

We eat as fast as we can and then head to the living room to peep the game. We usually watch the C's in the attic, but my parents just got a new TV for down here, and the games look way better with the extra six inches.

"That's an ill fort," Mar says to Benno. "Lemme climb in real quick?"

Benno pokes his head out and nods.

"Kinda comfy up in here," says Mar. "Lemme make a peephole to watch the game?" Benno agrees and Mar props up the front of the tent with Benno's horse-on-a-stick.

"Those pills you were taking at dinner—that was Prozac?" Mar asks.

Benno nods.

"They work on you?"

Benno shrugs.

"How d'you know about Prozac?" I ask.

"I just do," he says.

I go to my room and grab the good luck shrine me and Mar made together before the season started. It's the Bird-Magic card, now in a bolted plastic case, propped up on a foldout book stand with all kinds of crap from Benno's chest—a rubber cobra, some Mardi Gras beads, a Navajo dream catcher—draped over it. I place the shrine on top of the TV and take a seat on the couch.

"Yo, Green," says Mar. "Get in. Bring the shrine in here, too. This tent's good luck for the C's. I can feel it."

Now that Larry's retired, the C's are a disaster. The other dudes from the Big Three—McHale and Parish—are crumbling without him. The only bright spot on the squad is Reggie Lewis, and even he can't carry this team on his back. They're in last place, with a two-and-seven record. Throughout the slump, I've tried multiple prayer positions, rally caps, inside-out clothes, putting pins in Benno's Barbies—none of it works. If Mar thinks the tent is gonna bust the jinx, I may as well try it out. And I've gotta say, it *is* cozy in there. Benno set it up with just about every pillow and stuffed animal in the crib. Me and Mar lie on our stomachs, heads popped out of the front like Siamese turtles. Mar asks Benno to watch, too.

"With the C's," he says, "you gotta do everything in threes, just like the Big Three."

Pops walks through the door, smiles, and shakes his head. A second later, he comes back, snaps a photo, and says, "This one's going up in my office." Mar doesn't give one damn, so I let it go.

The C's lose their lead late in the game and are forced into overtime. With the Hawks up four and only four seconds left on the clock, I suggest *Spaceballs*—another Cramps favorite—but Mar refuses to stop watching until the game's actually over. By the end, pretty much everyone in the crowd is gone except for Superfan, whose black hair has gotten a little gray and who's still wearing that same shiny old-school C's jacket. Even though we lose our eighth game, Superfan sits there, clapping for the C's as they run off the floor.

"Realest fan they got," says Mar.

The buzzer sounds and the C's announcers come on for another depressing postgame analysis. It's the worst Celtics start in fifteen years.

I'm about to pop in *Spaceballs,* but Mar's in a bad mood from the C's and he's already trying to go to sleep.

"It's barely ten," I say.

"Test's a week away," Mar says. "I'm trying to get rested."

"I'm not tired at all. Let's watch a little more TV."

"Fine. Check 68."

"You like that channel, too?"

"Depends." He grins.

Channel 68's the last one before my TV resets to 2. Half of the time it's home shopping. The other half is a total grab bag.

"Word!" I say. It's *Sal and Al's Memorabilia Mayhem.* "You ever watch this show?"

Mar nods, chuckling.

I've been watching *Sal and Al* for years. Limited-edition collectibles are my shit—especially autographed ones. I've never been able to afford anything on the show, but if I ever get rich, I'm putting their 800 number on speed dial.

"Folks, you're not gonna be-*lieve* this next item!" screeches Sal, running around the stage and flapping his arms like a lunatic. "I practically crapped myself when it came across our desk."

Fat, sad Al silently yanks the white hanky off the pedestal and unveils a Reebok Pump signed by Reggie Lewis.

"Oh snip," I say. "It's only $499.99."

"We're talking about a *game*-worn sneaker, signed by the man who sweated all over it. Take a whiff of that, Al," Sal says, shoving the shoe in Al's face. "You're smelling grade-A Reggie DNA.

"Al, I know what you're thinking. *Gee, Sal, that's a once-in-a-lifetime collectible. But how do we know it's the real deal?* I've got your answer *right* here," he says, holding a piece of yellowed parchment up to the camera. It says, CERTIFICATE OF AUTHENTICITY.

"That's right, folks," says Sal. "Notarized *and* embossed."

"Oh *snip*," I say.

"What you getting all worked up for?" Mar says. "All that stuff's fake."

"What about the certificate?"

"That's pyrite, too."

"How do you know?"

"Man, everybody knows," he says, laughing. "You're mad gullible."

Benno cracks a smile, too, and I sit there steaming with shame.

After a while, it gets too hot in the tent, so me and Mar migrate to the couches. A few minutes later, Mar's snoring. I consider rousing him so we can go to my room—Benno's been sleeping in his tent lately, and Ma put fresh sheets on his bed for Mar—but I decide not to. I don't feel like going to my room alone, either, so I turn off the TV and try to fall asleep out here with them. Pretty soon, Benno's out, too. His snore sounds like a whistle tonight. Mar's is more of a snot-train rumble.

An hour passes and, as usual, I'm way too awake. I turn *Sal and Al* back on and study those charlatans for a while. At midnight the show ends, and I reach for the remote. But before I click it off, the opening credits to *Baywatch* fade onto the screen. You never know what's gonna pop off on 68. There she is, the blond goddess, racing into the riptide, hard nipples stretching her bright red suit. Instant wishbone. I suffer through ten minutes of Hasselhoff-centered plot about a cancer kid from Kansas whose dying dream is to see the ocean. Then the kid is swept away by a rogue wave and Pam springs into perfect, slo-mo action. I hear Mar stirring on the couch. I pull my hands out of my Hanes and scramble for the remote.

"Ugh, yo," he whispers. "That's *nasty.*"

"I was just flipping through channels," I say. I turn to PBS and the guy with the fro is on, painting a shack next to a pond.

"Mmm-hmm," Mar says, stretching himself off the couch. "Whatcha hands doing down there?"

"Down where?"

"You read the Bible, right?"

"Yeah," I lie.

"You read the part about Onan? My youth pastor said he's one of the wickedest in the whole Bible. He said you need to save up your stuff till you married. He said if you waste it, the devil comes up and collects it. He measures it, too, so he knows just how much you spilt."

Mar walks to the bathroom and a couple minutes pass. I assume he's taking a deuce, so I switch back to *Baywatch*. I'm salivating at another montage when Mar calls to me from the bathroom.

"Hold up," I say, transfixed by Pam but also, at this point, rooting for the cancer kid. "I just wanna see him finish this spruce tree."

"For real, Green," says Mar. "I think something's wrong with me."

I do the tuck move and walk to the bathroom. Mar points to his unflushed number one.

"So it's mad yellow," I say. "What's the big deal?"

"Nah, but *smell* it," he says. "Nasty, right? It's never smelt like this before."

"Now that you mention it, that piss is *funky*," I say. "That's, like, not normal."

"Don't play," says Mar.

"This could be serious. We should probably call an ambulance."

"Stop playing, Green."

"For real. My uncle's a doctor. My piss once smelled like

this and he told my pops I had to go to the hospital to get tested."

"For what?"

"Cancer."

"Nah."

"Dick cancer."

"Man, shut up," says Mar. His voice squeaks a little when he says it. I've never seen him this shook.

"Uh, guys," Pops says, standing in the doorway of his room in his tighty-whiteys. "It's way past time to hit the hay."

He walks by us and into the bathroom. Then he sniffs, closes the door, and flushes.

"How about flushing next time, Dave?" he says through the door. "Especially with asparagus pee."

We go back to the living room and I start rolling.

"Who's gullible now?" I say. "You didn't know about asparagus?"

Mar's not smiling. He storms back to the couch and whips his blanket over his body.

"I never ate that nasty-ass shit before."

"Cancer?" I say, mimicking his cracking voice. *"Nah!"*

"Man, fuck you," he says, rolling over onto his other side, away from me. He's cursing again. If he's actually mad about a lie this stupid, how's he gonna feel when he finds out I've been fronting about being Christian?

Five minutes later, Mar's snoring again. There's a plague in my pajamas and I don't know if I'll survive the night without a quick sesh. I look at Mar, sleeping so soundly. I wish I had what he has, what Bobby and the Rev have. I'm not saying it's easy being black, but at least they came up with answers. All I came up with was confusion. Pops says we're secular, but he's always preaching about nonviolence, telling us never to fight back, which sounds like Jesus. But then you start *why*ing with him, asking him why you should be so nice to people, even if they're dicks, and he says, "You never need a reason to be nice." And then later you ask him why the Holocaust happened—because there's got to be some reason all our ancestors got smoked—and he says, "Things don't happen for a reason. There's no purpose to the universe." And then you say, if there's no purpose to the universe, why do you care so much about us being nonviolent, and he says, "Because of what happened to our family in the Holocaust, for one." And then you become a kid who stays up all night wondering, *So the lesson of the Holocaust is to never fight back?*

Figuring out how to live in an atheist house is hard enough—but that's easy compared to thinking about death. In those first few days after Benno cut himself, when everybody was worrying he was gonna do it again, what really bugged me out was thinking about Benno's rotted body in a hole. If I believed Pops, he'd just be dust in the dark, until a million years later a comet detonated Earth and sent his particles into space. If I believed the Christian kids at school, he'd have a chance at heaven. He might go to hell for killing himself, but even hell seemed better than the horrible infinity of outer space.

Now I'm not sure what's worse, endless black boredom or getting jabbed in the dick by the devil. All I know is I'd rather go to heaven. I decide I'm gonna come clean to Mar about everything first thing in the morning, ask him how to convert without getting caught by my parents. Once I'm a legit Christian, Jesus will forgive me for all the tactics and everything will work itself out. I start to feel a little more relaxed, but I still can't sleep. Every time I close my eyes, I see Pam racing through the riptide. Then I open them back up and see the pictures of Pops's ancestors on the wall—all those Jews who ended up in the grotto—and I feel mad guilty about my plan to convert.

I turn the TV back on and watch Fro-man finish his chill landscape. My fingers tremble on the remote. The only time I've ever ached this bad was from growing pains. I take long, deep breaths till I feel light-headed. Fro-man dabs some white on the shack's window, to make it gleam in the moon-light. I sit on my hands till they get numb. There will be *no* tactics tonight.

I'm still awake when Saturday morning cartoons come on. Light starts straining through the curtains. The wood stands tall. I think about rats eating seagull shit. I picture Cramps playing nasketball naked. The best dick kryptonite fails me. I get up, walk to the bathroom, head hung in dis-grace, and yank away the pain.

CHAPTER 6

Tested

When I wake up, Mar's long gone. So instead of fessing up and finding out how to convert, I do the opposite, setting my record for tactics in a single day. On Sunday I break that record. I'm lying in bed that night, gutted by guilt, when I see a few flurries through my window. An hour or so later, the snow starts falling hard. I'm hoping it's a real storm, the kind that whitewashes the whole city—all the trash-strewn streets, the rat-stained alleys, the roofs of every filthy Onan.

I wake up extra early and flip on the news. Right at six, the bar starts scrolling across the bottom of the screen: ABINGTON—CANCELED. ACTON—CANCELED. ARLINGTON—CANCELED. ATTLEBORO—CANCELED. I call Mar.

"Throw on channel five," I say. "They're about to announce Boston."

"Already watching," he says. "And you shouldn't be calling this early. You probably woke up my moms."

BEVERLY—CANCELED. BILLERICA—CANCELED. BOSTON—AWAITING ANNOUNCEMENT.

"*What?*" we both shout into the receivers.

BROOKLINE—CANCELED.

"Brookline's *right* next to Boston," Mar says.

"The suburbs always get canceled first," I say.

"It's probably a conspiracy," Mar says.

"Definitely a conspiracy," I say.

The scroll restarts a dozen more times, and finally, right at the 6:59 buzzer, we see what we've been waiting for. Next to BOSTON, the best word in the English language: CANCELED.

Mar arrives a little while later and I bring him out back to show him the icicles. The rain gutter on our garage is broken, and when it snows we get icicles the size of elephant tusks. Benno sets up his camera and dusts off the trampoline. I spring off of it and karate-chop an icicle with my bare hand. The severed spike lands upright in the snowbank below. Mar goes next.

"You saw that?" he says to the camera. "Two in one swing!"

He sets up the trampoline for another jump, and I go into the garage to grab the shovels. I come out singing, "There's no business like snow business," and hand him one.

"I thought we were gonna watch C's tapes and get our study on," he says.

"We are," I say. "After."

"Why you always fiending to make money?"

"Why you always fiending *not* to make money?"

"I don't feel like it. I never shoveled before."

"I'll show you. It's the easiest loot out there."

"I told you I don't feel like it. Ain't everyone as greedy as you."

"Fine," I say. "I'm gonna go get paid. You can hang out here and make snow angels with Benno."

"How much you usually make?"

"Like ten per crib. I'm telling you—it's the hustle."

Mar agrees to a couple houses. He's rocking sweats and sneakers and when I offer up some extra snow pants and boots, he says, "I'm straight like this." Ma forces me to include Benno, even though there are only two shovels. He zips up his Lake Placid Junior Ski Jump Team suit, fastens his hockey helmet, and slides down his snowboarding goggles. I hand him a short broom and tell him his job is to sweep the snow out of sidewalk cracks. He agrees to a five percent cut.

By the time we get started, half the street's already been cleared by the competition. We walk to the far end of the block and roll up to Mrs. Murphy's. I've been clearing her walk for years, but when we ring the bell no one answers. I knock on the door, then the window. I see an upstairs curtain move, but no one comes to the door. We decide to come back later.

We hit four more houses and nobody's coming to the door. Mar suggests me and Benno ring the bell while he waits on the corner.

"For real?" I say. "This isn't, like, Mississippi."

But Mar's right. After a couple tries of the new method, we score an old lady.

"Do the driveway and brush the cah, too," she says. "And be cayahful not to scratch it. And don't put any salt on the cah, neithah."

"It's awright," I say in a Boston accent. "We nevah use salt anyway."

"Whattdya mean ya don't use salt?" she says.

"Bah fah the enviahmint," I say. The real reason is that our company doesn't have salt in its budget.

"This blawk sure has changed," she says.

The lady goes inside and I whistle to Mar. He comes running back.

"Told you that'd work," he says.

We snap into action, me plowing the path into a big mound and Mar furiously chucking the pile into the lady's yard. I grab the broom and scrape the car extra hard. We finish in about fifteen minutes and Mar goes back to the corner. I ring the bell and the lady takes a ball of rumpled cash out of her pocket. She straightens out a ten, a five, and four ones. She does some math and then slowly peels off the four ones and hands them over. They're old, worn ones, too, the floppy, faded toilet-paper kind.

"That'll be easy to split," she says.

"We usually get paid, like, ten," I say. "Minimum."

"You wanna get paid moah next time? Use salt."

We try a few more houses using the Mar method and I can tell he's getting tired of the operation. But I convince him it's worth pushing on for a few more. Up to now our total profits are barely big enough for a slice. As we get closer to the PJ-end of my block, a dude calls out to Mar.

"Keep walking," Mar says under his breath.

"You hear me, nigga?" the guy shouts across the street.

"What's he want?" I ask Mar.

"Why you actin' like you can't hear me?" the guy says. He looks at least sixteen. It's hard to tell just how big he is because he's rocking a black three-quarter-length Triple F.A.T. Goose that makes him look like a sideways storm cloud.

"Don't make me come over there and whoop you with your own shovel," he says. He gets closer and I make out the Hornets logo on his black snow hat.

Mar stops and turns to him.

"What you want?" Mar says, surprisingly hard.

"All I want," he says, "is for you and your little white boys to dig out my whip. That too much to fuckin' ask?"

"We done workin'," Mar says.

"No you ain't," says the dude, coming over to our side. He grabs one of Mar's ears, which look extra-Mickey because they're popping out of his headband, and starts pulling him down the street.

"Why you actin' all shook?" he says to me and Benno. "I ain't gonna hurt y'all."

We march in silence to the front of the Shaw Homes. Mar refuses to dig and watches while I get busy on the massive car. After some extra-careful brushing, a sparkling black Land Rover is unearthed. I silently mouth, *Mycanocopy.*

Just as we're finishing up, another PJ guy walks up and gives our guy dap. He's wearing a Hornets Starter jacket and a matching purple headband.

"Y'all doin' a real nice job," the guy in the Triple F.A.T. Goose says. "Matter of fact, clean my man's car, too."

Mar looks furious, but I'm not trying to get shovel-whipped, so I trudge over to the next car, a black Jeep Grand

Cherokee. *Mycanocopy*. I'm working so fast my back starts spasming. I ask Mar for some relief.

"Please?" I say, "I'll go forty-sixty."

Mar sucks his teeth and starts shoveling. A couple minutes later, three other PJ boys show up and start laughing at him. One of them has that same Hornets Starter jacket and another has teal laces in his Nikes.

"Git, nigga!" the one with the laces shouts, firing a close-range snowball at Mar's ass. "Git!"

Mar throws his shovel down and I start up on the car again. I'm almost done when I look over at the PJ guys and seize up. One of them, the only one not rocking Hornets colors, is younger than the others, smaller, and I can see from here that he has green eyes. He's wearing a leather snow hat with long flaps, so I can't tell if he's still got the mini-dreads, but it's definitely him: the one who jacked the Machine. I can't believe it. Dude said he was from down south! He's been *here* this whole time, only a football field away from my house. He doesn't seem to recognize me—yet. A snowball sails past my head and explodes on Triple F.A.T.'s windshield.

"Another one hits my shit and I'ma *fuck* y'all up!" Triple F.A.T. screams at the other Hornets boys.

I'm barely breathing at this point. When I'm done clearing the car, Triple F.A.T. asks, "How much money y'all make so far today?"

"Four," I say, eyes digging into the snow below me.

"Four what?" he says.

"Dollars," I say.

"Don't make me check your pockets," he says.

"He ain't lying," says Mar. "We only did one lady's house."

"Man, check this white boy's pockets," Triple F.A.T. says to the jacker. For a second, the jacker's eyes meet mine. My heart hammers as he flips out my snow pants pockets.

"Where it at?" he says, with that same stony look that's been frozen in my mind for months.

I point to the secret pocket inside the lining of my coat and he retrieves the four limp singles.

"Lemme get sump'n straight," says Triple F.A.T. "Some lady gave you four fuckin' bones to shovel her shit and y'all just took it, no questions asked?"

I shrug, shamed.

"Y'all gettin' played out there. And y'all doing a real good job, too. Y'all gettin' took."

He peels three twenties from a thick, rubber-banded wad. "That's for you," he says, handing me one. "That's for little man," he says, slipping Benno another.

"And that's for crack baby," he says, crumpling up the last one and throwing it at Mar. Mar refuses to pick it up and stares straight at the dude.

"You could do a lot wit' that. Buy yourself some new pants," says Triple F.A.T. "Maybe even cop some rock for your momma."

"Fuck you," Mar says under his breath.

"You say somethin'?" says Triple F.A.T., now in Mar's face. "Say it again, crack baby."

Mar looks into the distance and mist streams out of his nostrils.

Benno squeezes my sleeve and I stare at the snow. Snow

only makes the city look clean for a second. On the patch I'm staring at, there's a dog-yellow crater and a red smear from what looks like a peanut M&M.

Triple F.A.T. takes Mar's shovel, scoops up a heap of exhaust-stained snow, and slowly dumps it right onto Mar's head.

"Pick that money up and walk the fuck outta here," says Triple F.A.T.

Mar stands there defiantly, wiping the snow out of his hair. Triple F.A.T. picks up the twenty and shoves it down the neck of Mar's coat, and Mar snaps. He pushes back so hard, Triple F.A.T. stumbles into a snowbank. Then my jacker walks up to Mar and clocks him in the side of his head. Mar drops to the concrete, and my jacker spins back toward the other dudes and smiles, fishing for props.

Triple F.A.T. gets up and kicks Mar with his hard-toed Tims right in the ribs. The other boys form a ring around him and get their kicks in, one by one.

Benno's pulling my sleeve frantically now. I'm still staring at the snow, worrying about my glasses getting snapped, wondering just how bad a broken lip or a ripped knuckle would hurt, positive that nothing could be worse than the lifelong throb of knowing I was a pussy when it mattered.

"Fuck you think you is?" Triple F.A.T. screams, winding up like a punter for another full-force kick.

I'm standing outside the circle, still doing nothing. I wish I could scatter them through my presence alone. I wish I was a whale, too big to fuck with. Soft and enormous.

"Stupid fuckin' crack baby," says Triple F.A.T. He delivers one more blow to Mar's side and they finally leave.

Mar stands up, coughing and bleeding. He beats away the snow from his coat and sweatpants, reaches in his shirt for the twenty, and throws it in the direction of the cars.

"Just shut the fuck up, aight?" Mar says when I meet his eyes, and he limps away, back toward his corner of the PJs.

Me and Benno jet back up our hill, cheeks streaked with bitchwater. I can barely see because my glasses are so fogged, but we don't stop for air until we're back inside and the door's locked. Benno throws his twenty in the trash and I call Ma. We sit by the radiator and thaw till she gets home.

With Benno as a witness, I can't *not* tell Ma what happened. She wants to call Mar's grandma, but I beg her not to.

"You don't get it," I say. "If people think Mar snitched, it's gonna be way worse for him."

"You should at least call him and see how he's doing," she says.

"I don't think he wants to talk to me right now," I say.

"Call him, Dave."

After a few tries, Mar picks up. "What you want?" he says.

"Just, like, making sure you're straight?" I say.

"What do you care?"

"I'm sorry, okay?"

"You should be."

"How come you didn't just take the twenty?"

"How come you just stood there while I was getting fucked up?"

"I don't know. But if you'd just taken the—"

"That's *coke* money. Don't act like you didn't know."

I go silent for a while.

"You still there?" Mar says.

"Yeah."

"Least you coulda done was jump in. Benno's one thing. But you just watched me get fucked up."

"I was gonna call for help. There wasn't anyone around."

"And there wasn't nothing else you could do but stand there while dude was kicking me?"

"I wanted to."

"But?"

"I was . . ."

"Shook. As always. But just cuz you're shook don't mean you got the right to stand there."

Now I'm feeling a little defensive.

"The one who hit you first—that was *my* dude."

Mar gets quiet.

"The one who *jacked* me. The one who had the gun in his bag."

Mar's still saying nothing.

"Dude's been living right down the block from me, walking around in broad daylight, in *my* Machine. You must have seen him in it. You must have known this whole time."

"What you want me to do about that?" Mar says.

"You could've at least told me."

"And what then? Asked for it back?"

"I don't know. You knew the guy in the Triple F.A.T. Goose."

"It ain't like we're friends. You think I'm boys with ev-

eryone in the fucking Shaw Homes? Why don't you ask him
for it yourself? You know there ain't nothing to be done
about it. And you shouldn't have been wearing those sellout
Hornets colors to begin with. That's *their* colors—coke-boy
colors. That's why he took it off you."

It's quiet on the line again and Mar says, "I gotta study."

"How come . . . ?" I say, and then start to wonder
whether I should.

"How come what?"

"How come they called you crack baby?"

"Cuz they ignorant-ass bitches, that's why."

"But, like, what they were saying about your mom . . ."

"*What?*"

"Forget it."

"Nah, what was you about to say? Say it."

"What they were saying . . . Is it, like, true?"

"Fuck kinda question is that? Is *Benno* a crackhead?
Man, *fuck* you."

Mar hangs up and I stay on the line, through the silence,
the beeps, the *Please hang up and try again*s.

At night I can't fall asleep despite back-to-back tactics.
Benno can't either, and halfway through the night he moves
to the floor outside my parents' room. I turn on the radio to
relax, but the C's talk just makes me think more about Mar.
Now I'm wondering if he's more heated about me being a
bitch in front of the Hornets boys or because of what I asked
about his mom. I walk to the kitchen, and as I'm making
myself some ice water I eye the garbage can under the sink.
An hour or so later, I get up again, fish Benno's twenty out
of the trash, pocket it, and pray hard for forgiveness.

. . .

It's Friday, the day before the Latin test, and we're on the bus, on our way to meet another motivational speaker. I'm sitting next to Mar, watching the flurries through the window. He's barely said anything to me over the last few days. He's been buried in his three-by-fives, and when I try to snap his seriousness with the Rogaine face, he angles away. The last thing me, Mar, and everyone else needs right now is another adult to scream in our faces and tell us to pass the test or go directly to jail. This one's my fault, too. I was wearing a REELECT SKIP shirt the other week and Ms. Ansley started yapping with me about how she voted for him and I stupidly blabbed, "You know Skip Taylor went to Harvard?"

You'd think Boston City Hall would be some fancy old building with a golden dome, but it's actually a depressing upside-down pyramid made of concrete. There's a big barren plaza surrounding it, and on days like today the plaza turns into a wind tunnel, which means you have to watch out for high-speed trash. We get off the bus, zigzag through the elements, and walk into the sad gray barracks. Skip's staffer greets us in the lobby and marches us down a long, dark hallway to his office. We enter single file so we can shake his hand on the way in, and when Skip sees me his smile widens.

"You must be Liz and Lou's boy! I remember you from when you were *this* tall. Send them my regards, will you?"

Skip is huge. He looks like a black Paul Bunyan in big old baggy pinstripes. His bald head is shiny with sweat and he's got stains on his tie and crumbs in his long gray tornado beard. His hands are the size of those foam fingers they sell at Celtics games. He doesn't just shake my hand, he swallows it. We pack into his office and he stands behind a wood desk that looks like it was built *way* back in the day, with all sorts of birds and fish and shit carved into the legs. It's covered with newspapers, Chinese food cartons, half-drunk sodas, an END THE EMBARGO mug filled with chewed-on pens, a framed picture of him and Danny Glover, and an ashtray with a porcupine mound of cigarette stubs wedged into it.

He pulls a cigarette out of a pack, lights up, and says, "First of all, don't smoke. This cigarette right here—and that one, that one, and that one, too—all of those are gonna kill me. So do yourself a favor and don't ever take that first drag, because you're going to like it. I don't give a brown penny about whether you remember any of the words I say to you today, except these three: Don't smoke, dummy."

Smoke starts filling the room, so Skip walks over to the window and cracks it.

"That better?" he says. "Always gets too hot in here anyway. They keep saying they're gonna update the system."

Wind from the plaza moans through the slot.

"Now that we got that out of the way," Skip says. "I spoke to your teacher on the phone a couple weeks ago, and I know she brought you here so I could tell you my inspiring story about how I made it all the way from the mean streets to the lovely lawns of Harvard, and eventually to this very seat in City Hall. Well, with apologies to your teacher, I will do nothing of the sort this afternoon. Forget about Harvard."

Skip stops talking and stares into the room, like his speech is over.

"Sorry, Councilor?" says Ms. Ansley.

"Let me back up," he says. "Maybe a couple of you got a shot. Perhaps one or two of you will be the exception to the rule, who makes it out and moves on up to Harvard. But that's the first mistake—thinking because you got into some fancy school you made it. Getting in? That's the easy part."

Skip chuckles to himself, stubs out his cigarette, and plops into his swivel chair. Outside, snowflakes are whirling through the plaza.

"You came to hear about Harvard, so let me tell you a little bit about my time at Harvard. When I was growing up, I used to think only poor ignorant dummies could be racist. Well, I found out fast there's a whole lot of highly educated, rich racists out there, too. A whole bunch of folks who had a problem with this little program that had just started up called affirmative action—and had *no* problem telling me to my face I had no right to be at Harvard. A whole bunch of folks who asked me what sport I played, who thought I must have gotten in because I had hops, who couldn't conceive that I got in because I had a brain. You'll be hearing the same things at Latin, by the way, so get ready."

He takes a slow sip from his mug and eyes us. The snowy wind coming through the crack starts making a loud, rasping sound, like a recorder when you're not pressing any of the holes. Skip gets up and shuts the window.

"They had a special fund for broke kids like me who'd never been through a cold Boston winter before. At the beginning of the school year, they gave me twenty dollars to buy a winter coat. There was this one coat my roommate had, that every Harvard man had to have back then, a fine wool peacoat from a shop called J. Press. I went in there, tried on the coat, took a look at myself in the mirror, and very much liked what I saw. The gentleman rang me up and told me the coat cost a hundred dollars. I stammered out something about how I'd left my wallet in my room at Hollis Hall—I wanted him to know I knew the *proper* names for freshman dormitories at Harvard. I told him I'd be right back, but from the pained look in his eye I knew he knew I wouldn't be."

Ms. Ansley keeps checking her watch. I look over at Mar, and when he sees me his eyes dart toward the window. He's been sweating Harvard harder than ever, sketching *H* logos in his notebook, even following their teams in the *Herald*.

"You know Morgie's?" says Skip.

We all nod, and a few kids snicker.

"Back then, there was a store kind of like Morgie's, a couple train stops away, run by the Salvation Army. When I told my adviser that twenty dollars wasn't enough, he suggested I head over there. I found a coat that looked just like the J. Press coat, and I was delighted to see the price tag: sixteen dollars. Only after I'd left the store did I realize there was a small hole in the pocket. Within a week, one of the buttons fell off. The lining got all frayed, and the hole got bigger, too. I knew everyone was looking at me and my old, off-brand coat. One day I absentmindedly put my keys in the pocket with the hole, and when I got to my dorm the keys were gone. I remember standing by the door, waiting for someone to walk out so I could at least warm up in the lobby, thinking, *What am I doing out here? Why am I in Cambridge, freezing in this used-up coat, when I could be back home, minding my own business?* And then this man approaches—older man, professor for all I knew—and fixes his eyes on me as he walks by. One of those long, suspicious looks that says, *What are you trying to do?* Mind you, I'd been asking myself a similar question, but I didn't like it coming from him. I wanted to throttle that man. I wanted to grab him by the collar and shout, 'Hollis Hall. I *live* here!' But I told myself, *Skip, you can't lose it. You lose it, you lose your scholarship.* So I just stood there, shivering and irate. I ended up feeling like that a lot, actually, hot and cold at the same time."

Kaleem's nodding, but Mar's face is just hanging there, like someone pricked the air out of him.

"Thank you for that . . . perspective, Councilman Taylor," says Ms. Ansley. "I'm not sure if you're aware of this. But the Latin test—it's *tomorrow*. These kids have been studying for it, hard, since the beginning of the school year."

"By all means, study. I certainly studied hard. And dream big. I dreamed of a lot bigger than this when I was young."

He looks down and frowns at his desk.

"But don't fool yourselves. Don't look at me and start believing 'anybody can make it.' That's a doggone lie. And the longer you go on buying that lie, the longer this country's gonna coast on that lie. The truth is, this country's doing a whole lot to make sure you *can't* 'make it.' Any of you know *why* so many of us live in the 'hood'—why there's no white folks in Roxbury or Mattapan?"

"Racism," says Kaleem.

"Say more," says Skip.

"White people don't wanna live near us," says Kaleem.

"See, you're not wrong, son, but that's not it. It's more than individuals deciding not to live near black folks. It's bigger than that. It's about institutions, whole *systems* they set up to set us apart and keep us down. How many of you ever heard of redlining?"

Nobody's hand goes up.

"That's your homework from Skip tonight. Look it up. And explain it to your parents, because odds are they won't know what it is, either. What I'm trying to say is that the best—the only—way to think about things is systemically. That's a big, scary word, so I'll say it again. Sys-tem-ic-ally. I know you came here to ask, 'How did Skip make it?' But I'd rather you ask, 'How come hardly anyone else is making it?' What's the *system* doing to hold so many of us back?"

"Councilor, the storm's picking up," says Ms. Ansley. "We'd better start heading back to the bus."

"All right, now. Good luck. Don't think I'm not rooting for you. By all means, keep working hard, study for that test. I sincerely hope you get into Latin. But what I really hope is that no matter where you end up—even if you do end up at Harvard—you start thinking bigger than your own bootstraps. Pick up a bullhorn. Picket the system. When you're of age, vote in all the elections—especially the small ones—and yes, run for office, because as you've probably noticed, there ain't too many brothers and sisters up in here."

IT'S SPOOKY SILENT on the way back to school. Mar's hoodie is pulled over his head and his eyes are closed; one of them is still purpled on the lid. I wonder what he's thinking, or if he's trying not to think at all. I want to talk to him, say I'm sorry for real, swear I'll never drag him into another stupid hustle. But maybe he's sleeping, and if he is, maybe he's dreaming about something cool like the C's, and if that's the case, the last thing I want to do right now is wake him up.

THERE ARE DOZENS of test locations throughout the city, but the one closest to my crib, the one I'm assigned to, is English damned High. It's freezing cold out, so Pops drives me over and walks me to the front doors. English is a big, flat rectangle of brick with a concrete tower jutting out of its center. It looks like a factory, or a jail.

"I don't feel good," I say.

"You'll be okay," says Pops. "Just relax and remember the tactics."

"Is there some kind of makeup I can do? I don't think I'm ready."

"Why are you talking like that? You've been doing great on the practice tests."

On my last one, I hit the ninetieth percentile in every category, even reading.

"What if I choke, though?"

"Dave, you're psyching yourself out. No one test is gonna define your life. And no matter what happens, Mom and me are gonna help you figure things out."

"Like put me in a private school if I don't get into Latin?"

"We'll figure things out."

"I'd feel a lot better if you'd just tell me—"

"You're gonna be late if you don't get in there."

The testing room smells like Wise onion rings. I look for Mar; we were supposed to walk over together, but he's still icing me. I don't see him, so I take a seat near the front. The word SUK is scratched into my desk. Aside from me and Kev, there are only a couple other white kids in the room. I wonder where all the private school whiteys from Moss Hill—the rich part of J.P. on the other side of the park—are taking the test. Probably somewhere with chandeliers and stained glass.

"My name is Mr. Shaughnessy, and I'll be your proctah today," says our withering corpse of a proctor. He's easily as old as Cramps and appears to hate life just as much. He's got hearing aids in both ears and has a big red runny nose. He keeps dabbing at it with a hanky.

"You have three ow-ahs to complete the test," he says. "If you need to go to the rest-rum, you bettah go now, because you will not—I repeat, not—be allowed to leave again until the test period is ovah."

Mar walks into the room, out of breath, and takes the open seat next to me. A girl in the back sucks her teeth at him.

"Yah *late*," wheezes the proctor.

I notice that Mar's collar is lopsided, like he got dressed quick and missed a button.

The proctor passes out the test, waits for the clock to strike nine, and says, "You may begin."

Mar's pencil is trembling in his hand. Seeing him this shook stresses me even more. I'm spending as much time watching Mar and the thin red second hand on the big white clock on the wall as I am taking the test. Who the hell decided those clocks needed to be behind metal cages anyway? When's the last time someone tried to jack a wall clock?

I blaze through the vocab, but the reading section is killing me. C'mon, now—birdsong? It's too boring to even skim, so I skip to the next passage. This one's about Puritans. I decide to jump ahead to the math section. Everything's going okay, until about halfway through I look back at my sheet and realize that I missed a bubble. I'm erasing and rebubbling as fast as I can, and my foot starts to tap the floor uncontrollably. I'm already hard from the anxiety, and the way my leg's moving up and down makes the wood even worse. I'm so desperate, I consider telling the proctor I'm about to yack so he'll let me go to the bathroom, where I can resolve this situation with a quick sesh. But I've got way too much of the test left and I can't spare a second.

I finish the math, flip back to the reading section, and trudge my way through it. I'm finally starting to relax a little when I see Kev's cocky ass stride up to the front of the room to pass in his test—fifteen minutes early. He walks back to his desk, puts his head down, and pretends to fall asleep. I want to stab him in the neck with my number two.

With five minutes left, I make it to my last remaining reading passage—the Puritans. You'd think that reading about Puritans would help with the wood. The name Cotton Mather sounds like a synonym for soft dick. But picturing those frowners in their tall black hats shoots even more stress blood down there. My heel's drumming the floor and my thighs are whittling the wood. I glance back at that caged clock. Two minutes to go. As I sprint against the second hand, my body starts to tense up.

You know when you wake up in the middle of the night and feel a calf cramp coming on? You always stupidly hope the cramp will decide to chill and give you a pass this one time, but there's a zero percent chance of mercy, and you just lie there, awaiting your agony, an utter bitch of your own body? Same situation: nothing I can do to stop this. I'm actually going to nut during the Latin test. It takes tremendous mental deez not to flail or pant as the bolts rip through me. The wet warmth pools in my lap and I hear the proctor say, "Time's up."

I'm scrambling to fill in the last few bubbles, and the proctor says, "Ya hear me? I said time's *up.*"

The proctor looks away and I steal a glance at Mar's sheet. He sees me copying a couple of his answers and side-eyes me in disgust. When I try to take another peek, he flips his sheet over and smacks it on his desk.

Then the proctor walks right up to me and I freeze. He looks down at my sheet, then at Mar's, then back at mine. I cross my legs to block the dark spot in my jeans. I'm sure I look guilty enough already and I don't want him thinking

I pissed myself. Everyone in the room is watching. The proctor dabs his nose with his nasty rag and looks right into my eyes. I'm done. I'm going to English.

He leans down, collects my test, whispers, "Yah lucky it's my last year doin' this," and walks away. A sickening mix of relief and shame sweeps over me. Mar knows it and I do, too: I've been saved by the force.

CHAPTER 7

Saved

It's been a week since the test and Mar's icing me worse than ever. He won't even let me sit with him on the bus anymore, and Kev sits in the middle with one of his b-ball teammates now, which means I'm back on the White Bitch Bench, by myself. When you're by yourself, the WBB is a flashing, fluorescent FUCK WITH ME sign.

I'm reading *The Source,* trying to get my mind off the test, when Angel sneaks up behind me, snatches the mag out of my hands, rolls it up, and smacks me upside the head with it. He knows I won't hit him back, so he just stands there, with his pretty-boy smile, chomping a wad of smelly green-apple gum. When I try to grab it back, he holds it out of reach, tears out a page, balls it up, and pegs it at my face. He gets bored after a few pages and Frisbees the magazine back to me.

"You need to slap that retahd," says Vicki, the big white girl with braces, the only person who still talks to me on the bus.

"I think he might be a psychopath," I say.

"Nah," she says. "Just retahded. He got kept back, you know. He was in my math class. Every time the teacher asked him to do a problem on the blackboard, he'd try to make a joke—like draw a picture or something. Mr. Pimanti got fed up and, like, forced him to try to answer for real, and Angel just stood there with the chalk like a 'tahd. He got sent to remedial and he was all embarrassed, too. Looked like he was gonna cry. You should definitely slap him. If you want, I'll slap him for you."

"Thanks," I say. "I can slap him myself."

THE ONLY THING keeping me going right now is Carmen. Even though she's changed her steez a lot since the school year started—swapped the glasses for contacts, stopped sporting librarian gear, even started throwing lipstick on—there's still something about her that feels pure to me. Sitting next to her, I feel like I'm in a clean corner of a garbage world. Part of it's how quiet she is. Everyone else at the King's always hollering, snapping, stepping, but she never talks, and when she does it's in a whisper. I think she might be embarrassed of her accent. I overheard her tell someone she only came here from the Dominican three years ago. She said she learned English on her own, watching Saturday morning cartoons. You realize how smart you've gotta be to learn English from cartoons? I've been studying Spanish with certified teachers for four years and I can barely say *Me llamo Dave*. I've peeped her grades over her shoulder, too—she gets A's on all her assignments. Still, she never raises her hand in class, and when teachers call on her she shrugs even though she obviously knows the answers.

We've been presenting our science projects this week, and today Carmen's up. She's wearing an oversized Looney

Tunes sweatshirt and a thin gold chain with a cross, which is hanging over Taz's crazed face. She looks at the floor the whole time, whispering her presentation, which has something to do with the effect of water on flowers. When the teacher asks if we have any questions, I can't pass up the chance at an interaction. I raise my hand and ask her what her hypothesis is. "I already said what it was in my presentation," she says.

That brings our total exchanged words to about twelve. At this point, I pretty much love this shorty, and the fact that I'm rocking the tactics every night—always to Pam—makes me feel like a two-timing demon.

On the bus home I feel Angel breathing into my neck, and when I turn around, he says, "What you drawin', gringo?"

I've been practicing graffiti in my notebook. My tag is GREEN, but today, I've been drawing CARMEN with an arrow-shanked heart for the M.

"Lemme see it, *maricón*," he says.

I close my notebook and offer up my arm for an Indian burn.

"Nah, I just wanna see what you was drawin'," he says, reaching for the notebook.

I slide it under my butt and Angel takes out a knife. He smiles and starts stroking it with his pointer finger, like he's petting a small animal.

"Get the fuck up, gringo."

I spring onto my feet and Angel grabs the notebook. He flips through it and says, "*Te gusta Carmen*? I thought you was a *maricón*!"

He rips the page out of my notebook and shows his boy Hector.

"*Mira,*" Angel says, "Gringo got the fever."

"Carmen?" says Hector. "She is lookin' good these days."

"Right?" Angel says. "I should prolly get her to suck my dick."

THE NEXT DAY at lunch I tell Jimmy about Angel's blade. He asks how big it was.

"It wasn't huge," I say. I'd exaggerate to come off as less of a bitch, but Mar's here and he saw the whole thing go down. He still sits with us in the cafeteria—probably because he has nowhere else to sit—but he's been keeping to himself, reading, at the far edge of the table.

"Like, how big?" asks Jimmy.

"Like a small folding one. But still."

"Like a key chain?"

"Kinda."

"If he's coming with a nail file," Jimmy says, "just buy a bigger knife."

I assume Jimmy's playing, but he checks to make sure Rawlins isn't around, and then he motions for me to look under the table. Mar shoots me a warning glare. I drop my lunch bag as an excuse to crouch. Jimmy's gripping a harmonica. He presses a button and a three-inch blade pops out.

"Switchblade?" I whisper, trying to act casual, and he nods.

"Where'd you get it?"

"Connections."

"How much?"

"Sixty."

"Dollars?"

"No, cents, stupid. Cost a lot more than sixty, usually, but my cousin has a hookup."

In the moment—with a psycho on the bus, not to mention a jacker down the block—a blade is pretty appealing.

"I got forty," I say. I still haven't spent me and Benno's loot from the snowjack. The Hornets boys have me way too shook to buy a new Machine.

"Please," he says. "I'll get you a used Swiss Army knife for forty. You want one of these? Sixty."

"Don't have it," I say.

Jimmy dips a limp fry in a pool of ketchup water, chews, and considers.

"You still got that Bird-Magic card?" he asks.

I nod and Mar slams his empty Fresca can on the table.

"You should come play *Street Fighter II* at my crib on Friday," says Jimmy. "My cousin might come by."

Mar walks up to me in the hall on the way back to class.

"You best be playing," he says.

"I don't know," I say, avoiding his eyes. "I mean, if no one else is gonna catch my back, I gotta catch my own."

"Don't even joke about catching people's backs. And don't even *think* about selling the Bird-Magic. How many times we gotta go over the Curse of the Coke? You're gonna fuck up the shrine. The C's are on a roll right now."

"C's-Pacers tonight," I say. "You wanna peep it at my spot?"

"Benno still got the tent up?"

"Yup," I say. "And the C's *aren't* on a roll anymore. They lost last night. If anyone's jinxing them, it's you. You're the one who said the tent works best when all three of us—"

"I got shit to do."

"Like what? We barely have any homework. The test's over."

"Ain't everything about the damn test," he says, and we head into class.

JIMMY'S BEEN INVITING me over since the beginning of the year and I always make excuses, because my rep is swiss enough already and I don't need people thinking I'm out-of-school homeys with a four-foot Vietnamese dude. But Mar says he's busy again, and I'm not down for a solo Friday. Plus, I actually like Jimmy.

Ma writes me a note so I can get on Jimmy's bus after school. It's half-sized because he's from Chinatown and only a few other kids at the King live anywhere near there. Mar sees me walking past our bus and asks where I'm going.

I nod toward Jimmy and say, "Think I might make that deal."

"Fuck's wrong with you?" Mar says. "You brought in the Bird card?"

"Nah," I say. "I wanna scope out the merchandise first."

Jimmy's stop is on Washington Street, right in the middle of the Combat Zone. That's what everyone calls this part of Chinatown, because gangsters used to get lit up out here all the time. Pops says it's not that dangerous anymore, but it's still grimy. There's peep shows and porno shops all over the place, even some actual hoes. We walk past Pho Pasteur, one of the few spots in the universe where my fam eats out. The restaurant is the size of our kitchen—just four wobbly tables and a tiny bathroom with a busted, plastic accordion door—but the grub is delicious. I ask Jimmy if he's ever been there and he shakes his head.

"How 'bout there?" I ask, pointing to the Glass Slipper, a strip club with a naked neon lady sign.

"I wish," Jimmy says.

We turn down a skinny side street and walk into Jimmy's building. It's one of those smog-smudged tenements, the kind with rusty, busted fire escapes on the front. The hallway smells like the mixed piss of six different species. We trudge up five flights to his place and it's the smallest crib I've ever seen. There's a kitchen that's also a living room full of oily steam, where his mother is cooking spring rolls. She looks more like a grandma with her curled-in fingers, spotty skin, and missing canine. Jimmy's big sister is sitting on a white leather couch watching Vietnamese music videos, and she's so locked in she doesn't even nod hello. All that's on the walls is a calendar with nature pictures from, I guess, Vietnam, and a family photo in a brass frame, where nobody is smiling except for his sister, a little. His mom presents me with a spring roll wrapped in paper towel and I accept it. It's crunchy, greasy, great.

Jimmy's sister won't let us use the bigger TV, so he hooks his Sega up to a thirteen-incher on top of the dresser in the other room. We sit on the floor in between two beds, which are pressed up against opposite walls.

"Which one's yours?" I ask.

He nods toward the one next to the window.

"Your parents sleep there?" I ask, eyeing the other one.

He nods and he doesn't even seem embarrassed.

"How 'bout your sister?"

He pauses and looks away, seeming a little ashamed now, and points to his own bed. I wonder how Jimmy deals with this setup. What happens if he has to rip wind in the middle of the night? Does he hold it in and let it burn until it bursts inside? How does he deal with morning bones? How can anyone live so cramped?

Jimmy wants to go up against me in *Street Fighter II*, but I tell him I prefer to watch. He plays with Chun-Li. Nobody else I know ever picks Chun-Li, because she's the only girl in the game, but if you know the codes Chun-Li is by far the best, and Jimmy knows all the codes. "Check this," he says, and I watch his fingers dance across the controller until he slams one last button and then lifts his hand like a maestro. The controller crashes to the floor and we watch as Chun-Li turns upside down and helicopter-kicks her opponent to hell. Until now I'd only read about that move in *Nintendo Power*.

"Why you biting your nails?" Jimmy says. "It's Friday, son."

"Can't stop thinking about the test."

"The reading shit was hard, right?" he says.

"Mad hard," I say. "I barely finished."

"You're fucked," he says. "Especially with those quotas. White boys gotta get nasty on the test. Asians too."

"Where'd you hear that?" I say.

"About the quotas? My cousin told me about 'em after he didn't get in."

"Where'd he end up?" I ask.

"Dorchester High," Jimmy says. "Most of the dudes in his crew go there."

"Like a *crew* crew?" I say.

"Yeah, yo, Vietnamese dudes be cliqued up," he says. Jimmy talks extra-hood sometimes. When Kev and Simon talk like this, they always sound pyrite to me, but Jimmy sounds legit. Now that I've seen his crib situation, it makes a little more sense: He *is* hood.

"I was at Teddy Bear's with them a couple weeks ago— you know, that arcade, with all those pool tables? This white dude made the slant eyes at one of them and they straight *swarmed* on him. My cousin's boy Ray broke a pool cue over the dude's back."

"Damn," I say. "Right in front of everyone?"

"They don't give a fuck. This other dude, Nguyen, took this long gym sock out his bag, grabbed a pool ball, and stuffed it inside, started *wailing* on him."

"You, like, jump in?"

"Nah," he says. "My cousin wouldn't let me. He's tryin' a get me to go to MIT, stack megabucks, buy him a Lambo and shit."

"You know my grandpops works there, right?" I say.

"At MIT? Stop lying."

"He's a math professor," I say. "Topololology or some shit."

"Shut up. *And* your parents went to Harvard? If you got so many geniuses in your fam, why you such a dumbass?"

"Why do you think?" I say. "Cuz my parents keep sending me to schools like the King."

Jimmy laughs as Chun-Li kicks a bony Hindu in the neck.

We play for another hour or so and then Jimmy asks, "So you want that shank or what? My cousin's gonna come through soon."

I tell him to let me think on it and ask where the bathroom's at. I don't like deucing in someone else's crib, especially a new spot, but this isn't one I can put on hold. I walk through the kitchen to the bathroom. The shower is a mildewed casket and I see a centipede scamper into one of the cracks in the plastic floor. I don't mind that the toilet bowl is stained green, but there's no heating in here and the seat is ice-cold. What makes it even harder to go is the fact that I'm like two feet away from the stove and there's a big slit at the bottom of the door, so anything I drop is gonna mix with the kitchen smells.

Jimmy knocks on the door.

"Yo, you done yet? My cousin's here."

I suck in with all I've got. I'm off the hook for now, but I know it's gonna be constipation city later. Shit's a dictator like that. Forces you to go when you don't want to, and then later, when you're actually down, it's like, nah, we're good right here.

I walk back to the bedroom and Jimmy's cousin introduces himself.

"Dang," he says, holding his hand out for dap. He looks like the kind of guy who would kick the shit out of you for making fun of his name. He's tall, hunched, has one of those all-chin faces with no fat on it at all and a long lock of copper-dyed hair that curves around his cheek.

"You tryin' a get strapped?" he asks. He pulls a switchblade out of his pocket, the same kind Jimmy has, and places it in my hand.

"Go 'head and test it," he says. I slide the button and the blade springs out. I reload it, shoot it back out again. There's something addictive about the snap and the rush of steel. It's way better than a normal knife—almost like a gun. I once had a dream that some jackers rolled up on me, told me to run my shit, and then I pulled a gun out of my waistband and said, "No, run *your* shit." I extend my arm out sideways, like a gangster, and slide the switch again.

"You got that rookie card on you?" Dang asks.

"Nah," I say. "I'm not trying to trade it."

Dang starts to look angry and says, "So sell it to me."

I look down at the blade. *Sell.*

"It's, um, not for sale."

"How about I throw you twenty right now *and* let you take home that shank. You could bring the card to Jimmy on Monday."

I hand him back the knife and say, "Let me think on it."

"You got them niggas on you, huh?" he says. Outside of *Roots,* I don't think I've ever heard a nonblack dude say the n-word. He didn't use the hard *er,* but he might as well have—he definitely meant it that way.

"You need to start packin'," he says. "Only way to get 'em off you."

THIS SMILEY CORPORATE rep from Polaroid and a hippie-looking documentary filmmaker from Emerson College visit our art class today for some kind of public-private partnership. They give each of us a camera and a box of film and ask us to go home and document our communities. The filmmaker says telling our stories can be empowering.

On the way home from school, I stretch my arms out in front of me and take a self-portrait. If I have a story, this is it: sitting alone on the White Bitch Bench, Mar looking out the window a couple rows back, Angel in the aisle, coming my way. I offer up the camera with zero resistance, because I don't want him pulling his shank. First he photographs the back of the bus driver's head, trying to figure out how it works. Then he jabs the camera down his swishy pants and takes a picture of his dick.

"Check it, gringo," he says as he shakes the photo. "Might have to give this to your girl Carmen."

I turn away, but he twists my head back and forces me to stare at his art. I close my eyes, so he peels one of them open and I watch the swirling browns slowly settle. The photo's so blurry and crappily lit that I can barely make out the dick. But I can see a pube jungle, which makes me feel swiss. I'm still Mr. Clean down there, unless you count the one long hair coming out of the mole on my pelvis.

"Why you lookin', *maricón*?" he shouts.

"I'm not."

"Yo, gringo lookin' at my dick!"

"I wasn't—"

"You like it, gringo?"

"Nah."

"You wanna *suck* it?" he says, smearing the photo all over my face. "I'ma make you suck this every single day, gringo."

He stands on the seat and turns to his crowd.

"*Suck*-my-dick," he chants. "*Ev*-ry-day. *Suck*-my-dick. *Ev*-ry-day."

Vicki leans over to my seat and whispers, "I thought you were gonna slap his ass."

"I was. But he has a—"

"*Suck*-my-dick," Hector and a few others join in. "*Ev*-ry-day."

Angel stands over me, places the photo between his legs, and starts rapid-fire thrusting in front of my face. I turn back to Mar and beg him with my eyes to intervene. He looks back out of the window. Angel screams as he fake-nuts in my face.

I GET OFF the bus and charge up my hill, determined to do business with Jimmy's cousin. But when I look for the Bird-Magic in its usual spot, on the shrine, it's not there. I check every shelf, tear through every drawer, flip every rug and cushion in my crib. At first, I assume Benno's been messing with me, but after a long interrogation I'm convinced he really has no idea where it is. Nothing else in our house seems to be missing, so I rule out a random robbery. It had to be someone who came for the Bird-Magic. Maybe Kev or Simon, because Kev knows where we keep the extra set of

keys in the garage. I tactic a couple times to cool off, wait
for him to get home from ball practice, and call him.

"Did you take my Bird card?"

"What are you *talking* about?" he says.

"I can't find it."

"You check Benno's ass? Maybe he put it up there."

"Did you take it or what?"

"Fuck no. I don't even like Larry—"

"Did Simon?"

"Why the fuck would—"

"Did he?"

"You're wiling. Neither of us wants that gay-ass Bird
card. Even if we did, we could buy one in a second."

I hang up and the thought in the back of my head gets
harder to ignore. On a few different occasions, when I've
had a dentist or doctor appointment or whatever, Mar's
come over and chilled with Benno alone.

"Did Mar come by this past Friday?" I ask Benno.

He pauses to think, then nods.

"You didn't see him take it?"

He shakes his head vigorously.

I dial Mar's number and hang up when he says hello. I
search my whole house again and then call him back.

"How would I know where your Bird card is?" Mar
says.

"I've been looking for it for an hour," I say. "I can't find
it anywhere."

"That's on you."

"Well, Benno said you were here on Friday. If you *happen* to know where it is, and can help me get it back—"

"What you want me to say? I *don't know* where it is."

"I just said if you happen to—"

"I didn't take it, aight?"

I want to believe him. But two words keep tapping at my dome's door—*then again*. It's the knock-knock of the force and I'm trying not to let it in. Mar wouldn't gank my prized possession. He's the one who saved it from Kaleem, who stopped me from slinging it to Buck. Then again, maybe he was just scheming for it himself all along. I thought I knew Mar, but he's been acting mad shady ever since the snow-jack. Maybe he's not the goody two I made him out to be.

"I was just saying maybe you *know* who did."

"I *don't* fuckin' know," he says, his voice breaking a little. Things go silent and I hear him breathing heavy.

"Okay," I say.

All the Jesus stuff, all his talk about hell. He won't even stroke it. How could he steal? Then again, maybe someone put him up to it, *made* him take it.

I start to say something to break the silence and he says, "If you believe me, why you keep asking me?"

"I wasn't," I say.

Then again—no, *fuck* then again. He said he didn't do it. "I believe you."

WHEN MA GETS home from work and asks how my day was, I stare at the TV, determined to stand tall and say, "Fine." But my mouth won't cooperate, and just seeing her look back at me makes me buckle. She holds me for a while and I start to feel bad for snotting all over her shirt, and when I pull back I notice that her eyes are a little wet, too, and this makes the flow even worse. She makes me ramen noodles (the one wack snack exception in our crib, I guess because it's ethnic) and we watch a rerun of *Family Ties*. I love this show; Alex P. Keaton is my favorite TV white dude of all time. He's basically a young Perot in a house full of hippies, just like me, except he's never scared to step to his parents.

"You want to tell me what happened?" Ma says during a commercial.

I don't answer.

"Dave. What's up?"

"If you're so worried about me," I finally say, "why'd you send me to the King in the first place?"

She's quiet for a while now, too, but says, "We looked at a lot of schools. I know the King's not perfect, but Dr. Jackson's doing a lot to turn it—"

"Can't you just put me in a private school?"

"Why don't we try to talk to Dr. Jackson about what's bothering you?"

"*No.*"

"Then talk to me," she says. "I can't help you if you won't tell me what's wrong."

"Being the white boy—that's what's wrong."

"Is someone giving you a hard time?"

I stay silent.

"What about Marlon? I haven't seen him around. Is that what you're so upset about?"

"No," I say.

"Dave? Is something going on between you guys?"

"No. There's just a kid on the bus."

She waits. No way I'm bringing up the knife—that's an automatic call to Dr. Jackson.

"It's too embarrassing."

"Well, I think we need to talk to Dr. Jackson about it."

"No, just—*please*. Put me in a private school."

"Sweetie, we're not going to just pull you out of the King without at least trying to work things out with the principal."

"That'll just make things worse."

"What do you want us to do?"

"You never should have sent me there."

WHEN POPS GETS home, Ma brings him into their bedroom. I'm hoping they're having some sort of private school powwow. Maybe they can borrow the loot from Cramps.

They walk back into the living room and Pops picks up the cordless.

"What are you doing?" I say.

"Calling Dr. Jackson," Pops says.

"You have his *home* number?" I say. He starts dialing.

"Seriously," I say. "Put the phone down."

"Relax," he says.

"*Please* hang up."

"Hi, Dr. Jackson. This is Lou Greenfeld—Dave's father?"

THE NEXT MORNING in school, I get called down to Dr. Jackson's office. His desk is so clean I can see my nose freckles in it. There's one stack of paper, piled neatly in a wire-mesh tray in the corner, and at the center there's a yellow legal pad lying on a leather mat and a gold pen angled up out of a wood stand. The walls look recently painted and are bare with the exception of two diplomas, one from Morehouse College and the other from the Harvard Graduate School of Education, and a framed photo of Martin Luther King marching with a nun, a rabbi, and a bunch of other guys in black suits. They're all wearing flower necklaces.

"Take a seat, Mr. Greenfeld," he says.

He sees me looking at the photo and says, "That's the march from Selma to Montgomery. I was there for part of it. Drove all the way down from Boston."

"Did you, like, meet him?" I say.

"Dr. King?" he says. "I wouldn't say I *met* him, but I got to shake his hand."

"How come they're all wearing those flower necklaces?"

"The leis? A reverend from Hawaii sent those in solidarity."

"You get one?"

He smiles and says, "Only the bigwigs got the leis."

A minute later, Angel walks in. Dr. Jackson directs him to sit in the chair next to me.

"Mr. Martinez," says Dr. Jackson.

"I didn't do nothing," Angel says to the floor.

"We can do this the hard way or the easy way," says Dr. Jackson.

Angel doesn't respond.

"That's where you say, 'What's the easy way, Dr. Jackson?'"

"What I gotta do?" says Angel.

"You can start by apologizing to Mr. Greenfeld."

"I was just playing," Angel says.

"Not good enough," says Dr. Jackson. "Give him your hand. Look him in the eyes. Now apologize sincerely and shake it out."

"Sorry," says Angel. His hand is cold and damp and his eyes say, *I'ma slice your* huevos *off this afternoon.*

"This is your warning, Mr. Martinez. I hear about any more harassment and you're going straight to the Barron Center, you hear me?"

Angel tilts his head down and to the side, a sort of half nod, half shake.

"Now get back to class," says Dr. Jackson. "And Mr. Greenfeld, hold on for a minute."

He gets up, waddles with his cane to the door, and shuts it behind Angel.

"I need to know what's going on in my school," he says. "It would really help if you gave me some specifics about the bus."

"Nothing happened," I say. "I don't know why my parents even called."

"Well, listen," he says, clearly not buying it. "I want you to feel safe here. I spoke to your bus driver, told her to report even the smallest incident to me. Spoke to Rawlins, too. He'll be keeping an eye out during lunch. We're gonna make this work, okay? But I need one thing from you."

I look up from my lap.

"I need you to stand up for yourself. I don't mean with your fists. I mean *say* something. Anything starts up, with anyone, bring it to my attention right away, okay? Don't bottle it up. I've got your back."

WORD SPREADS WITH the quickness. At lunch, kid after kid walks by our table and coughs out, "Snitch." On the bus, when Angel passes me, he whispers, "Snitches get stitches." Mar overhears and shakes his head. I've broken the only rule: Step, don't snitch.

"YOU KNOW WHAT they say about snitches?" I scream at Pops during dinner. *"Snitches get stitches!"*

"Did you tell Dr. Jackson people were saying that to you?" says Pops.

"I'm not gonna snitch on people for calling me a snitch!"

"Then maybe I should call him," Pops says. "If you still don't feel safe—"

"No! Forget it. No one actually said it."

"You're scaring us, Dave," says Ma.

"Nothing happened. And if anything ever does, I'll tell Dr. Jackson myself, okay?"

Ma turns to Pops, looking a little skeptical.

"So you feel safe?" she asks. "That's the most important thing to us."

"Not really," I say.

She turns back to Pops.

"I mean—yeah, I do," I say. "It's fine. I just—can you, like, let me take the day off tomorrow?"

"I don't think so," says Pops.

"It's the day before break. Half of it's gonna be taken up

by the Mistletoe Jam. They're not even gonna teach us anything!"

"Come on, Dave," says Pops. "You're about to have a whole week off."

I DON'T SLEEP at all that night, and the next morning I plead with Ma privately. Considering how badly she burned me, I figure there's a chance she'll let me stay home. Plus, my parents have let Benno take mad days off recently. Nowadays, Benno's extra shook of everything, even leaving the house. He was kind of like this before the snowjack, but he's gotten way worse since. One day last week, Pops had to peel his fingers off the doorframe, put his arm into a twist-hold, and drag him, kicking and weeping, into the Whale so he could chauffeur his ass to school. Pops is a gentle dude, a nonviolent dude—he's never even spanked us—and I could tell the twist-hold was ripping him up inside, because he kept saying, "Why are you making me do this?" I guess Benno broke him down, because yesterday and today, Pops just gave in. So yet again Benno gets to chill at Pops's office, swipe Cup O' Noodles from the supply closet, and watch Nickelodeon in the conference room while I'm forced to tough it out at the King.

Once they're out the door, I plead with Ma, but as usual she stands tall with Pops. This is what I get for not being as psycho as Benno. Fuck my sleeplessness, my friendlessness, my freakish bloody nails—I'm the *normal* one.

A FEW MINUTES into second period, I get called down to the office. Incredibly, Ma is there to pick me up. She doesn't say anything at first, and I'm starting to worry there's a family emergency—maybe something with Benno—but when we get to the car, she gives me a big hug and tells me we're going to the movies.

We drive to this mall in the suburbs and Ma lets me pick the movie. I go with *Malcolm X*.

"You sure?" Ma asks. "It's three and a half hours long."

"Everyone at the King's been hyping it."

X turns out to be the movie equivalent of an entrance exam—so slow and fact-full I wish I could fast-forward to the credits. A half an hour in, I ask Ma if we can bounce, and we sneak into *Honey, I Blew Up the Kid*. Moranis is max corny, but Ma rolls at every gag and I do, too, because hearing Ma laugh always makes movies funnier for me.

The day gets even better. For lunch, we hit this spot I've been fiending to try my whole life: Chili's. With Pops, it's always ice water and entrees only, but Ma says I can order anything I want. I go with a char-fried chicken roll, some Southwestern steak-blasts, and a never-ending soda. I'm too full for dessert, but I order it anyway—a brownie mega-bowl. There's a miniature American flag speared through one of the ice cream scoops. I wolf the whole thing and pocket the flag as a souvenir. Best meal of my life.

As I'm washing it all down with my fifth Sprite, Ma asks if everything's okay between me and Mar.

"Why do you keep asking that?"

"Well, I never see him anymore."

"I think he hates me."

"I actually spoke to Alma last night."

"What the *hell*, Ma?"

"I just called to say hi. Anyway, if Marlon's being a little . . . you know, try not to take it personally. He's going through some stressful stuff at home."

"Like, with his mom?"

She takes a sip of her coffee before answering.

"Alma's very private about this, so don't go talking to him about it. But yes."

"She's the lady who walks around on Centre Street with those purple socks, right?"

Ma nods.

"I saw her with Mar once. He wouldn't even introduce me."

"Well, it sounds like she's got some pretty serious problems."

"Like . . . what?" I say.

"Alma wouldn't get into details. From what I can tell, it seems like some kind of—some sort of mental illness. Apparently she's going through a rough patch right now. I'm only telling you because I want you to be sensitive to Marlon."

"Okay." I stare into my soda.

"Alma said he misses you, by the way."

"For real? He's the one who—"

"That's what she said."

On our route home, we pass by Morgie's. Ma can't resist.

"I need some winter boots," she says. "Five minutes."

I've never set foot inside Morgie's for obvious reasons, but I don't feel like sitting in the car alone. Besides, school's not out yet, so it's not like anyone from the King'll see me.

We walk in and it smells like mummified ass. Ma peeps the shoe rack while I scope the toy section. It's mostly stuff like bent Barbies and headless Legos. But something on the top shelf catches my eye. There are trophies up there—real ones, not chumpstumps. As I read the etched names, I picture these proud champions bounding onto spotlit stages, mobbed by backslapping teammates and hair-mussing fathers.

Mike Shminski—MVP 1983—Shrewsbury T-ball.

Ed Haggerty—1988 All-Star—Beverly Youth Basketball.

Alice Everton—Highest Overall Score—1979 Floor Competition—Needham Gymnastics Club.

How did these trophies even get here? Did Mike's get lost in a move? Did Alice Everton die? Who deliberately dumps a legit trophy? I ever got one, I'd clutch that shit for life. There's a Geto Boys song that's pretty much tailor-made for me, called "Trophy." It's about how they never win Grammys—never even get nominated: *Sold a lotta records / and a lotta people know me / Now where's my goddamn trophy?*

The last trophy on the shelf is the shortest of the bunch, and it's not as flashy as the others. The stand isn't made of disco ball material; it's a solid red column. The golden guy at the top isn't holding a bat or a basketball. He's standing up straight, his head is bent back, and his arms are stretched to the sky. All the plaque says is FIRST. There's no name or anything. I take it off the shelf and the price sticker on the bottom says $0.50.

I go up to Ma and ask her if she'll buy it for me.

"Sure," she says, smiling. "I found something else you might like, too."

She leads me over to the coatrack and pulls out one of those old-school shiny green C's jackets, the same one Superfan rocks to all the games.

"Whoa," I say.

"I'm telling you," she says. "Morgie's is the best."

I try it on and it fits perfectly.

"How much?" I say.

"Nine bucks," she says. "You can have it as an early Hanukkah present."

"Actually," I say, "let's get this for Mar."

Ma kisses me on the hair.

"Happy holidays," the cashier says as we walk out.

"Happy holidays," I reply, and when I say it I actually feel happy. I'm almost embarrassed by the feeling—definitely not used to it.

As we're driving home, I ask Ma, "Would you say you're happy or sad?"

"Right now?"

"Like, in general."

She thinks about it for a minute and says, "Both."

Ma never gives good answers when I ask this kind of question. For example, when I ask, *Family Ties* or *Full House*? she says, "Neither." Skittles or Twix? "Don't really care." Harvard or MIT? "Why are you always trying to get me to rank things? I don't think that way."

This time I press her.

"Like, what percent happy and what percent sad would you say your whole life has been?"

She thinks about it for a sec and then says, "Fifty-fifty."

This seems mad depressing to me, but she just stares

ahead at the road with a soft smile. We sit quietly and I turn on JAM'N 94.5. Ma doesn't even mind; on normal days it'd be Woody Guthrie, NPR, or nothing. I keep looking over at her, and she doesn't seem sad about her answer.

"Half of life sucks?" I say.

"For a lot of people, way more than half. If only half sucks, you're pretty lucky."

"How 'bout Dad?" I say.

"You'd have to ask him."

"You think he's, like, depressed?"

"No. But we both know he has a hard time relaxing."

"Maybe he'd be more relaxed if he took us to Chili's once in a while."

"Well, it wasn't easy growing up with your grandfather—or your grandmother, for that matter."

"How come he never talks about what happened to her?"

"You can ask him about that, too, if you want."

"I have."

"He'll tell you. It's just, with everything that's happening with Benno, he wants to wait until you're both a little older."

"Sometimes I, like, hate having him as a brother. I feel bad saying that, but it's true."

I thought this would make Ma angry. For some reason, it makes her smile. One of the few songs she likes on JAM'N comes on, Bell Biv DeVoe's "Poison." We're both dancing along to it, and she keeps turning to me, grinning. "That girl is *poooiii-son*," we sing. I'm glad Pops isn't here to mess it all up by harmonizing.

When the song ends, I say, "How about today? Like right now. What percent happy are you?"

"Exact percent?"

"I want a number."

"Somewhere in the high nineties."

"How come?"

"Because you're fun to hang out with."

This is one of our inside jokes. A couple years ago, she gave me a valentine that had a picture of an orangutan on it, dangling from a tree. She wrote *You're fun to hang out with* on the inside and I've been clowning her about it ever since.

"And there's something else, too. Dad and I were gonna wait to tell you—"

"You're sending me to private school?"

She laughs and says, "You're gonna make it through sixth grade just fine."

We pull up to a stoplight. Ma looks over at me and smiles even bigger.

"You know how you always say you wish you had another little brother?" She starts patting her belly.

"Wait," I say. "For real?"

She laughs.

"It's a boy, too?"

"We won't find out for a little while. I don't know why, but I have a feeling you're gonna have another little brother."

I've always wanted another brother—one I could mold into a don from day one. I was only three when Benno was born, too young to understand my brotherly burdens. I let him do his own thing and look what happened. Here's my chance to start fresh—to bring up a little bro proper—to teach him how to dress, dance, and ball, so he can have it better than I did. This white boy's gonna make it anywhere, even at a place like the King.

When we get home, I slide the new trophy on my shelf. It stands out like the Hancock in my chumpstump skyline. Then I call Mar and leave him a long message, like everything's normal between us, about how amped I am to have a new bro on the way, how I'm gonna teach him how to hold his bottle lefty so he'll have a head start as a baller. I also tell Mar I copped him a really dope Christmas gift that he can come get whenever. I figure he won't call back, but it feels good just to say that stuff.

A couple hours later, my bell rings. I open the door and Mar's standing on the porch, blowing into his fists. I raise my chin for a whattup, trying to front like I'm not hyped he's here.

"You said you had something for me?" he mumbles.

"I still gotta wrap it," I say. "You wanna come in for a sec?"

He looks away but says, "Aight."

I ask him to wait on the couch while I get the jacket ready in the kitchen. I don't know where Ma keeps the wrapping paper, so I grab the sports section of the *Globe*. It's hard to get the jacket to stay stiff as I'm wrapping, and the pages keep ripping as I try to tape it up. After a minute or two, Mar calls out from the living room, "Yo, Green."

"One sec!" I yell back.

"You were sick today?" he says.

"Yup," I say. "Feeling better now, though."

I want to ask if everything's okay with him, too, but I

know I shouldn't start nosing into his shit again. I walk back to the living room and hand him the hideously wrapped gift. I used about a half a roll of tape, and Mar struggles to unravel it.

"You see the game last night?" he says.

"Of course. We're still peeping all of 'em in there," I say, nodding to the tent. My parents haven't made Benno take it down.

"Told you that thing would work," he says. It's true. Since we started watching from the tent, Reggie's been on fire and the Celtics have climbed from last to third place.

"Figured this might help bust the curse, too," I say. "Just rip it."

He finds a small tape-free opening and tears. His eyes go giant when he sees the silky green.

"Oh *snip*," he says, fingering the stitched letters. "Where you *find* this?"

"Memorabilia shop, downtown," I say.

He slides his arms through and looks into the antique mirror in my hallway.

"Been wanting one of these joints my whole *life*," he says.

"Merry Christmas, dog," I say.

He holds out his hand for dap and I extend it into a dap-hug. He pulls back pretty quickly, and it's awk for a second. Mar starts balling up the wrapping paper and I'm thinking of something to say. I want to talk about my new little brother, but Mar's not bringing it up.

"So," I say. "Was everyone talking all day about me snitching?"

"I didn't hear nothing about it. Far as I could tell, no-body said shit."

My heart double-pumps with relief.

"Today ended up being mad fun," he says. "Ms. Ansley showed that Grinch movie and gave out candy canes. Then everyone got their dance on at the Mistletoe Jam. Got me all in the Christmas spirit."

"Word," I say. "I'm starting to feel the spirit myself."

"You should come by my church on Christmas Eve. I'm singing in the Nativity show. Got one of the lead parts this year. Now that the test is over, you got no excuse. Unless you got something going on at your own church."

"Nah," I say. "I'm down."

MA LETS ME off at the address Mar gave me. We're in a fairly hood part of J.P., right on the border of Roxbury, so she waits for me to walk inside. The church is in a row of storefronts next to a bodega. I'm afraid to knock, because I'm late and I don't want to interrupt anything, so I turn the knob slowly and glance back at Ma anxiously. She motions for me to go in, and when I push the door a crack someone inside pulls it all the way open.

The church looked tiny on the outside, but it feels huge on the inside. There's gotta be at least a hundred people packed into the pews. It's bright, too, from the fluorescents in the styrofoam ceiling. The walls are sky blue and the car-peting is purple and the only real decorations are a couple of wreaths and the big cross at the back of the stage. I walk up the aisle in Pops's oversized suit and sneakers and get plenty of glances, but mostly the curious-friendly kind. I see Mar's grandma sitting in the second row, in her big flower hat, by herself. I look around to see if Mar's mom is sitting somewhere else, but she's not here. Alma motions me over to her, squeezes my hand, and says, "Merry Christmas, sweetie."

Out of instinct, I respond, "Happy holidays." It's like I'm trying to blow my own cover.

"It's real nice of you to join us. Marlon says your family goes to St. Thomas. They going to midnight mass over there?"

I have no idea what midnight mass is.

"Yup," I say. They're going to Pho Pasteur, like they always do, and after that watching *National Lampoon's Christmas Vacation* with Cramps.

I eye the red Holy Bible in the pew slat in front of me.

"It's a wonderful book, isn't it?" she says.

"My favorite" is all I can think to say.

"Mine too," she says with a chuckle. "If you want to read some before the show starts, I don't mind. Go right ahead."

I scan around for the Onan section, but before I can find it the lights go down. We sit in total darkness for about five seconds. Then Mar's voice shakes the silence. "Goooo tell it on the mountain . . ."

A chorus walks into the room, faces brightened by the electric candles they're carrying, and joins in.

> Over the hillllls, and everywhe-ere.
> Go tell it on the mountain
> That Jesus Christ is born.

The pace picks up and eventually the whole church stands, sways, claps, and sings along, and I can't help joining them. The Jesus love lifts the Jew right out of me, and I feel, for once in my life, in sync. Mar closes the show with a solo that draws a standing O and Alma's eyes pool with pride. As I'm watching him up there, bowing under the big cross, I feel terrible for accusing him about the Bird-Magic. I decide I'm never gonna bring it up again. I'm not saying there's no chance he did it, but I'll never know for sure, and even if he did I pre-forgive him. It's the least I can do. He's let everything I've ever done slide—he never even brought up the test-copying thing.

A collection basket goes around, filled with ones and a few fives. I pull the forty dollars from the snowjack out of my pocket. I can't think of a better way to spend that tainted loot. Alma looks shocked when I drop my donation in the basket, and a little ashamed, too, when she only slips in two bucks.

Mar emerges from backstage, hyperventilating, and hugs Alma.

"I had no idea you could sing like that," I say. "You shoulda invited Maurice Starr."

"Man, shut up," he says. "I got you something, by the way. Didn't have time to wrap it or nothing, so close your eyes and put your hand out."

I feel metal edges in the crease of my palm and open my eyes.

"How'd you know?" I say. I reach under my shirt collar and untuck the low-karat gold chain I got for Hanukkah. "I just got this for—from my mom, for Christmas. This goes perfect with it."

I unclasp the chain and slide it through my new Jesus piece.

A COUPLE DAYS after Christmas, my parents are back at work and I'm stuck babysitting Benno. I know there's only one way to get him out of the house: the Arboretum. It's his favorite spot in the world, and it used to be mine, too. Coming up Nintendo-free, the Arbs was all we had. We'd spend hours out there together, mining the lawns for four-leaf clovers, scoping the grounds for freaks of wildlife. We had a whole point system: one for a yellow ladybug, two for some even rarer shit, like an all-black squirrel or an albino pigeon.

I call Mar and ask him to roll with us. He meets us at the big stone entrance gate and I point out a plaque that says PROPERTY OF HARVARD UNIVERSITY.

"I didn't know Harvard was in J.P.," he says.

"On the down-low, Harvard's everywhere," I say, with no factual backup.

We walk in, and right beyond the entrance there's a weak slope that a bunch of Moss Hill–looking whiteys are sledding down.

"That looks mad fun," says Mar.

"You never been sledding?" I say.

"You got a sled?" he says.

We find some plastic bags in the garbage can but they don't work, so we decide to bust hill rolls, which are more fun anyway. We go for a few rounds until some lady yells at me for nearly steamrolling her precious little softy on the way down.

"This place is ill," Mar says.

"You never been here?" I say.

"I been past here a bunch of times," Mar says. "I didn't know you could just, like, go in."

"But why didn't you try?"

"I don't know," he says.

I hate it when he says, "I don't know," but I leave it there.

Benno tugs me toward the woods. Mar asks where we're going and I fill him in on Benno's box. A couple years ago, Benno put all of his prized possessions into an old cigar box and buried it in the Arbs. The box, and most of what's in it—hawk feathers, shark teeth, pyrite chunks, train-flattened pennies—are things I've passed down or traded to him for Tater Tots.

What I don't say is where Benno got the idea to bury his box, because then I'd have to tell him the truth about Cramps, and I still don't feel like getting into the Jew stuff. Cramps gave me the box for Hanukkah a while back (he has about a hundred of them, which he salvages from his local liquor store), and it came with this whole story about how his fam ran a little candy and cigar shop back in Germany, basically a Jew bodega. Great-Cramps was all stingy about giving Cramps free samples of the candy, but he let him collect the empty cigar boxes. Then one night a bunch of Nazis came through, smashed up the windows, jacked the cash register, and threw all of the cigs and candy onto the floor—

like, hundreds of dollars' worth. They did the same thing to the Jew store next door. Cramps watched the whole thing happen. His family lived right across from the store, and when the Nazis were finished he snuck out of his house and followed them down the street.

The only reason he had the stones to do that is because he had blond hair and blue eyes like I do. So Cramps walked around all night watching shops get smashed and temples get torched. He followed a crowd to this park, where there was a big rally, and he even cheered along with everyone so no one would suspect him. He said that before things got really bad, he saw Hitler speak at that same park. He was around my age, so he slid through the crowds and stood right near the platform to get a better view. He realized he was close enough to peg Hitler with a rock, and that he could've, too, because there were plenty of rocks around in the park. He went back to that park and saw Hitler like five more times, learned all of the Nazi chants and everything, and one time he picked up a rock the size of a tennis ball and was squeezing it, turning it around in his hand, thinking he could throw it, maybe crack his skull and knock him off the podium. He couldn't sling it, obviously. The odds were almost zero, he said, and hit or miss, the crowd would have pulped him. (When I first heard this story, I told Kev about it. He said it was no wonder where I got my bitch blood, and that if he'd had the chance he'd have smoked Hitler without hesitation.)

Once the Nazis started putting Jews on trains, Cramps packed his top valuables in his cigar boxes, brought them to that same park, went to a spot deep in the trees, dug a hole, and buried them. And then, after he got his visa, right before he got on the boat for America, he went back to the park and dug up the boxes. Now here's the part that sounds pyrite to me, like a trick to get me to sweat reading. He said he was only allowed to bring one bag on the boat, and with his clothes and papers and snacks and stuff he could only fit the contents of two of the cigar boxes inside. So he ended up leaving behind a box with a solid gold desk clock in it and took the other two, which held his favorite *books*. He says he's never going back to Germany, but he swears the clock is still buried out there and that he even remembers the exact tree it's under. The first thing I'm gonna do if I ever go Perot is buy a first-class flight to Munich and haul that thing home. If Cramps is ghost by then, I'll give it to Pops. That shit's going back on a Greenfeld shelf.

We walk through the woods and come to this spot on the top of a hill, which is totally bald except for a massive cork tree. It's perfect for climbing, because the bark is soft and full of fingerholds and the branches are thick as barrels, so they never snap, no matter how far you scoot upward. Of all the trees in the Arbs, this is my favorite, Benno's, too. Pops has his chestnut; Ma has her Japanese maple with the fiery leaves; me and Benno have our old, ugly cork.

Benno takes Pops's garden shovel out of his backpack and unearths the box, which is sealed in a plastic freezer bag for extra protection. He lets Mar hold a shark tooth and Mar tucks it into his upper lip, bugs his eyes out, swerves his head, and hums the *Jaws* tune.

Mar takes the tooth out and says, "I should do my own box."

"What you gonna put in it?" I ask.

"My C's tapes, prolly."

Benno drops the Reggie Lewis Starting Lineup toy I gave him for Hanukkah into the box, closes it, kisses it, reseals it, puts it back in the earth, and pounds the dirt. We all pound the dirt.

We climb the cork tree and inch our way toward the edge of the biggest branch. You can see the skyline from up here.

"Oh snap—the Citgo sign!" says Mar. I never noticed it before, but he's right: You can see the bright red tip of the triangle. "This view is tight."

"You should see New York, though. I went there with my fam once. Compared to Manhattan, this skyline ain't shit. Once I make my loot, I'm moving there."

"Man, fuck New York. Why you always trying to sell out Boston? This skyline's plenty dope. New York ain't got a Citgo sign."

It's quiet for a second, and then he says, "Only other city I'd even *think* about's Miami."

"I'd move to Miami," I say. "Dope honeys down there."

"What you know about the honeys down there?"

"Saw this bikini calendar at Borders."

Mar laughs. "Dumbass."

"Why do you feel it?" I say.

"What?" Mar says.

"*Miami,* dumbass," I say, smiling.

There's another long pause and I'm worried I made him uncomfortable with the bikini talk.

"I don't know," he says. "Just heard good shit about it."

A second later, he adds, "Plus, my pops lives down there."

I've been wondering about Mar's pops for a while, but I learned to mind my bees about this kind of thing in elementary. Still, I figure he's cracking the door.

"What's he do down there?" I say.

Mar acts like he didn't hear and climbs higher, trying to get a better view.

On our way back to my crib, Mar stops by his spot and grabs his C's tapes. By the time we get home, our fingers and toes are throbbing numb. We move Benno's tent next to the radiator, grab my parents' big comforter, huddle under it, and thaw. Benno leaves the tent and comes back fifteen minutes later with a steaming pot of ramen and three spoons. We slurp away and watch the C's, and pretty soon Benno's snoring.

"Lemme ask you something?" I whisper to Mar.

"Sup?"

"If someone wants to, like, convert—like, to your kind of Christianity—how does it work?"

"They just gotta believe in Jesus."

"That's all? You don't have to take classes or a test or anything?"

"Nah. Believing's enough."

"There's no ceremony or whatever?"

"I mean, they'll dunk your head underwater. But that's pretty much it."

"The pastor?"

"Usually, but it could just be someone else at the church. And it doesn't even have to happen at the church. I seen someone get baptized in Jamaica Pond."

A few minutes later, Mar's snoring with Benno. I prod him awake and he snaps at me for messing up a good dream.

"I gotta tell you something," I say.

"Spit it out, yo."

"I don't think I ever got baptized."

"I thought you went to St. Thomas. How come they didn't baptize you?"

"I dunno."

Mar squints skeptically.

"But, like, I wanna. You know. Get baptized. To be sure."

"So come to my church and do it."

"You think we could do it here instead?"

Mar laughs. "You a weird-ass dude sometimes. But yeah, I'll baptize you right now, that's how you want it."

I fill up the tub and get in with shorts and a tee on. Mar crouches over the side of the tub, cups the back of my head with his hands. I repeat a bunch of stuff he tells me to say about how I accept Jesus as my lord.

"You ready?" he asks.

I clutch my cross as he lowers my head. Once I'm all the way underneath the water, nose and all, he pops me back up.

"Okay," he says. "You're good."

Mar heads into the tent and I change into dry clothes. By the time I crawl back in, he's already deep into his nap again. I lie between Mar and Benno and let my lids slip. For the first time in weeks, I don't even need tactics to fall asleep.

CHAPTER 8

Players

It's been over two months since our beef went down, and everything's cool between me and Mar. We're chilling every afternoon and it's more or less like it used to be. But something's off, something small. We argue less than we used to, and that sounds like a good thing, but it's weird. We don't even scrap about sapien shit like animal facts anymore. We're quieter now. Sometimes I wonder if Skip Taylor put a crack in what me and Mar had—a tiny one, just big enough for a bit of the force to blow through.

THE SPRING SEASON of my musical theater group, the Jamaica Players, is starting up soon. They recently kicked off this new diversity initiative, offering scholarships to local youth, and Ma suggests I invite Mar to sign up. I'm hesitant, because the only nonwhite in the Players is our director Milt's Guatemalan daughter, who was adopted and lives in Moss Hill. I figure if Mar's shook to even walk into the Arbs, there's no chance he'll want to be a Player. But the second I mention it to him, he says yes.

Mar comes to tryouts in his church suit and patent leather kicks. I tell him he's way overdressed, but he assures me it's always better to be suited. This season's show is *The Pied Piper*. The way tryouts work is everybody reads a monologue from the play and then sings a song of their choice. If it's a classic show tune, Milt will play the piano accompaniment, but if it's some newer shit, you have to bring your own tape. Now, I don't mind acting in front of heads, but singing is a different story. I was fine with doing solos two years ago, because at ten a falsetto is all good. At twelve a falsetto is like a public service announcement that you have tiny balls.

They call us up by last name, and to avoid discriminating they start with Z. Cornballs like Milt think they're being all revolutionary doing it this way, when at least half of my teachers and counselors over the years have been Z-firsters. If they really wanted revolution, they'd start with some random letter, like G. Anyway, Mar's last name is Wellings, so he goes first.

Mar walks up to the stage, stares into the crowd, and reads his monologue mad stiff. It's the part where the piper vows revenge after the mayor rips him off. Milt tells him to try again with a little more anger. But Mar does it in the exact same monotone, barely glancing up from his shaking sheet. I'm surprised at how wack his performance is. From the very first time he stood up to Kaleem, made his eyes all buggy, and convinced him that he was actually dangerous, I felt like he had Player potential. I'm starting to feel kind of bad for bringing him, but then he pops in his tape. His song is Whitney Houston's "I Will Always Love You"—the same one I brought.

He stands under the spotlight, eyes closed, hands clasped in prayer position, and starts in a vibrating near whisper. As the stanza builds, he gets looser and louder and he finally opens his eyes. He gets this look of crazed confidence, pacing around the stage, and as the chorus starts up he thrusts his baggy jacket from his shoulders down to his elbows and flings it to the sofa on the side of the stage. The song goes quiet for a second and he freezes. When it starts up again, he shoots both of his arms out and sweeps them across the crowd. His huge voice fills the room: *"And III-I-III . . . will al-ways love youuu."*

It's the first time I can remember shorties screaming for a tryout performance, and I can tell Mar's gobbling it up.

"Marlon!" cries Milt. "That was *phenomenal.*"

My turn comes, and my strategy is to start as baritone as possible so that once I get to the chorus I at least won't have to put the falsetto on full blast. But when I try to hit the low notes, my throat gets all choppy and tickled and I start coughing.

"You want to try something else?" Milt asks.

I stick with Whitney and when I finish, no one claps. All Milt says is "Good job, Dave. Good effort."

After tryouts, Meghan Frank, a seventh grader at Latin who gets the lead role in every play—the one Mar said was cute when he saw her in my home video—comes up to us. She holds out her arms for a hug. Most of the dudes in the Players fiend for Meghan. I can't stand her. Not only does she look like a Hitler youth—with her straight blond bangs and iceberg eyes—she acts like one, too. If she decides she

likes you, she'll ply you with hugs, invite you to hot tub parties at her Moss Hill mansion. If she decides she doesn't,
she'll go Doberman on your ass. Last season, this nerd
Nancy wore makeup to practice, and Meghan said, "You
look too pretty today." Then she took a pen, drew a line
down Nancy's face, and said, "That's better."

I always promised myself if Meghan ever did offer me a
hug, I'd give her the one-eighty. But over the past year,
Meghan's gone through a serious cup spurt, and when she
approaches in a stretched V-neck, it's hard to resist. I don't
have a lot of practice—this is my first non-Ma shorty hug
ever—so I give her a quick double back tap and try to pull
away. But she goes for a hold-hug and when I feel them
pressing up against my chest, it's just as I imagined: water
balloons not quite full enough to burst. I feel a bone-rush
coming on.

She pulls away, turns to Mar, gives him a little wave, and
says, "Hey."

"Sup," Mar says with a cocky nod.

"You were *so* good," she says.

"I know, right?" he says. Mar's loving it.

"I'm Meghan, by the way," she says, and then leans in
for a hug. Mar looks at me with wide eyes as he pats the air
behind her back.

"So how do you guys know each other?" she asks.

"From the King," I say, sucking in my pelvis.

"Wait, you go to the *King*?" she says to me. "Your parents actually sent you there?"

I look over at Mar, who's keeping a poker face.

"Not that there's anything *wrong* with the King," she says. "But isn't it supposed to be, like . . ."

"What?" I say. "Ghetto?"

She bites the side of her lip.

"It's not, like, Iraq," I say. "But it gets real sometimes."

Mar smirks.

"You go to Latin, right?" he asks Meghan.

She nods. "You guys gonna be there next year?"

"The letters haven't come out yet," Mar says.

"Well, after you guys get in, you should come for a tour. Have you heard about the auditorium?"

"Nah," Mar says.

"It's insane. They have the names of all the famous alums on the walls in gold letters. The first day you get to Latin, they bring you in, and the principal—we have to call him *headmaster*—points to each name and tells you about them. Like a million of the Founding Fathers are up there—John Hancock, Sam Adams, even Ben Franklin—and all these inventors and businessmen, too. My favorite one is Leonard Bernstein. You know—*West Side Story*? So, like, the whole point of the headmaster's talk is that there's one empty spot up on the wall, and he's like, 'Perhaps one of *you* will be the one to fill the last slot.' He's been giving the same speech for twenty years. Whatever, it totally worked on me. Now I'm like, shit, *I* wanna be up there. Especially because there's no women on the whole wall."

"Any black dudes up there?" Mar says.

"Not yet."

Meghan smiles and Mar's eyes go big.

"Anyway, Marlon, that was seriously amazing," she says. "The cast list'll be up next week. I heard the main roles have a make-out scene."

On our walk home, I clown Mar for trying to act down in front of Meghan.

"Please," he says. "I wasn't the one talking about how ghetto the King is."

"*Sup, Meg'n,*" I say in an Ice Cube twang. "*Any black dudes up there?*"

"Man, shut up. You're the one who dragged me into the Players. I don't even know if I'ma go back next week. Play seems weird as hell. What's the piper doing with all those kids? I don't know if I'm feeling it."

"You felt it when all those shorties were screaming," I say. "Admit it."

"You're wiling," he says.

A COUPLE DAYS later, Mar shows up to the bus stop with a haircut that's so close-cropped he almost looks bald.

"Oh snap," I say. "Someone needs the *Ro*-gaine!"

I try to rub his dome and he swats me away.

When Kev gets on the bus, he lifts his headphones off his ears and says, "Cut looks dope."

Kev's right. Even with his big ears, Mar looks way smoother. But it's the first time I can remember Mar doing something bold with his steez—actually, doing *anything* with his steez—and it feels a little suspect. Mar's whole thing is not giving a what.

"How come you got it like that?" I say.

"Felt like coming fresh," he says.

When we get to school and Ms. Ansley sees him, she says, "Who's this handsome young man?" and at lunch, this girl Chantel says he looks mad cute. Mar beams the way I must've when I debuted the Machine.

THAT WEEKEND, MA takes me to my annual eye appointment and I decide I wanna come fresh, too. I've been getting new glasses every year since I was six, and my lenses are already shark-tank thick, so I ask my doc about contacts. Ma flinches at the price tag, but the doc says we can buy a few months' worth and make our minds up from there. To sweeten the deal, he offers to throw in a free pair of color contacts. I choose brown.

When I rock the lenses in school on Monday, barely anyone even notices. Carmen doesn't bat a lash. But when I show up to Players practice, Meghan cocks her head to the side and looks me over.

"Did you get contacts or something?" she says.

"Just doing a trial run."

"Well, you should keep them," she says. "Wait, did you get *color* contacts?"

"They look fake or something?" I say.

"I just remember you had blue eyes," she says. "You should go natural."

Milt reads the cast list aloud and it's pretty much as I expected. Meghan gets the lead, Mar gets the second-biggest dude part, and I get a loser-ass role with three lines. Twenty-three words total, all of which are corny follow-up jokes to real characters' lines.

Meghan comes up to us, congratulates Mar, and hugs him. Then she makes a pyrite sad face at me, opens her arms, and leans in. I hold on a little longer this time.

On our walk home, Mar complains about not getting the main role.

"Seriously?" I say. "You have seventy-two more lines than I do."

"You counted my lines?" he says. "What's wrong with you?"

"You wanna be Nobleman Number Three?" I say. "I'll trade you."

"Nah, I just wanted, I was hoping I could, you know . . ."

"What? Be in a make-out scene?"

"Didn't you?" he says.

"You know she was just messing with us, right? There's no make-out in *The Pied Piper*."

"I know," Mar says. "I was just playing."

"You wanted to french Meghan, didn't you?"

"Man, shut up."

There's a long pause.

"She's fly, though, right?" he says.

"I don't really feel white girls," I say.

"You're bonk," he says.

"Nah, for real," I say. "You know who's looking fine, though? Carmen."

"She's aight, but Meghan's way finer," Mar says. "I might try to kick it to her next practice."

We never talk about girls. I don't want another Onan lecture, so I've been keeping all my fiending to myself. It's a little surprising—relieving, even—to learn that Mar's inno-cent ass is fiending to get some, too.

"Do your thing," I say.

BEFORE OUR FIRST rehearsal, Milt makes us do bonding exercises. First he has us do trust falls. Mar refuses to par-ticipate and Milt lets it go. Then he asks us to sit in a big circle, hold hands, and close our eyes.

"This is called 'Passing the Squeeze.' I'm going to squeeze the hand of the person to my right, and that person is going to pass the squeeze, and after a little while you'll begin to notice something really cool."

Meghan's cold fingertips sink into my palm. I feel the pulse and pass it on to Mar. About five seconds tick before it comes back around, and then, after a couple more rounds, the squeeze is instantaneous. The pulse is quick and con-stant, like a shook heart.

"That feeling," whispers Milt, "is unison. It's you disap-pearing into *we*. Every performance lives or dies on unison or the lack of it."

Milt asks us to open our eyes and get ready for rehearsal, and Meghan's still holding on to my hand. She gives me one final squeeze and I can't deny it. Volts shoot through my veins.

After practice, Meghan gives me my longest hug yet.

"I'm so stressed right now," she whispers, still hugging. Mar's watching us.

"About the play?" I say.

"About my Bat Mitzvah. It's on Saturday. I totally don't

know my parashah yet. Plus, I have a Latin test *and* an English paper due this week."

"Hold up," I say. "You're Jewish?"

"Uh, *yeah,*" she says. "That surprises you?"

"Your last name doesn't sound very Jewish."

"My mom converted. And Frank is like the most famous Jewish last name ever."

I give her a confused look and she says, "Don't tell me you've never read *Anne Frank*?"

"Oh yeah," I say. I've definitely heard Pops hype it before. "Good book."

"I'm obsessed with that book," she says. "I was convinced for so long that I was related to her. I even made my dad do all this research. You're Jewish, right?"

I look back at Mar, who's chatting with Milt now.

"Yeah," I say. "Sorta. My dad is."

"So your mom converted?"

"I'm not sure. She's, like, an atheist. So's my dad."

"Well, if she didn't convert, then you're not Jewish."

I'm not sure what this means, but it kind of pisses me off. If I was half-black, I wouldn't want someone telling me I didn't count.

"You been to Israel?" she asks.

"Nah," I say. "I don't think my parents feel Israel."

"That's insane," she says. "Israel's amazing. I'm going back there this summer. My grandma's taking me for my Bat Mitzvah gift. You have to go."

"I'd be down."

"I literally cried when I saw the Wailing Wall for the first time—like, kissed the ground and everything."

"Word," I say. "What's that, again?"

"Um, the *Western* Wall? From the Second Temple?"

I've never heard of any of this shit. It's making me gnaw on my pointer.

"You don't have a clue what I'm talking about, do you?" says Meghan. "You're seriously the least Jewish Jew I've ever met."

If someone at the King said this, I'd be happy. But hearing a Jew tell me I'm not a Jew makes me heated.

"My grandfather's a survivor," I say.

Cramps hates it when people call him a survivor. He says that word makes him feel even guiltier about not dying. Even though he went through six straight years of the worst shit ever under the Nazis, he got out in 1939. So he says he doesn't count.

"Seriously?" she says.

"Yup."

"Was he in a camp? Or, like, hiding?"

"I think a camp," I say. "He doesn't like to talk about it."

"Wow," she says, grabbing my hand. "I'm, like, so sorry."

ON THE WALK home, Mar asks about my chat with Meghan. I tell him she was just giving me some acting advice.

"Must've been some specific-ass tips," he says.

"Yeah," I say.

"Stop fronting. You know she's feeling you."

"I don't know what you're talking about," I say. Sure, something's going on. But the idea that Meghan Frank could feel *me*—even with the contacts, even with the one and three-quarters inches of height I've gained this year—is some opposite-day shit.

"You should man up and make her a valentine," he says.

"I'm already working on one for Carmen."

"Fine. Then I'ma give Meghan one myself. You think I should get her a carnation, too?"

"Hell yeah," I say.

"How come I'm not getting a Bar Mitzvah?" I ask Pops over dinner.

"Since when does Johnny Christmas care about being Bar Mitzvahed?" he says.

"I was just curious," I say. "This girl in the Players is about to have one, and Simon had his a couple weeks ago. Seems like it'd be fun."

I leave out my main interest: Simon's claim that he hauled home over three g's at his Bar Mitzvah.

"Trust me," Pops says. "Studying Hebrew in a basement while your friends are out playing stickball—not what I'd call fun."

"Did you have to, like, read the Torah in front of everyone?" I ask.

"Sure did," he says. "Check this out."

He pulls a book called the Tanakh off the shelf. He flips through the pages, half of which are in English and the other half in Hebrew. He leans in close to the book, runs his fingers along the tiny text, and starts bobbing and chanting. I had no idea he still knew Hebrew.

"This was my Torah portion," he says. "The Akedah—the Binding of Isaac. It's an amazing passage. Very intense."

"I thought you hated religion," I say.

"Will you cool it with that kind of talk? Nobody said they hated religion. We're secular humanists, okay? We don't take this stuff literally. It doesn't mean we can't appreciate the Bible as a book."

"Hold up—that's the Bible?" I say. "I didn't know we had a Bible in the house. Like, with Jesus and everything?"

"No Jesus in the Tanakh," he says. "Just the good Ol' Testament."

After dinner, I open the Tanakh and look for the part about Onan. The way Mar talked about it, I figured it'd be some long chapter, but it's just a tiny mention in a paragraph about how he "spilled his seed on the ground" whenever he went over to his brother's wife's crib. I can understand why G-dash put the dude to death.

I flip to the page Pops was reading from—the part about Isaac. I'm not sure why Pops sweats this story—it's even more depressing than Onan. It's hard to understand all the old-school language, but from what I can tell, Abraham talks to G-dash and G-dash tells him to take his son Isaac and burn him to a crisp on top of a mountain. The saddest thing about it is how long it takes Isaac to realize what's up. Isaac's walking around with the kindling Abraham's gonna use to torch him, still thinking Abraham's gonna sacrifice a lamb instead, maybe even thinking it'll be dope to burn the lamb with his pops—because co-flaming a lamb is their version of bonding over s'mores. And Abraham straight lies to him, says a lamb's on its way, while he loops the rope around his sad dupe son and gets ready to knife him.

Thankfully, G-dash calls the whole thing off at the last second after he sees that Abe is actually willing to go through with it. I don't usually get worked up by books—I don't usually open books—but this one riles me. The Jewish G-dash seems like such a dick, at least compared to the chill, forgiving Christian one. And Abe—what kind of sick father would do that? Why the hell does Pops think this is a good story?

Hours later, in bed, I'm still thinking about it. And now I'm thinking about Angel's knife, about all the other hidden blades at the King, about how shocked Meghan was when I told her I went there, and about how she must think Pops is some kind of Abraham for sending me there. Maybe she's right. He never gives me a straight answer when I ask him if he's gonna make me go to English.

Eventually I roll into my parents' room and wake up Pops.

"What time is it?" he groans.

"I read the Isaac story," I say.

"Nice. Let's chat about it in the morning."

"You think Abraham was right?"

"That's a big question. We'll talk about it tomorrow."

Why won't he give a straight answer?

"Do you or not?" I say.

Pops takes a deep breath, props himself up a little, and looks me in the eye.

"No," he says. "He was a fanatic. I can't imagine a father doing that. Now go get some sleep."

"Okay," I say. "Just checking."

I start to walk back to my room, but then I turn around and ask, "Can I, like, sleep in here? Just for tonight?"

Pops sighs. "You're a little old—"

"Sure," Ma says.

She grabs me a comforter from the closet and I curl up at the foot of their bed.

I ONCE SAW a Pert Plus ad, where these white dudes prepped together before their prom, and it seemed like fun, so I invite Mar to come over early on the morning of the Valentine's Dance. Even though he's not planning to ask any shorties to dance at the Love Jam, we've got Players practice after school, and he wants to look extra-fly for Meghan. Mar shows up at my crib at five-thirty A.M. carrying a foil-wrapped carnation.

We play some pump-up jams on low volume and do push-ups. I max out at four and Mar does seven. When he finishes he jumps up at the exact moment in that song where the guy goes, "You're unbelievable," and instead, sings, "*I'm* unbelievable." We flex in the mirror and I'm all ribs and red nipples. Mar's mad skinny, too, but when he makes a bicep, a baseball pops out. Mine looks like an anthill.

"You should flex for Meghan," I say. "Bet you we'll get invited to her hot tub party."

"I ain't about to let anybody see my ex," he says. Mar has eczema and he's shook for people to see it, so he's always rocking long sleeves and pants, even in gym class. Once, Kaleem saw him changing and called him *ash-pits*. He takes a huge bottle of skin cream out of his backpack, squirts a puddle into his palm, and rubs it into his elbows, knees, and armpits.

We're supposed to wear red or white to the dance. I dig through my drawers, looking for the least wack option, and settle on the Harvard '72 shirt I snagged from Ma's reunion gift bag. Mar pulls a white silk dress shirt, still in the plastic wrap, out of his bag.

"Got this for Christmas," he says.

"That's fresh. Matches the C's jacket, too. How come you haven't been rocking it?"

"That's a collector's item. I keep it under plastic at the crib."

We roll to the bathroom to do a final mirror check. Benno tries to film us and I slam the door on the Handycam. I bust out Pops's store-brand yellow mouthwash. Yellow's the nastiest flavor, but Pops says it's the most effective. I take a big swig and genocide my mouth germs. Mar asks if we have any cologne around. We don't, so I look for a magazine, hoping for a fold-out sample, but all I can find are old issues of *The Nation*—and the only ads in there are hotlines for sex-crazed geezers.

We head down to the bus, and since I'm with Mar we take the direct route, past the PJs. On our way down my hill, we spot one of the Hornets boys walking ahead of us across the street.

"What's he doing up so early?" I whisper to Mar.

"What do you think?" Mar says.

"I don't know," I say. "I figured most of those dudes were, like, dropouts."

"Nah," Mar says. "Most of them go to English."

"How do you know?"

"It's right around the way. A lot of Shaw heads go there."

"You think the dude who jacked me goes to English?"

"Probably," he says.

WHEN WE GET on the bus, I put some finishing touches on my card for Carmen. Vicki reads it over my shoulder and shakes her head.

"You gotta do this over," she says. "Compliment her. What do you like about her?"

"I dunno," I say. "Everything, I guess. The whole package."

"You gotta get specific or the card won't work. And cut the Spanish," she says. "*Tu gusta* means '*You* like,' dumbass. Just be yahself. Be confident for once. You look a lot cuter without those retahd goggles."

I'm working on my revisions when Angel gets on the bus with a handful of roses and two big silver balloons. He leans down to this blazing Dominican girl, Yennifer, hands her one of the balloons, and gets a cheek kiss back.

"Friggin' player," says Vicki. "Wonder who the other balloon's for."

Secretly, I've always wanted one of those big silver balloons. My parents hate the helium kind, so all me and Benno ever get are Pops-blown balloons that drift depressingly down to the floor. When I was little, I got a helium balloon at this kid's birthday party, bit through the ribbon, and watched it fade into a red pinprick before the blue erased it, hoping it would float up to an astronaut. When I told Pops what I'd done, he said it probably fell into the ocean and choked a whale.

I look back at Angel. He's sitting a few rows behind us, in the aisle seat, and little green flecks are shooting onto the floor in front of him. It takes me a second to realize what he's doing. He's shaving off the rose thorns—with his knife. He's still bringing it in, even after the talk with Dr. Jackson.

THE LOVE JAM is an even bigger deal than the Mistletoe Jam, because it's the only dance of the year where sixth, seventh, and eighth graders are all together. Kev's already out on the dance floor with Kaleem, rocking the one move he knows how to do. He makes a fist with his right, hooks his left in front of his stomach, hunches forward, and punches down like he's beating an invisible dude he's got in a headlock. At least he *has* a move. Every time I try to dance, I end up doing capoeira. (I took cap lessons for a couple years, learned how to do cartwheel kicks and everything, but quit to focus on basketball.) I know I'm just supposed to shake my hips, but I can't help moving my arms and legs all over the place, like I'm trying to block blows.

Me and Mar stand by one of the giant speakers and nod to the beat. My game plan is to wait for the very last song, which is probably gonna be a slow jam, and summon the stones to ask Carmen. I guess Mar's scared to dance, too. Jimmy rolls up to us, rocking a long white tee that looks like a dress on him and a red bandanna with the knot in front. He bobs his arm to the beat, like he's dribbling an overin-flated basketball.

"Yo, we need to get *down*!" Jimmy yells over the speakers. "Everyone's dancing but us."

Kaleem's pulling crazy complex break-dancing moves and a crowd forms around him. When the song changes up, Kaleem heads back into the crowd, and Jimmy jumps into the circle. He immediately nose-dives to the floor, and at first I'm shook he passed out or something. But then he flails his upper body off the floor, catches himself with his hands, and springs his legs up. He's actually nasty.

"Oh snap!" shouts one kid. "Chinaman doin' the Worm!"

"Bruce Lee be choppin' up that floor!" says another.

Jimmy's still going at it, slithering back and forth, tee flapping like a sail, but the circle breaks up and no one's watching his ass anymore except for me and Mar. The next song is this joint that just came out—"Jump Around." Even though the song is by a bunch of Shamrock-sporting white dudes, everybody bugs out when the beat starts up. The chorus comes—*Jump around! Jump around! Jump up— jump up—and get down!*—and everybody jumps with their hands in the air and I realize, oh shit, now *this* is a move I can definitely do, and I go pogo on that dance floor. I don't give a what—I'm jumping, Jimmy's jumping, even Mar's jumping. It's all good, I'm feeling great, and then—"What the *fuck*, white boy!" I've accidentally landed on an eighth grader's brand new Adidas—*white* Adidas. All of a sudden I'm in the middle of a mosh pit, a little white Ping-Pong ball getting paddled and slammed every which way by sweating eighth-grade titans. I'm using all of my strength to stay on my feet, because if I fall my ass is getting trampolined.

Thankfully the next song is "End of the Road," the exact slow jam I've been waiting for. Everyone spreads out and tries to find a shorty. Chantel, the one who propped Mar for his haircut, asks him to dance. Kev finds his rally girl. Jimmy hangs by the speakers, and I walk off to look for Carmen. I'm scanning the room for her when I hear a dude behind me say, "Check out white boy, scopin' all the honeys."

The dude next to him laughs and says, "Tryin' a *cream up* that coffee."

I spot Carmen lingering near the wall on the opposite side of the gym. Her long black hair's sparkling under the glow of the disco ball. I walk toward her, feeling fresh in my contacts and Harvard '72 tee, gripping my card and mouthing my opening line, *Sup, Carmen*. I'm a few feet from destiny when I spot Angel from the corner of my eye. He's looking for a shorty to give his balloon to; the ribbon is bow-tied around the thornless roses. Angel watches me for a second, realizes who I'm heading for, and starts speed-walking in the same direction. He zooms past me, hands his evil gift to Carmen, and puts his arms around her waist. Without stopping my stride, I change direction, ball up my idiotic card, dunk it in the bin, and head for the exit.

"Where you going, white boy?" I hear a voice say from behind me.

It's Vicki. She's dressed, as usual, like a dude: black jeans and a red Champion hoodie. But today she's got huge silver hoops in her ears and bright pink on her lips.

"Nurse," I say, continuing to the hallway.

"Get back here and dance with me," she says.

"I don't feel good."

"Put your arms around me, you friggin' lose-ah."

I submit. Vicki's a big girl, a few inches taller than me, and when I reach up to her shoulders, she sighs and drags my hands down to her waist. Her hairspray smells like grape soda.

"Will you slow down?" says Vicki. "And stop movin' us in a friggin' circle. Just sway a little, all right?"

I do my best to follow her instructions, but I've got Carmen in my peripherals. Her head's on Angel's shoulder. His hand slides down to her ass and she doesn't even brush it away. C'mon, Carmen.

"Will you stop twirlin' like that?" says Vicki. "And loosen up your grip, for God's sake. What're you so afraid of? Relax. Jesus."

I loosen my grip, but I can't help going in a circle. Not a full circle—more like long swoops, like Carmen cursive. Angel leans in for a kiss and Carmen *lets* him. And there we are, me and Vicki, the only white couple on the dance floor, a blob of cream swirling in a sea of coffee.

On the bus home, Angel grabs Yennifer's booty as she passes his seat. She smacks him hard enough to hear from rows away, and Angel just laughs, holding his cheek. He catches me looking at him, makes crazy eyes back at me, and waves his tongue like Taz.

"Just ignore his ass," Mar says. "He doesn't even care about you anymore."

"Yes he does," I say. "He swooped in on Carmen, fucking *got with her* right in front of me. He's just doing it to fuck with me."

"So step to him."

"I'm not stepping to that psycho," I whisper. "He's still packing a blade."

"Then maybe you should forget about Carmen," Mar says all coldly.

It's quiet for a few minutes. Mar twirls his carnation between his fingers.

"Yo, let's make a plan," he says. "I feel like you should start talking to Meghan after rehearsal, keep the vibe casual. Then I'll roll up with the flower."

"I'm not going to Players practice today," I say.

"Oh, hell no," he says. "I ain't trying to do this alone."

"I feel nauseous," I say.

"Don't sell me out," he says.

I give in. Mar carefully tucks the carnation in his bag as we walk toward the theater. During warm-ups, I see him biting his nails. I wonder if he got that from me. Rehearsals start and Mar's in the first scene with Meghan and a few other Players. Mar stammers out his first line and blanks completely on his second. His hands are shaking—I haven't seen him this shook since the Latin test. He pulls the rolled-up script out of his back pocket.

"Dude," Meghan says. "Are you gonna start memorizing your lines or what?"

Mar stands there, frozen, and Milt says, "She's right, Marlon. This scene's supposed to be off-book by now."

After practice, Meghan corners me backstage and starts blabbing about her Bat Mitzvah and how awesome her DJ was.

"He wasn't just a DJ," she says. "This guy literally

knew how to do everything. He could juggle, unicycle, do magic . . ."

I edge away, trying to make room for Mar.

"He even freestyle-rapped for us," Meghan says. "It was incredible. Have you ever seen anyone do that?"

I turn to Mar and give him a little head tilt. He takes a deep breath and walks toward us, holding the flower behind his back.

"Wait, can *you* freestyle?" Meghan says to Mar.

Mar doesn't answer. The carnation's in plain view now, dangling upside down on his leg.

"Seriously, can you?" she says.

"Nah," he says. "I don't flow."

"Stop being so shy," she says, grabbing his wrist and pulling the flower up to his mouth, like a microphone. "Let's hear it."

"I can freestyle," I say, trying to get her off Mar.

"*Shut* up," she says.

"If someone kicks me a beat," I say, "I'll flow right now."

"'Kay," she says. "Let me try."

She makes slow fart noises into her hands and I spit some elementary rhymes about how hard I am, how I'll step to anyone, and then I close things out with a line that rhymes "Say ya prayers" with "Jamaica Players."

"Holy shit! How did you do that?" she says. "I guess you *have* learned some things at the King."

"Ha," I say. I can't believe Mar feels this dumbass.

"What's with the flower, Marlon?" Meghan asks. "You got a date tonight?"

"I gotta be out," Mar says to me.

"Who's the lucky lady?" Meghan calls as Marlon walks off. He turns back to me for a second and flings the flower into the darkness behind the curtains.

"What's up with him?" Meghan says.

Meghan hugs me goodbye and I try to jog after Mar, but he's long gone. I don't really want to call him when I get home, so I don't. I feel bad, but not that bad. *He's* the one who forced me to go to practice. I got burned today, too— where was his pity for my ass? He couldn't have given fewer fucks about Angel and his knife. If I don't get into Latin, I'm gonna be stuck at the King, fending off shank-packing maniacs for another two years. Then it's on to English—where I'll be stuck with a bunch of Hornets boys, including my jacker—for *four*.

I don't need tactics every night anymore, but I need them bad tonight. For the first time, Meghan flickers into my visions.

CHAPTER 9

Ghetto

Over the next month, Mar misses four days of school. Even though he still comes over, we've been spending way more time watching TV than talking, and he won't tell me what's up with the absences. He's out again today but shows up to Players practice.

"Angel started with me," I say. "He fucks with me whenever you're out."

"What you want me to say?" he says. "You wanna tattle on him again? Do it."

"I'm just saying I wish you'd been in school," I say.

"You act like you're the only one who got shit going on," he says.

I start to respond, but Mar widens his eyes for me to shut up. Meghan's rolling up to us.

"So . . . ?" she asks with a big, expectant smile.

I stare back.

"You guys get your letters yet?"

"From Latin?" I say.

"My cousin got her acceptance yesterday," she says.

"I didn't get a letter," I say.

"Huh," she says.

"I got mine," says Mar.

"And?"

"I made it," he says.

Meghan squeaks and throws her arms around him, and instead of doing an air-pat Mar holds on for real.

"How come you didn't tell me?" I say.

"I was *trying* to tell you," says Mar.

"I'm sure you'll get in, too," Meghan says to me. "But still, knock on *wood*."

When I get home, I scour my house for the letter. I call Ma and Pops at work and they say they haven't seen anything. Then I call Kev. Not only did he get into Latin, he got a perfect score on the test. I call Jimmy next. He got his letter, but it was the wrong kind of letter.

THE NEXT DAY, Mar shows up late to homeroom, looking like he got no sleep. Kaleem holds his letter up and says, "Booyah! You make it or what?"

"Yup," Mar says.

"Congrats, homey," says Kev.

The laid-back way Mar keeps delivering the news makes it even harder to take. Both of us wanted this so bad, and now that he's gotten it he's acting like it's no thing.

"WHAT DID MARLON get on the test?" Jimmy whispers to me while Mar's waiting in the lunch line.

"I don't know," I say.

"Ask him. Bet you I got a higher score."

"How do you know?"

He looks around and whispers furiously, "Marlon, Kaleem, they only got in because of the quotas."

"Nah," I say. "Mar's mad smart."

"So ask him what his score was! I guarantee it's the fucking quotas."

"Well, even if it is—"

"I know. America fucked black people. You know who else America fucked? The motherfucking *Vietnamese*. And we get jack fucking shit."

I know it's the force speaking through Jimmy. Then again, maybe he's onto something. We feel mad guilt about all the shit we did to black people, Native Americans, too, but we don't give a doggie bag about what we did to Vietnam. And all those Vietnamese heads whose lives we ruined and who had to jet from their homes to America? We just let them fade off in their own grimy grottoes and forget about them.

MY LETTER ARRIVES that afternoon. I tanked the reading section.

I'm on the wait list.

When Ma gets home, she finds me in bed stabbing into a cuticle—a stubborn bit that I can't pry out with my teeth— with a thumbtack.

"What are you doing to yourself?" she says.

I keep at it, and she grabs the tack out of my hand.

"Jesus, Dave. You're bleeding," she says. "There's probably germs all over this thing."

"Good," I say.

I show her the letter and she tries to console me with some ramen, but I tell her to take it away. Then Pops gets home and tries to get all huggy. I can't even look at his cheap ass. I barricade myself inside the tent and refuse to come out. He's the reason I'm still at the King. If it was just Ma's decision, she'd have come up with the loot for private school a long time ago. He's the one who always says no—to new sneaks, to new cars, to anything other than homegrown grub. Dude never, ever bends.

"Why don't you come out so we can talk about it?" he says.

"Why don't you take me out of the King?" I say.

"Let's just see what happens with the wait list, okay?"

"Or you could put me in Benno's school *now*."

"Dave," he says. "You know Benno's a special case."

"Well, I'm sick of being the unspecial case!"

I know what he's gonna say—*Of course you're special, too, but we believe in public schools*—so I wrap a pillow around my ears and wait till he walks away. Eventually the lights start going out and I decide to stay the night in the tent. I shoot into a sock and I'm still feeling tense, so I start right in on a doubleheader. Even after round two, I'm nowhere near relaxed. I'm lying in the soiled tent, surrounded by Benno's beady-eyed animals, when the obvious occurs to me. Tactics aren't the answer—they're the problem. I got what was coming to me. I'm lucky G-dash even put me on the wait list.

I decide the next morning: no more tactics, ever again. I figure it'll help my chances even more if I do some Good Samaritan shit, so over the weekend I go to the Arbs and spend an hour scraping cig butts out of cracks in the pavement. When I get home, I hear Benno crying in our room and instead of saying something like "Shut it, sapien," I make him an egg sandwich and slip it under the door. That stuff feels good and is actually pretty easy, but the tactics ban is a next-level struggle. I'm back to sleepless nights and they're lonelier than ever, especially since Benno's made a permanent camp in the hallway outside my parents' bedroom. As soft as this sounds, I miss having his chubby ass around. I like hearing him shift in bed, fluff his pillow, sigh and groan in frustration. It calms me.

Pam and Meghan creep into my thoughts constantly, little taunters whispering, *Just this once*. I try to crowd them out, thinking about Carmen and her cursive, but I'm not even sure she's pure anymore. So I've been thinking about my little brother—the one on the way—to get my mind clean. He's started squirming in Ma's belly, and whenever he moves Ma calls me over and lets me touch him. I like to press my face against the bump and feel him flapping around in there, like a fish in a bag. His hand poked out today—at least, that's what it felt like, a fist—and I pressed my fist to his. I can't wait to chill with him, but I also wish he didn't have to leave that dark, snug sack. Better to just stay there, ignorant and satisfied, unaware of pyrite and knives, fiending for no shorties, no Machines, no Latins, utterly untouched by the force.

I'VE HELD OFF for a week now, and each day it gets a little less agonizing. But then Meghan rocks this outfit at Players practice—one of those stretchy leotard-looking tops. It's white, which means straight-up bra strap visibility. And this isn't some dull beige granny bra, either. This shit is *red*. Halfway through practice, a bit of lace pokes out. Just a shred of red, but I can see the best part of the bra now, the centerpiece, the motherfucking *clasp*. I bite the inside of my cheek so hard it bleeds.

That night, I'm up late with a raging Lincoln Log and I know that freedom from agony is just two tugs away. But I take a deep breath, clutch my Jesus piece, and run my thumb over the nails on his tiny palms. Eventually, I go cotton and slip off into sleep. And that's when I have my first wet dream.

I'd love to tell you that the dream went like this: I unclasp Meghan's bra, watch the red lace fall away in slo-mo, spin her around, still in slo-mo, and dive into second base. But it doesn't go down like that. It doesn't go down that way at all.

Instead I'm sitting at my desk in Ms. Ansley's room alone, no Meghan, Carmen, or Pam in sight. The bell rings and I walk to my locker. There's a flyer taped up on it:

BAKE SALE

CAFETERIA

TODAY

I roll to the caf. No one's around and the tables are covered with uncut sheets of Rice Krispies Treats, pyramids of brownies and pies, rows of cupcakes the size of softballs. A friendly old black woman appears and says, "Where you been, Dave? What took you so long?"

"Just got out of class," I say. "Came as soon as I saw the sign."

"Don't you realize?" she says. "I've been waiting for you. This bake sale—it's for you."

"For me?"

"Just for you."

"How much for a Krispies sheet?"

"Why, Dave, nobody told you? It's free. All of it."

"All of it?"

"Every last bite. Better hurry, though. The sale ends in a minute."

For some annoying dream-reason, I don't have my backpack with me, so I'm stuffing my pockets and using my T-shirt as a net, gathering in as many snacks as I can. The old lady is smiling and saying, "Go right on, son. As much as you please." And the goods look so delectable and I'm starving—probably because, as usual, I barely ate any of the swiss lunch Pops packed me—but I can't waste valuable seconds, so I don't stop, even for one nibble. The woman says, "Time's almost up," and I'm flying down the tables, arms extended like tollbooth barriers, knocking as many sweets as I can into my shirt-net, and she says it again, "Time's almost up," and all of a sudden my legs freeze and I can't move anymore, and before I get the chance to sink my teeth into a single sweet morsel I'm awake, exploding.

It's four A.M. I'm too ashamed to fall back asleep. I lie there, in the mess of my nutmare, pondering and loathing who I am. The only light in the room is coming from the Day-Glo galaxy on my ceiling. I got those stars at the science museum gift shop, stuck them up there years ago with Pops, before all this madness began. Pops sweats stars and I used to love them, too, especially the Big Dipper, because it looked like a basketball hoop to me. I used to be inspired by the Dipper, dream about dunking on it. Now it just depresses me. I'm stuck down here, always will be, fiending for unreachable rims.

I OVERSLEEP AND Pops barges into my room.

"You're gonna be late," he says. "Up and at 'em."

I spring up, shirtless, and Pops eyes the Jesus piece on my chain. I've been rocking it inside my shirt around him to avoid a beef.

"Where'd you get that?" he says.

"Marlon gave it to me."

"You've been wearing that to school?"

"So?"

"It's not a fashion statement, Dave. You might offend an actual Christian."

"Who says I'm not Christian?"

"If you want to keep it around the house, that's fine, but I don't want you wearing it in public."

"Mar said as long as you believe in Jesus, you're Christian."

"How many times are we gonna go over this? You're Jewish."

"Did Ma convert?"

"What does that have to do with anything?"

"Did she?"

"No. Why would she?"

"This girl in the Players told me half Jews on the dad side don't count."

"That's absurd."

"She said if I want to have a Bar Mitzvah, I'll have to convert."

"You are going to have a Bar Mitzvah—a secular one."

"Well, what if I want to have a real one?"

"What does that mean? You want to have an *Orthodox* Bar Mitzvah? I suppose you'll have to convert. You'll have to get circumcised, too."

"What? I'm already—"

"That's right. Just like you're already a Jew. But some idiot rabbi, probably the same one who taught your friend who is and isn't a real Jew, is going to tell you yours isn't a *real* circumcision, and that if you want to be a *real* Jew you're gonna need a do-over."

"You mean he's gonna take a knife—"

"More like scissors."

The last thing I want is less of a dick.

"Forget it," I say. "I'm just sick of being nothing."

"You *are* something. Anyone who says you don't count is a moron. You certainly would've been Jewish enough for Hitler. The Nazis weren't checking with the rabbis to see who had a real circumcision."

MAR'S NOT ON the bus again today. He shows up halfway through second period and he's got crust in both eyes. At lunch, he takes yesterday's *Boston Herald* out of his bag, flips it over, and reads the sports section.

"You're not getting lunch?" I say.

"Not hungry," he says, buried in the *Herald*.

"You know you can get, like, pre–kicked out of Latin if you have too many absences and late days?" I say.

Mar scowls and turns back to his paper. Jimmy shoots Mar a bitter stare and chews his taco with his mouth open. I slurp my yogurt silently, waiting for the bell, when I hear a loud crash at the other end of the caf. Two kids race by our table. Someone shouts, "Fight!" and now everyone's out of their seats.

Jimmy gets up and says, "Fight!"

"You coming?" I ask Mar.

"What you wanna look for?" he says.

He sits there with his paper and I run with Jimmy and everyone else to get a better view. The crowd around the beef is too thick, so me and Jimmy stand on the bench of a nearby lunch table. Two eighth graders are headlocking each other. One of them is rocking a yellow hoodie and the other's in a black White Sox tee. The dude in the yellow wriggles his arm out, grabs on to the Sox guy's high-top, and yanks it, hard. The Sox guy screams and the dude in the hoodie lets go of his hair and starts punching him in the face. He gets at least five direct blows in before Rawlins rips him away. One of the teachers on lunch duty, a tiny Haitian lady named Ms. Noel, rushes over to the kid in the Sox shirt, who's lying all fetal, cupping his bleeding face. Rawlins twists the kid in the hoodie's arm and everyone watches and oohs as he marches him out of the caf.

All of a sudden, the Sox kid is back on his feet with something shiny in his hand and rushing toward the dude who beat his ass. Rawlins and the kid in the hoodie don't even realize he's behind them, and the Sox kid plunges his blade right into the other dude's back. Instead of running away, the stabber drops his knife and just stands there, trembling and crying, screaming, "What? *What?*" Rawlins slams him into the floor and pins him down with his knee.

Ms. Noel screams, "We need an ambulance!" and the dude in the hoodie staggers to a bench and tries to pat his wound, but he can't reach it. Ms. Noel holds his hand and the kid sits there, eyes shut, breathing fast but not crying as a brown splotch expands across his yellow hoodie, like rot spreading on a banana. The bell rings, but nobody moves.

"Everybody get to class! I want you to *walk* out of here *quietly*!" booms Dr. Jackson from the entrance of the caf. My heart's machine-gunning and I'm starting to get shook that I'm having some kind of panic attack.

"Mr. Greenfeld," Dr. Jackson says. "Move it!"

I tag up with Mar in the hallway.

"That was fucked up," I say, voice squeaking on the *up*. "I feel sick."

"That's what you get for looking," he says, speed-walking now.

"You think he's gonna, like, die?" I say.

"Just shut up about it," he says. "Stop thinking about it."

"You ever know anyone who died?"

"You serious right now?"

My fam's tiny. Ma's cut off from her peeps, except for her gay little brother, and pretty much all of Pops's relatives got smoked in Germany. I don't even have any cousins. I've never been to a funeral.

"I mean, you ever known someone who got killed?" I say. "Like, actually murdered or whatever?"

"Yeah," he says, looking at me like I'm corked. "More than one. Like three different dudes."

"Jesus," I say. "That's fucked up."

"That's normal," he says.

We walk into class and Ms. Ansley asks us to put our heads on our desks and take a long moment of silence. I hear the sirens crying in the distance. We just saw a piece of steel break through a sweatshirt, a T-shirt, a body. Normal is a cold, an elbow cut, a bad dream that eventually ends. What the fuck is normal about this?

A couple minutes later, over the loudspeakers, Dr. Jackson calls the whole school into the auditorium.

He limps onto the stage with his cane and says, "It goes without saying that stabbing someone in the back is a cowardly act. But what I want to say, loud and clear, is that every act of violence—back, front, or sideways—is a cowardly act. Any of you with a knife, or God forbid a gun, in your pocket or locker is nothing but a coward. My hope is that nobody's even entertaining the thought of payback. Because if you are, I don't want you coming back in here tomorrow, through these doors, past the name etched above them. This is the Martin Luther King Middle School. You want to do the brave thing? If you're angry or hurt or scared, come talk to me or your teachers. That's what we're here for. Now, let's all bow our heads. We've got a student at Beth Israel right now, and he needs our prayers."

. . .

THERE'S A FOX25 news truck waiting outside after school. A reporter sticks his mic out as we're boarding the bus, asking if anyone knew the kid who got stabbed. Mar puts his hand in the lens and boards, but I stop, stare into the camera, and say, "I didn't know him personally, but I saw it happen. . . ."

"You have a minute to talk?" the reporter asks.

"Green," Mar says through the window. "Don't even—"

"I guess I could do something real quick," I say.

For all I know, I could die tomorrow. I could get stabbed by Angel. I'm not trying to pass up my last chance at prime time.

"Great," the reporter says. "Stand over here?"

The cameraman positions me so he can get the MARTIN LUTHER KING, JR., MIDDLE SCHOOL sign in the background. Before I can even think of a good sound bite, the reporter says, "So, it must have been pretty scary, seeing that?"

Dude's trying to get me to go soft on TV. No chance.

"I mean, not really," I mumble into the mic.

"I'm surprised to hear you say that," says the reporter.

"This kind of thing happens sometimes," I say, palming my curls down as casually as I can.

"So you've seen other incidents—"

"Not, like, stabbings," I say. "But I've had a knife held up to me."

"Well, *that* sounds pretty scary," he says.

I'm not about to let this dude lure me into his bitch trap.

"It's normal," I say.

"Normal?"

Mar gets off the bus and waves me in.

"You know," I say. "For a ghetto school."

The reporter tries to pump me for more, but our driver honks and I bounce onto the bus with Mar.

"Probably shouldn't have done that," I say to Mar.

"Ghetto, huh?" he says.

I CALL MA as soon as I get to the crib and tell her about the stabbing. She leaves work early and comes home to be with me. Pops does, too. They're trying to get me to talk about my feelings; they even ask if I want to go to Benno's shrink. The truth is, the stabbing hasn't fully sunk in—and right now what's really stressing me is that interview. I said *ghetto*—out loud—on FOX25. In my house, calling a school *ghetto,* especially on FOX25, could get you disowned. Still, I decide to tell my parents in advance that I'm gonna be on TV. Then we'll watch together and I can explain, blame my blabbing on the trauma. I'd rather them find out from me than from one of their hippie-ass friends.

The news comes on at six. I'm in the tent with Benno, channeling anti-jinx vibes, praying that the *ghetto* part will be edited out of the broadcast. About ten minutes in, there I am, nibbling my nails, blatantly doing my hair, looking like a Guinness-level sapien. I bury my head under the pillow to block it all out. When I come up for air, the TV is off and Ma is crying.

"*Jesus,*" says Pops.

"I'm sorry," I say. "It just came out. I didn't mean to say that word—but it's kinda *true,* okay? You sent me to a school where kids get stabbed—"

"Why didn't you tell us?" Pops says. He looks horrified, but not *at* me.

"What are you talking about?" I say.

"You had a *knife* pulled on you?" he says. "When did this happen?"

A thousand *fuck*s erupt inside of me. I was so shook about *ghetto*, I blanked on the way worse move. I got tricked into snitching on the six o'clock news.

"It was a while ago," I say. "It wasn't a big—"

"Dr. Jackson needs to know about this," he says.

"It was a tiny knife!"

Pops heads for the cordless.

"Are you trying to get me killed?" I say.

"We're trying to keep you safe!" he screams.

"Then take me out of the fucking King already!" I scream back.

"Dave—" Ma starts.

"Hang up! I'll save you the trouble and just kill myself," I say, plunging under the pillow. Pops pulls it off me and I cover my face with my hands.

"What did you just say?" he says.

"You heard me! I said I want to fucking *kill* myself."

I'm expecting Pops to get big, flail, and roar like a grizzly. Instead he shrinks.

All trembly, he whimpers, "Don't *ever* say that again."

He's staring at me, inches from my face. Benno's cupping his ears and crying now. Pops grabs my wrist and says, "Don't even joke about that."

The phone rings. Pops picks up, clears his throat, says hello, and then, "Hi, Dr. Jackson. Yes. We saw."

. . .

DR. JACKSON ASSURES me he'll keep my tip confidential. The next day, during first period, Rawlins clips Angel's locker and finds the knife. Dr. Jackson calls me into the office to let me know that Angel's been sent to the Barron Center. I'm expecting SNITCH carvings in my desk, an avalanche of fists at lunch, but no one says or does anything. No shit talk about the FOX25 interview, either. A few heads stop me in the halls, say they saw me on TV, and one girl even says, seemingly serious, "You did good on the news."

I guess everyone's too focused on Curtis Monroe, the dude who got stabbed. It turns out he's got a punctured lung. He lost mad blood, kids are saying, and he's still in the hospital, on a breathing machine.

A COUPLE WEEKS later, during last period right before April break, Dr. Jackson makes an announcement over the loudspeakers: "This hasn't been an easy time for the King. But I've got some good news to share. It'll take a little while, but Curtis is on his way to a full recovery. No matter what anyone says about the King, I believe more than ever that *the dreamers united can never be defeated*. Now, enjoy your time off, and let's all say it one more time, together."

We all say it, loud—"The dreamers united can never be defeated!"—and Dr. Jackson rings the bell, releasing us into break. The only person who doesn't seem amped is Mar. I ask him what he's doing with his week off. He shrugs and asks if I'll be around.

"Nah," I say. "Gotta go on this stupid trip with my pops."

Kev's mom is taking him and his sister on a Caribbean

cruise. Pops is taking me to the grand opening of the Holocaust Museum. At least we're staying at a hotel, which means unlimited continental and free cable.

"Aight," Mar says. I'm sort of relieved that he seems upset.

ON OUR FIRST day in D.C., we ride around in the Whale and Handycam the White House, the huge, sad Lincoln, and the Vietnam Memorial, which makes Pops all blinky. The next day we wake up early and roll to the Holocaust Museum. There's a line around the block and a bunch of people are waiting in wheelchairs.

"This is a big deal," says Pops. "When I was your age, people didn't talk about the Holocaust. We didn't even have a word for it."

"It's *all* Cramps talks about," I say.

"He only started recently," says Pops. "For years it was 'I don't want to get into it.' Same with my mother."

It takes a couple hours to get inside and my feet are already killing me. There's way too much to read and I'm doing my best to speed Pops along. The first thing I actually stop for is this exhibit about the ghetto. I didn't know any of this, but it turns out that, back in the day, there were Jews in Venice, who were making solid loot, and the Christians got jealous and forced them into the most hood part of the city, aka the Ghetto. I didn't know there were Jews from gangster countries like Italy. I always assumed they all came from cold potato-and-borscht spots like Poland and Germany. I definitely didn't know they invented the ghetto. I'm starting to feel proud of my Jew side for the first time—and

I feel even prouder when I get to the part about the Warsaw Ghetto, about all these Jews who stepped to the Nazis.

"This is where Cramps's family got deported to," Pops says, pointing to the Krakow Ghetto on the map.

"You sure it wasn't the Warsaw one?" I ask.

"Positive," he says.

"What about your mom's side?" I ask. I don't say "Grandma," because she died before I was born. Pops never talks about her, but I remember him saying her fam was from Germany, too. I'm hoping I've got some steppers in my blood.

"I don't think so," Pops says.

We walk through the rest of the museum and it's one long blur of swastikas and bones. The thing that stands out for me is the mountain of shoes. You'd think kicks might stop smelling after fifty years, but they don't. And the funk makes it feel like everything just went down, like all these Jews just got their shoes jacked, and I wonder if any of the funk is Greenfeld funk. I think about the photos in my living room—all those Greenfelds sitting there, trying to look fly for the camera, in their suits and ties and dresses and hats—and I wonder what they were wearing when the Nazis made them strip. Did they get new prisoner gear or did they stand around naked and ashamed for the last seconds of their lives? Thinking about this hits me harder than the pictures of the body piles.

AT THE HOTEL that night, I can't sleep. I watch ESPN on mute and think about Mar. I wonder what he's doing right now, why we keep drifting, whether we'll still be boys in a year. If I don't make it off the wait list, will he just move on to Latin and forget about my ass?

Eventually Pops wakes up, turns off the TV, and says, "Why don't you read something?" So I stay up half the night with this comic book called *Maus* that he bought me at the museum shop. It's about this kid, Artie, who grew up exactly like Pops did, in the fifties, in Queens, with Holocaust survivor parents. The dad mouse is just like Cramps, too: cranky and cheap as hell, especially about food. At one point, he freaks out on Art for shaking too much salt out of the shaker. He even tries to return a half-eaten box of cereal to the grocery store. Cramps has pulled that stunt, too.

The next morning, Pops wakes me up mad early and we're back on I-95 as the dawn starts creeping.

"I feel like the guy who wrote *Maus* must've met Cramps," I say.

"A lot of survivors are like that," Pops says.

"You mean cheap?" I say.

"I wouldn't say cheap. They just sort of can't accept it's over. You get to the part about Art's mother yet?"

"You mean, when he finds out she killed herself?"

He nods and then, like it's no thing, says, "Your grandmother took her life, too."

He glances over at me and then turns back to the road. He's waiting for me to respond, and I don't know what to say other than "I didn't know that." Technically I didn't. But I feel weirdly unsurprised. I guess I've somehow always known that she didn't just die in an accident. What does surprise me is how calm he seems. No tears, no pulling over to the side of the road, nothing.

"A lot of people who escaped took their own lives," he says. "They felt guilty they got out."

The way he's talking, so matter-of-fact, reminds me of how Mar said he knew three dudes who've been murdered—like it's *normal* for a mom to kill herself. I ask how she did it and he tells me, still totally calm, that she turned her car on in the garage and sucked in the poison air.

"Sorry about saying I wanted to kill myself," I say after a long silence. "I was just kidding. You know that, right?"

"I know," he says.

"I feel guilty."

He touches my knee and says, "You didn't know," which makes me feel even more guilty.

We flip the radio on and I doze off for a while. Pops taps me awake as we pass the Camden exit. We've driven past here a bunch of times, on the way to Philly, where Pops's best friend from college lives. We have this tradition of waving when we pass, because before Pops's family moved to Queens, they lived on a farm near there. Pops took us there once, but now the land is filled with satellite dishes.

"What did you grow there?" I ask.

"I never told you?" he says. He has told me, but I always zoned out whenever he talked about that farm. "We raised chickens, for the eggs. I used to help my mom sandpaper blemishes off the shells. The customers didn't want them if they had any brown spots on them. They had to be perfectly white."

"That's kind of racist," I joke.

Pops laughs. "That's a good point."

A couple seconds later he says, "My mother let me keep

one of the eggs in my own little incubator. I still remember watching the chick peck its way out. It was pretty cool."

Hearing this reminds me of something I did when I was little that I've never told anyone about. I'd forgotten about it for years, but watching Ma's belly grow and feeling my new brother kick around in there, it came back to me. And the longer I wait for my little brother—not to mention a letter from Latin—the more that shit haunts me. I decide to just get it off my chest and tell Pops.

When I was in second grade, our teacher, Ms. Ross, brought a caterpillar in, and everyone wiled out when it turned into a cocoon and eventually burst out and spread its slimy butterfly wings. So then Ms. Ross brought in an incubator and an egg. Everyone was amped for it to hatch, especially me. After a couple weeks, the egg started shaking a little, then cracking. Ms. Ross said it was only a matter of time till we'd get to meet the chick. During recess, I told the teacher I had to go inside to pee, and instead of going to the bathroom I snuck into our classroom. By that point, there were cracks all over the egg, and one crack was so big, you could even see a little bit of feather sticking out. I couldn't wait any longer. I reached into the cage and slowly peeled open the egg. But the chick didn't raise its head or kick its legs. It just stayed curled up. I went back out to recess and when we got back, this girl Tameka screamed, "Ms. Ross— it's dead!" and started crying. I waited until I got home to cry because I didn't want anyone to suspect me.

"I still feel bad about that," I say.

"You were a kid," Pops says. "You shouldn't be so hard on yourself."

A few seconds pass and I say, "You shouldn't, either."

"What do you mean?"

"I dunno. You don't, like, ever treat yourself. You're not as bad as Cramps, but you never wanna eat out or get take-out—"

"What do I need to take out for? I like growing my own food. I like cooking."

"Fine, but you never buy new gear. You keep driving this old-ass car."

"That stuff's not important to me," he says.

"Yeah," I say, "but it's fun."

He doesn't respond. He just smiles like I said something funny. I can't tell what he's thinking, and there's a million extra things I want to ask him about his mom and the Holocaust and the real reasons he never spends money on himself, but I don't. Eventually he turns the stereo back on and pumps Woody Guthrie, and for a second I remember I'm still mad at him—for sending me to the King instead of ponying up for private school, for all the Nintendo-free years, for every swiss lunch he ever packed me. But the longer he hums, the harder it is to stay mad. My poor pops. Your mom sucked in poison air. How the hell do you even hum after that?

WHEN WE GET back to Boston, Pops turns off at the wrong exit and parks the Whale.

"What's going on?" I say.

"Follow me. We gotta hurry."

We jog down Lansdowne Street toward Fenway.

We get to the ticket window and Pops asks for two in the

bleachers. Bleachers tickets cost five dollars each and are behind center field. They're the absolute nosebleeds—not just because you need binoculars to see the ball but because all the rowdy drunk dicks, the kind who will punch you in the face for knocking into their beer, sit out there. Still, this is the first time Pops has ever taken me to a Sox game, so I don't complain. We hike up hundreds of stairs till we get to our row, which is underneath the huge overhanging scoreboard. Our seats are in the middle, so everyone has to stand up with their beers and dogs as we butt-rub our way past them. Pops is wearing his usual Birkenstocks with socks and one guy says, "Go back ta Woodstawk," as we edge by.

A vendor comes around slinging Fenway Franks. Without me even having to ask him for one, Pops raises his index finger and says, "One dog. Extra mustard." He passes the bills down the aisle and tells the vendor to keep the change. I don't even like mustard that much, but I smear on both packets for Pops's sake and the dog is still delicious.

"You're not getting one for yourself?" I ask.

"Nah," he says, "I'm good."

He pulls a baggie of trail mix out of one of the twenty pockets in his safari vest.

The Sox start losing big in the fourth inning and can't recover. By the time the ninth rolls around, about half of the crowd is gone and I'm ready to bounce, too. But Pops is like Mar, I guess, when it comes to staying for the whole game.

"Let's start the Wave," Pops says.

"No way. It's not the right time for it."

"Come on," he says. "The Sox need a little juice."

"I'm leaving if you do it."

Pops stands up, shouts, "One—two—three—*wave!*" and flaps his arms above his head.

A guy behind us laughs.

"One—two—three—*waaave!*" Pops says louder.

"One—two—three—*gay!*" the shithead behind us shouts.

"Dad, *please,*" I say.

"Who gives a crap?" he says. "This is always how things get started."

"Nothing's getting started. You're the only one standing up."

"That's how it works. You get over the embarrassment, and then the next guy stops being embarrassed, and then it happens. It takes a second, but it always happens. Watch. One—two—three—*waaaave!*"

And then a couple kids a few rows down stand with their mom. And then the geezer next to us gets up, too. And then, like magic, the whole bleachers are standing and raising their arms, and I watch as the fans in right field ripple up like dominoes in reverse, and then it surges across home plate, and around left field, past the Green Monster, all the way back to us, and this time I halfheartedly stand, too. All of a sudden ten, maybe fifteen thousand people are passing the squeeze—all because of Pops.

I look up at him and he's got this *Is this awesome or what?* gleam in his eyes as the human tide continues to roll around us. Each time the Wave starts up again, he erupts in squeaky, astonished "Ha!"s. After a half-dozen rounds, people fade back into their chairs and Pops turns to me and holds up his hand for a high five. The planet seems to stop for a second. I feel the faces of fifteen thousand fans lasered into me like shame-seeking missiles. I picture the whole city of Boston, peering out of skyscraper windows, ogling us from planes and hot-air balloons, scaling trees and streetlights to get a better view, all watching, waiting, to see if I'll meet my father's hand.

He's standing there, with the whitest, most open-jawed smile anyone's ever seen. It's the exact kind of dimpled-out glee I've tried to iron off of my own face for most of my public life. And I'm kind of amazed, actually, not just at the lack of shame but at how someone whose life has been so swiss—whose actual mom offed herself—is even capable of that softness. I raise my head and glance up at him, my father, bespectacled, Birkenstocked, but kind—someone who took me to a Sox game even though he hates sports, someone who copped me a dog and asked for extra mustard—and I feel like telling him that even though I'm still pissed about the King, if he ever committed suicide I would, too.

I high-five him and no one notices. Nobody—other than Pops—cares.

CHAPTER 10

Drama

When we get home, Mar's there, in the tent with Benno. "C's won again," he says. "I'm telling you, this tent's gonna bust the Curse. We gotta watch all the playoff games in here."

Benno nods and Mar gives him pound. "I'm down," I say.

I ask if he wants to sleep over. I decide I'm gonna finally come clean about all the Jewish stuff, but I figure I'll ease into it, in the wee hours, tell him about the museum and the Sox first. Mar says he has to bounce, though, so I walk him to Pops's garden at the edge of the PJs. I try to tell him there, but I can't quite transition out of C's talk, and Mar starts walking into the gates.

"Hold up," I say.

Mar turns to me.

"I, um—well, actually, my pops. He um . . ."

Mar's looking at me suspiciously now. I don't even have to say, *I'm Jewish.* All I have to say is *He's Jewish.*

"He *what*?"

"His mom committed suicide," I say.

"For real?" Mar says. "Like recently?"

"Nah," I say. "Before I was born. But I just found out."

"Your pops just told you?" he says.

"Yup," I say.

"Prolly didn't want people knowing about it," Mar says.

"Yeah," I say. "Kinda shook me up. Like, knowing that shit's in my blood."

Mar looks into the dark garden.

"You ever get shook about that kind of thing?" I ask.

"What kind of thing?"

"Like, you ever worry you might turn out mental or something?"

"Why you saying that?"

"I dunno," I say. "It's just like, Benno's got his shit, and sometimes I wonder if I might have mental stuff, too. Like, how I'm always shook and nervous, biting my nails bloody, and doing other stuff I shouldn't be doing . . ."

"What other stuff?"

"Just, like, calm-down rituals so I can fall asleep. But I always need to do them, because being up at night, by myself—I don't know—it fucks with me. You remember that time at Kev's when we stayed up all night together?"

"Yeah, I remember." He fiddles with the worn straps of his backpack. "I get shook about it sometimes, too.

"About the blood stuff," he says a couple seconds later.

I want to push for more, but I ride out the silence.

"Cuz of my moms," he finally says. "And that's why it pisses me off when people say she's a fiend."

"So why don't you just, like, tell them what's really up with her?"

"Ain't like crazy sounds better than crackhead," he says.

"She take pills?" I ask. "I mean, like Benno's?"

"She's supposed to. She doesn't like 'em, though, so me and my grandma have to . . ."

A car slowly pulls around the bend and we squint in the light.

"Forget it," he says.

"Have to what?" I say. "It's cool. I'm not gonna say anything."

"I gotta be out," he says. He walks off and I hear the C's tapes rattling in his giant black bag.

ON THE MONDAY morning after break, I try out a new piece in front of the mirror. It's a mini–Torah pointer that Cramps brought me back from one of his trips to Israel. It's way bigger than the Jesus piece, and when it's tucked in, it looks like I'm smuggling a kiddie cone, but I'm feeling it. I slip the cross into my pocket in case I change my mind.

Mar's out again today, and on the bus ride home Angel comes at me, fresh from the Barron Center.

"You dimed on me, gringo?" he says. I stare out the window.

"Li'l snitching motherfucker," he says, shoving me on the side of my head.

"Chill," says Vicki, which just makes things worse. Angel sees the bulge in my tee, pulls out the Torah pointer, and yanks it.

"Get *off* him," says Vicki, standing up now.

"Sit ya ugly ass down," says Angel.

Vicki cocks her arm back and swings a closed fist— hard—into Angel's ear.

"Fuck was that, *bitch*?" Angel screams.

The second he raises a fist, Vicki windmills her arms around and paddles his face with both palms. She looks like a *Street Fighter II* character under the spell of a complex code. She's getting so many blows in, so fast, that all Angel can do is crouch for safety. She probably has twenty pounds on him, she's got him trapped in the little space between the seats, and she's stomping him. She's wearing Hi-Tec boots, too—they're like budget Tims, with hard-ass soles—and he's shrieking from the impact. Everyone's standing on their seats, whooping and laughing, even Angel's boy Hector. The driver does nothing until she gets to Vicki's stop, and then shouts, "Off my bus—now!"

Vicki wipes the sweat from her forehead, smooths her hair back, gets one more stomp in, and says, "Little *bitch*."

Angel gets up and hobbles back to his seat. There's blood streaming from his lip and dirt all over his white tee. There's even a bit of boot print stamped onto his pretty boy face. I tuck my Torah pointer back in, clutch it through my shirt, and breathe.

MAR SHOWS UP to Players practice that afternoon and immediately spots the bulge.

"You wearing a new piece?" he says.

I knew Mar was gonna notice. I guess I even wanted him to so I'd be forced to tell him I'm a Jew, straight up, once and for all. After our chat near the garden a few nights ago, I'm not so shook anymore. I feel like things are different between us now. Talking—and getting him to talk—was easier than I thought it would be. I untuck the Torah pointer.

"I was gonna explain this shit the other night," I say to Mar. "It kind of has to do with what I was saying about my grandmother. Like, the whole reason me and my pops went to D.C. was to go to this museum."

From across the room, Meghan says, "Is that a *yad*?"

"I dunno," I say. "My grandfather got it for me."

"Why are you, like, wearing it?" she says. "That's for reading the Torah—in a *synagogue*."

Mar's forehead gets all lined up. I can't tell if he's just confused or if he's heated, too, and I lose my train of thought.

"You ever read *Maus*?" I ask Meghan.

"I've heard of it," she says.

"You should read it," I say. "It's even better than *Anne Frank*."

"No it ain't. And stop fronting like you've read *Anne Frank*," Mar says. "You've never read a real book in your life."

"Yeah I have," I say.

"Name one."

"*Tom Sawyer*," I say.

"What happened at the end?" he says.

"I've read *Drive*," I say.

Meghan laughs. "By Larry Bird? My dad has that book. He's obsessed with the Celtics—has season tickets and everything."

"Damn," I say. This shorty's even more looted than I realized.

"You ever go to games with him?" Mar asks all casually, like season tickets are no thing.

"All the time," she says. "We're supposed to go to the playoffs together on Thursday. If he gets back from his stupid business trip."

"Where's he at?" Mar asks.

"Dallas," she says. "His office always makes him go out there."

"They fly him first-class?" I ask.

"I think so," she says. "Who gives a shit? I'm just hoping he gets back in time. Last year he had to miss all three shows. I was so pissed."

"I wish my parents would miss a show," I say. "They come to everything."

"How about your parents?" Meghan says to Mar. "They coming?"

"My grandma," he says. "And my mom."

"Your dad can't make it?" she says.

"Nah," says Mar. "He's down in Atlanta."

"I THOUGHT YOUR pops lived in Miami," I say to Mar on our walk home.

"Nah," he says. "Atlanta."

"Remember? You said he was in Miami."

"*You* said you were Christian."

"I am. It's just . . . my pops is Jewish, so I'm sort of Jewish, too."

"You can't be both. Ain't no such thing as part Christian. You said you believe in Jesus."

"I do believe in him," I say, pulling the Jesus piece out of my pocket for proof.

"Then you ain't Jewish. The whole point of Jews is they *don't* believe in Jesus. That's the whole reason the Pharaoh-sies killed him."

"I thought the Pharaohs were the ones who killed the Jews," I say.

"The Pharaoh-*sies,* stupid. That's the Jews."

I look down at the Jesus piece. Seeing those tiny nails in his ankles and wrists, I feel queasy.

That night, I ask Pops about it. He smiles awkwardly and tells me that Mar probably didn't mean anything by it but that saying Jews killed Jesus is anti-Semitic.

A COUPLE NIGHTS later, Meghan calls and tells me her dad's not gonna be back in time for the C's. She asks if I want to go with her. To a motherfucking playoff game.

"I gotta ask Mar," I say.

"What do you need his permission for?" she says.

"We were gonna watch together. We have this whole tradition with my little brother."

"These are sixth-row seats," she says.

Mar's obviously heated when I call and fill him in.

"You can still watch it with Benno," I say. "We'll peep the rest of 'em together."

"Fuck that," he says. "We had a plan. You're gonna jinx the whole thing. Might as well buy another Machine and root for the damn Hornets—I know you *want* to."

"I told you I'm over the Machine," I say.

"Well, you obviously ain't over Meghan," he says.

Nothing quick comes to me.

"Hello?" he says.

"I told you, I don't feel white girls."

I hear him suck his teeth.

"You really expect me to turn down free playoff tickets? I mean, *you* got into Latin. You're gonna be able to afford your own playoff tickets someday. This could be my only chance."

"Fuck it," he says. "Sell me out."

I MEET MEGHAN at the Green Line stop and we ride to the Garden on the elevated tracks. I'm pretty nervous—I've never been alone with a shorty for this long in my life—and Meghan isn't making things easier for me. She won't say anything, and when she's not checking her pager she's looking into the window reflection, dabbing at her eye makeup and messing with her hair. I'm trying to come up with a convo topic, but nothing feels right. What do white girls like to talk about? The Gap? Horses? I feel like I have more in common with homeless Jerry.

Meghan finally breaks the silence. "You hear anything from Latin yet?"

"Nah," I say. "Pretty much gave up hope at this point."

"So you're just gonna stay at the King?"

I shrug. "I'm kinda used to it by now."

"You must be pretty pissed at Marlon, huh?"

"Nah. Why?"

"You guys have been, like, super-catty lately. You're obviously jealous he got in. He's obviously jealous of you, too."

"Why the hell would he be jealous of me?"

Meghan rolls her eyes and turns back to her pager. A few minutes later, we get off the train and head into the Garden.

Our seats are close enough to hear the parquet rattle. I look up at those sixteen championship banners and those retired numbers—6 for Bill Russell, 14 for Bob Cousy, and now 33 for Bird—hovering like ghosts in the rafters. There's a few empty spaces left. Someday Reggie's gonna be up there, too. It reminds me of the final slot in the auditorium at Latin. At least Mar's in the running for that shit.

There's a couple Irish dudes sitting next to us; they both have big Bird mustaches and skin the color of the Bud Light they're drinking. Reggie scores on the first possession and I give them both high fives. Over the next six minutes, Reggie drops nine more points. He's unstoppable, on target to break Larry's playoff scoring record, and Meghan barely cares. She's buried in her pager.

"Let's start a slow clap," I say to her.

"That's way too embarrassing," she says.

"Nah, it's cool," I say.

Clap. Clap. Clap. Clap.

"Stop it," says Meghan. "Let's just watch the game."

"Wait for it," I say.

Clap. Clap. Clap. Clap.

The guys next to us join in and within seconds the whole Garden is thundering.

"That was actually amazing," says Meghan.

"Let's do a 'Let's Go, Reggie!' together," I say. I grab her hand and stand up. She's still sitting and I start the chant without her.

"Let's go, Reg-gie!" *Clap-clap, clap-clap-clap.*

The white dude next to me stands up, spilling his beer on us, and then his buddy joins in. I watch the whole section rise. Meghan finally gets up, squeezes my hand, smiles, and joins in, too. I turn my back to the court, face the crowd, lift my palms toward the rafters, and scream, "Louder! Let's go, Reg-gie!" *I'm* making this happen, *I'm* gonna be the one to will Reggie to win, to break Bird's record, and I'm screaming, "Let's go, Reg-gie!" louder and faster, "Let's-Go-Reg-gie!" and clapping and flapping and sparkplugging the whole entire Garden—and then Meghan yanks my hand and twists me around and I realize I'm the last one chanting. Reggie's on the floor, flat on his face.

"What happened?" I ask.

"He just, I don't know," says Meghan.

"He just *what*? Why isn't he getting up?"

"He just fell. No one was even near him."

It's quiet as a Catholic church. Most people are cupping their mouths, but my hands are pressed together. I close my eyes and pray to G-dash until I hear a mild applause and see Reggie get up and walk off the floor. He's not limping, but we're close enough to see his face. He looks stunned, like he has no idea where he is. He sits out the rest of the game.

The C's win without him and Meghan hugs me to celebrate, but I'm in no mood to hold on. All I can think about is what happened to Reggie.

His diagnosis comes the next day: a messed-up heart. His doctors won't let him play for the rest of the playoffs and we lose the next three games. The Curse of the Coke continues, and Mar blames the whole thing on me.

"You never shoulda bought that Machine and rocked Hornets colors in the first place. You never shoulda put that damn finger on your chain. You never shoulda left the tent."

"I didn't jinx anything—I did the opposite. You shoulda seen me leading the slow clap."

"You never shoulda been at that game. They're saying Reggie might never play again. That's on *you*."

I don't sleep at all that night. Mar blamed me for fucking up my favorite player's heart. He pretty much said *I* was cursed. And it's one thing for him to hate on me for leaving the tent and rocking the Machine back in the day, but what the hell did my Torah pointer have to do with anything?

I WANT TO talk it over with him in school on Monday, but once again he doesn't show at the bus stop. He's missed eight days since I started counting. He really might get pre–kicked out of Latin and it's pissing me off how he's taking it all for granted. I show up to this shitty school every single day—and for what? I look over at Jimmy, who's drawing graffiti on his desk. He's been acting way harder these days. He recently bleached this long lock of hair he grew out. He told me that's a thing cliqued-up Vietnamese dudes do. He hasn't asked me to chill for a while, and I wonder if his cousin let him join the crew now that he's not going to Latin. I'm still thinking about what he said about the quotas. America fucked the Vietnamese and they don't get shit. You know who else America fucked? The Jews. They only hooked Cramps's family up with one damn visa and let the rest get gassed. And yeah, the Holocaust happened a while ago, but my fam's still getting fucked by it. And I know most

Jews are looted these days, but it's not like anti-Semitism's over. Shit, *Mar* might be anti-Semitic.

I grab my pen and draw a swastika on my desk. Since rolling to D.C., I've started seeing swastikas everywhere— on brick walls and bathroom tiles, even in the parquet at the Garden. I've started scribbling them in my notebook, too, and they're almost as addictive to draw as sharks. Yesterday I drew two interlocking *Tetris* pieces. On my desk, I draw one with Nike Swooshes on the tips. I make sure to erase it before class ends because I know it's messed up and I could get in serious trouble if I got caught. But I figure if black dudes are allowed to say the n-word with an *a,* Jews should be allowed to draw weird swastikas. Anyway, maybe getting caught wouldn't be such a bad thing. What's the worst that could happen—getting booted from the King?

The next day in class, I'm back at it, and when Ms. Ansley looks in my direction I stop drawing but make no effort to conceal the swastikas.

"David," she says, eyeing my desk. "What do you think you're doing?"

"Doodling?"

"Erase it, and see me after class."

Ms. Ansley's pissed.

"What was going through your mind, drawing those things? Especially after our World War Two unit. You know better."

I don't know why, but my mouth curls into a grin.

"This isn't funny, David. That symbol has no place in our classroom. It's *hateful.* You could get sent to the Barron Center for this kind of thing—you're aware of that, right?"

"I was just playing," I say, which makes her angrier. Getting kicked out of the King is one thing, but I really don't want to risk going to the Barron Center. From what I've heard, it's basically a juvie prison. So I tell her straight up: "I'm Jewish."

An awkward second passes and I add, "My grandfather's a survivor."

"A Holocaust survivor?"

I nod solemnly.

"Why didn't you mention that during our World War Two unit? We could have had him come in and speak about his experiences."

That's exactly why I didn't mention it. There's nothing Cramps likes better than speaking to classrooms about the Holocaust. He's visited schools all over the city. Last year, he came to my class at the Trotter and spent half the time crying in that same seal-bark way Pops does. It's not like anyone made fun of him, but it embarrassed the shit out of me. Still, after everything that's been going down, now I'm thinking having Cramps come to the King wouldn't be such a bad idea. I wouldn't mind having people feel *my* pain for once.

"You want me to ask him to come in and speak?" I say.

"If he's willing, I'd love to have him."

A FEW DAYS later, Cramps comes to the King. He refuses to even use a walker, so Pops and me each have to take an arm and basically drag him through the hallways. Mar passes us on our way into the classroom, stops, and says hi to Cramps.

"Nice to see you, Marvin," Cramps says.

"*Marlon,*" Pops says, and Cramps waves him off.

"Heard you got into Latin," Cramps says, shaking Mar's hand. "Congratulations."

"Thanks," Mar says shyly.

"When are you gonna find out about that wait list?" Cramps says to me.

"Dad," Pops says. "He'll tell you when he has news."

We enter the room and the class hushes. I think I hear someone snicker, probably Kaleem.

"We have a very special guest today, David's grandfather Professor Heinrich Greenfeld. We've all been studying World War Two and we learned about the Holocaust, but the realest history—the kind you can feel in your bones and actually remember—isn't something you can get from a textbook. We've learned all about primary and secondary sources, and you all know how I feel. . . ."

"*Primary is primo,*" a few kids drone.

"That's right. But do you know what's even more primo? A live human source—because unlike letters, diaries, and artifacts, Professor Greenfeld can talk back. He can answer our whys. Enough from me—why don't we hear from the source himself. Professor?"

"Thank you, Ms. Ansley," says Cramps. "I was up late last night thinking about what I wanted to say to you, and I decided it would be more beneficial for me to tell you about America than about Germany. Very bad things happened over there, but very good things happened over here, and I like to try to stick to the positive."

Cramps smiles and Pops pats him on the back.

"Let me tell you about the first thing I ever saw in America. I was on a boat for about three weeks with hundreds of other refugees. I was all alone and had no one to talk to, but eventually I made a friend, a boy named Viktor. He was sixteen, just like me. Everybody called him Eggplant because he had a big purple spot on his face, and nobody wanted to go near him because they thought he was diseased. I had a cousin with one of these on her face and I knew it was just a birthmark. Viktor brought a small folding chessboard with him from Frankfurt, and we played dozens of games a day to make the time pass. Sometimes the ship would make a quick turn and the pieces would fall to the floor and we had to scramble to pick them up before they slid into the sea, and then we had to restart the game, because neither of us could agree on where the pieces had been before the spill. At the time I was ticked off and cursed the captain. I later found out he was swerving from German submarines. Anyway, one morning out on the deck there was a real commotion. Everyone started running to one side of the boat shouting, 'Look, look!' It was dark and foggy and I couldn't see what they were talking about. And I had Viktor's queen already.

" 'Should we go see?' Viktor said.

" 'Let's finish the game,' I said.

"But so many people ran to that side of the boat that it began to tip, and half of our pieces slid off the deck. I walked over to the crowd to curse the idiots.

" 'Look!' a man said, with his daughter on his shoulders. He was pointing to a tall metal structure poking out of the mist.

" 'The Statue of Liberty!'

"We got closer and the fog lifted a little. It turned out to be some kind of oil tower in Jersey. But seconds later we saw the real thing, holding up that torch, welcoming us to our new home. I'll never forget it. We got to Ellis Island and waited for hours in line. They made us answer so many questions and did all kinds of tests on us. I passed and Viktor was behind me, so I waited for him right beyond the gate. They took one look at his face and sent him into a cage on the other side of the room for further inspection. The rumors were if you went into the cage you'd almost certainly get sent back to Europe. There was no use in arguing with them. I saw a man who argued when they turned back his wife and they sent him back, too. So I shut my mouth and boarded the ferry to Manhattan. I don't know what happened to Viktor. I ran into a lot of the people from the ship later on, but I never saw Viktor again."

Cramps pauses and takes a big, loud breath. I look around the class, scanning for smirks, but everybody's sitting upright, listening closely.

"I was angry about Viktor and I cursed America. I cursed it some more when the only job I could get was sewing tablecloths for a dollar a day in a cellar on the Lower East Side. Can I say *damn* in here? Good. Every night I went home muttering, 'God damn this place. God damn America.' I missed Germany: the music, the shops, the Weisswurst, my sister, my parents. I wanted to go home. I knew things were terrible over there, but at the time I didn't know how terrible. When Roosevelt finally went to war, I signed up like everybody else. I finally got to go back to Germany and saw a million of the worst things I ever saw, but I stopped damning America, because we beat Hitler when no one else could. And when the war was over, I didn't have to slave away in a sweatshop anymore, because the army paid for me to go to college. I stopped damning America, because I saw that when you worked hard here, your life changed."

Cramps lets out a couple seal barks and straightens himself in his chair. I look over at Mar and his lips are quivering a little. I guess he's inspired or something.

"I stopped damning America and started hitting the books, and guess what? The sweat turned into a PhD. That's not the American dream. I don't buy that silly phrase. I'm a mathematician and I could care less about dreams. That's the American *formula:* You get what you put in. If you end up a have-not," Cramps says, directing his gaze on me, "it's because you have not worked."

Mar doesn't seem inspired anymore. A tremor is spreading across his face, slowly, like cracks in thin ice. Is he gonna cry? I don't see why he's getting all emotional. If anyone should be crying, it's me.

"All right, Dad," Pops says. "Maybe it's time you open it up for questions."

"We'll get to questions. I have one more thing to say. I know many of you in here come from tough lots. I know something about rough luck myself. But rough luck is not a lifetime pass for making excuses. Look at me. I've got every excuse on the planet. Look at my back. I walk around like a good-for-nothing chimpanzee. I weigh a hundred and ten pounds without an ounce of muscle. Every joint in my body throbs when I crawl, literally *crawl,* out of bed each morning. But I still show up to work every day, fifteen minutes early, because I learned in the army that early is on time, on time is late, and late is inexcusable."

"Dad, it's really time for questions," Pops says.

"I just want to leave you with this. You want to succeed? Burn up your excuse card as soon as possible—in other words, now. Do your homework and study for your tests and I promise things will work out for you. You'll get into college, and if you don't you can always join the army like I did. The army could be an excellent option for some of you."

Mar gets up and hands Ms. Ansley a bathroom pass. She signs it and he quickly walks out.

"Did I say something?" says Cramps. Pops reddens, closes his eyes, and runs his fingers through his hair.

"The class prepared some questions for you," Ms. Ansley jumps in. "Tanya, would you like to start things off for us?"

"Mr. Greenfelt, why did you survive the Holocaust?"

"Look, I don't know who told your teacher I was a Holocaust survivor. I got out before the camps. But my parents and sister and all of my other relatives . . . they weren't as lucky."

"Were you happy at least you made it out?" asks Tanya.

"No. I felt terrible. I still do."

After a couple more questions, Mar comes back into the room, takes his seat, and puts his head on his desk. I still don't see why he's acting so upset. Sure, Cramps said some bonk stuff, but Mar already knows Cramps is crazy. Besides, from the thousand conversations I've had with Mar about Latin and Harvard and making loot, he basically agrees with everything we just heard. He voted for Perot in the mock election last fall.

The period ends and everyone claps for Cramps, and when I ask Mar what's up on our way to lunch, he says, "Nothing."

"I've got some announcements," says Milt a couple days later at Players practice. "We're going one hundred percent off-book next practice and I don't want to hear any whining about it. I also want to give you a heads-up about our service show."

Everyone groans. Last year we did a show at the VA and this toothless vet whistled through his fingers every time Meghan came out.

"This year," says Milt, "we'll be performing at the Robert Gould Shaw Community Center. The folks I've talked to there are thrilled to host the Players."

The Shaw Center is a couple blocks away from the PJs. We might as well be performing *in* the PJs, because it's pretty much the go-to free after-school program in our neighborhood. I pull Milt aside.

"Have you been to the Shaw Center?" I say.

"Personally?" he says. "No. But I've had some terrific chats with the staff."

"Did you tell them we're a musical theater group?"

"Of course."

"I don't think this is a good idea."

"Dave, you really need to watch your assumptions. Musicals aren't just for people in Moss Hill. By the way, what's up with Marlon? We're in crunch time here. This is the second rehearsal he's missed in a row."

"He wasn't in school today, either."

"I hope everything's okay," Milt says. "I want you to get ready as his alternate, just in case."

WHEN I GET home from Players practice, Ma meets me at the front door, grabs my hand, and leads me into the kitchen. There's a big purple star-shaped balloon floating above the kitchen table. The ribbon is tied around an envelope that's been opened and taped back together. Ma, Pops, and Benno applaud while I slide out the letter. I assumed if this moment ever came, I'd be all *Price Is Right,* pumping my fists in the air and kicking my heels into my ass. But I just collapse onto the couch and close my eyes. I've felt my heart speed up a billion times. This is the first time I can remember feeling it slow down.

"How 'bout we celebrate at J.P. Licks?" says Ma. Benno nods enthusiastically. J.P. Licks is the expensive-ass ice cream shop on Centre Street.

"Sounds good to me," says Pops. "I'll pick up Cramps."

"Can I invite Mar?" I ask.

"Of course," Pops says.

I think about how I want to tell Mar before I call him. I wanna say something about how dope it's gonna be, rolling together for the next six years, and how after that, we'll be roommates at Harv, and how after that, we'll start a business together, build an empire and shit. But the answering machine picks up, and I play it cool. I tell him to call me back in ten if he wants to come with us. I know he's still heated at me, but I figure he'll be down to make up, especially over sundaes. We wait for the phone to ring, and it doesn't.

At J.P. Licks, Ma says me and Benno can get anything we want. I go with a root beer float, and Benno copies me as usual. I've never had one, and I've been curious about them ever since I saw this old pic of Pops and his fam where they're drinking floats on top of Mount Washington, looking like happy all-Americans, even Pops's mom.

"We're proud of you, buddy," Pops says. "You too, Benno."

"To the first big milestone of many," says Cramps, raising a glass of water. He's sitting at the end of our table in his new wheelchair. Pops finally convinced him to get one.

"To hard work paying off," Cramps continues, and the guilt starts to seep in. I wonder if I would've gotten in without copying those last couple answers off Mar.

"*L'chaim,*" says Cramps.

"*L'chaim!*" we all say.

Benno starts on his float, but I keep staring at mine. I wish Mar was at least here to split it with me. Pops asks me what I'm waiting for and I stab my straw through the vanilla scoop. I suck down a cream-and-soda bullet. Then another, and another, without even taking a breath.

"Savor it, you gourmand," Cramps says. "Savor it!"

"Instead of telling Dave how to eat his," Ma says, "why don't you get your own?"

"That's not a bad idea, Dad," says Pops.

"No way," says Cramps. "Thing's an absolute rip-off. There's less than fifty cents of materials in there."

Cramps keeps staring, so I reluctantly offer him a taste. He hesitates before dipping in his pinkie tip.

"Now that," he says, "is premium stuff."

Pops gets up and returns with three more floats: one for him, one for Ma, one for Cramps.

"I can't," says Cramps.

"You can," says Pops.

"Mmm," says Ma.

"My blood pressure," says Cramps.

"Your blood pressure's fine," says Pops.

Cramps pokes at his straw, sighs, and lowers his mouth for a sip.

"This really is premium stuff," he says. He goes in for another long, slow suck.

We sit there slurping, a family of freaks, sapiens, hippies, and immigrants, huddled together in a red padded booth. Pops is sitting between me and Cramps; he puts his arms around our shoulders and lightly pulls us in.

"I shouldn't have done that," Cramps says.

"Here we go," says Ma under her breath.

"You absolutely should have done that," says Pops.

"No, no, no, no," he says, shaking his head. "I should not have done that."

"It's okay, Dad," says Pops.

"No, it's not," says Cramps. "It's not okay."

WHEN I GET back home I try Mar again, and he finally picks up.

"You get my message?" I say.

No response.

"It came," I say.

"The letter," I say. "I'm *in*."

"Cool," he says.

"You don't seem too amped for me."

"Can't really talk right now."

"Everything cool? Milt's kinda worried about you."

"He needs to mind his bees."

"So's Meghan," I lie.

"Everyone needs to chill the fuck out," says Mar. "I got this."

THAT FRIDAY, THE day of opening night, Mar's not in school. I'm realizing I might actually have to be his stand-in and I start to feel my throat dry up. I passed out once, because I was dehydrated, and the last thing I want to do is faint onstage. So to be safe I do something I never do at the King: hit up the fountain. The water's bath-hot and there's two-toned snot blocking the drain. I close my eyes, imagine I'm sipping from a pure mountain stream, and glug. Ten minutes later, I have to piss. I manage to hold it in for an entire period before resigning myself to a bathroom visit.

One of the two urinals is taken by an eighth grader. The toilet is clogged, an inch or so from overflowing, so I wait. I hate whizzing next to other dudes, especially older ones. Whenever I try to—no matter how bad my bladder's burning—I can't squeeze out a drop. The dude finishes, walks out, and just as I'm getting going, someone else walks in and rolls up to the other urinal. It's Angel.

I know he's been waiting for his chance to wail on me.

Did he spot me in the halls and follow me in here? Or is this some kind of omen? Maybe G-dash doesn't want me to be Mar's stand-in. Maybe he sent Angel to cripple me before the big show. I keep my head as still as possible and shift my eyes toward him, careful not to look downward. His eyes dart in my direction, too, but then, instead of talking shit or shanking me, he shifts his body away from mine and unzips. I need to get out of here before he snaps, but I've got a gallon left in the tank, and the harder I push, the more it feels like I'm pulling in the piss. A few seconds pass before I realize how quiet it is in here. I glance back at him and he sees me clocking, but he looks more ashamed than angry. He pivots some more. A couple seconds later, I'm still not hearing any trickle or splash at his urinal.

I can't believe it. Angel's got the same problem. He can't pee, either—he's been waiting for *me* to leave. And the craziest thing is, I actually feel bad for him. I zip up, walk out, and wait in the hallway. A minute later he emerges, avoiding eye contact, and I head back in to finish my business.

I'M BACKSTAGE WITH the rest of the Players and everybody's bugging. We've got fifteen minutes till curtain and Mar's still not here. I keep calling him from the phone in Milt's office and I keep getting the machine. We do a few final voice exercises and then we gather in a circle backstage.

"Go ahead and grab your neighbors' hands," Milt whispers. "Take a belly breath. In. And *out*. For many of you, this is your first show-must-go-on moment. Almost everyone in the theater dreads these moments, but I'll tell you what. I *live* for them. This is the magic of live performance. This is what makes us feel *most* alive. Dave has been prepping the whole season for this and we all know he's gonna be a kick-butt understudy. We're gonna miss Marlon tonight, and I can understand how upset many of you are."

Just then, Mar creeps in, mad quiet. Milt doesn't see him.

"None of us knows why he's not here tonight and I'm sure he's got his reasons."

"I'm here," says Mar.

"Mar!" Meghan squeals. Everyone jumps around him in celebration.

"I'ma need that costume," Mar says to me.

"Curtain's in five—go!" says Milt.

I strip out of the costume, relieved. Mar speed-changes and we jet back to the circle.

"It's time to pass the pulse," says Milt. I let Mar sit next to Meghan.

When the curtain opens, I scan the crowd for my fam. From my third-row perch in the chorus bleachers, I can see all the way to the back of the audience. Pops is rocking his usual butterfly hunter gear but Ma's wearing a dress, which makes me proud and embarrassed at the same time. She's chatting with Alma, who's in one of her church outfits and holding a bouquet. I don't see Mar's mom. Benno's in the aisle, wearing black pants and a tucked-in black button-down, panning the Handycam across the crowd.

I'm doing okay in my tiny role; Mar is killing it. He gets a standing O after his first solo, something I've never seen in my Players career. He's feeding off the crowd now. I can tell the confidence is surging in his bones as he twirls across the stage. He's louder, lighter on his feet, so much looser than I've ever seen him in practice. His face is pearled with spotlit sweat, and as he holds a long note his eyes and smile are stretched wide. His look reminds me of Pops during the Wave—one of those looks that says, *I don't give a fuck, I love this shit, I'm soft but free.*

The rest of the show is flawless and when the curtains close, the cast starts screaming. I forgot to tell Mar about this. Screaming after curtains close on opening night is a Players tradition, and even though I thought it was sapien the first time I saw it, I stopped clowning once I tried it. Mar looks a little tentative, but Meghan runs up to us, shrieks in our grills, and gives us a group hug, and Mar tips his head and screams to the rooftops. I throw my head back and howl with him.

When the yells die down, Meghan says, "I'm having a super-small cast party after the service show. You guys wanna come?"

"I don't know," says Mar.

"We'll be there," I say.

"Cool," she says. "Bring sleeping bags."

"Can we bring anything else?" I ask, because that's what they say on TV.

Lowering her voice, Meghan says, "Maybe you can swipe some booze from your parents."

We walk out from backstage and my parents are yapping with Alma. She wraps Mar in her arms and says, "I'm so proud of you, baby. So proud."

When we get outside, a lady rolls up to us and shakes Alma's hand.

"Your son was terrific tonight," she says. She tells Alma she runs this sleepover camp in New Hampshire called Wilderwood Arts Academy and that a bunch of the Players are campers. Ma tried to sign me up for Wilderwood once, but I was way too shook to go.

"Maybe Marlon could join us this summer," the woman says.

"We'll think about it," says Alma.

She leans closer to Alma and quietly says, "We do have scholarships available. And we'd love to have Marlon. He's very talented."

On the walk home, me and Mar lag behind my fam and Alma, and he asks, "What you know about this camp?"

"I know Meghan goes there," I say.

"For real? You ever been?"

"Nah. But I'd roll this summer if you're gonna."

"You sure Meghan'll be there?"

"Positive."

When we get to the PJs gate, I ask Mar if he wants to grab some C's tapes and come over.

"I got shit to do," he says.

"On Friday night?"

"I gotta help out my grandma with some shit."

When we get home, I complain to Ma about how Mar keeps icing me, and as usual she reminds me not to take anything too personally.

"Still," I say. "I don't see why he has to be so shady."

"You saw his mother wasn't there tonight?" she says. "Alma told me she's been in and out of the Shattuck."

The Shattuck is the mental hospital near Franklin Park.

"So she, like, had a breakdown or something?" I say.

Ma raises her eyebrows but doesn't respond.

"I won't say anything to Mar."

"Okay, Dave. I'm going to share this with you, because I think you can handle it and I think it'll help you to know what's going on with him. This is serious and I'm trusting you to keep it discreet."

"I promise."

"Apparently, Mar's mom ran out into the Jamaica Way the other day. Alma says this isn't the first time. The police found her standing in the middle of the road."

"Was she trying to get hit?"

"Alma doesn't know if it was that or if she was seeing things and thought she was somewhere else or what. But it's been pretty scary for Marlon. So just try to be supportive."

A WEEK LATER, we roll to the Shaw Center for our service show. We walk into the gym and it's classic recess-level chaos. A bunch of kids are running after one another, playing tag with their fists, and one of them careens into Milt, who tries to laugh it off. A girl in a Hornets jersey walks up to Mar, raises her eyebrows, and says, "What you doin' here, Marlon? You ain't wit' them, is you?"

He looks down and she sputters into her hands.

"Miss Shirley!" another girl shouts across the gym. "Miss Shirley! White people here."

Meghan giggles and Mar looks mortified. Miss Shirley turns around, grabs the whistle around her neck, blows the crap out of it, and the whole gym is zapped into a hush. She's wearing gym-teacher wind pants and a matching breaker with a white towel around her shoulders and she looks like a mean female version of James Brown, from the parted perm to the popping chin. She walks over to Milt and extends a hand. It feels like it's a hundred-plus degrees in the gym, which has no AC, just a couple of clacking ceiling fans. She wipes her forehead with her towel.

"Sorry about that," she says. "It's been pretty crazy here the past few days. The kids get a little juiced up around this time, when the school year's almost over."

As she's yapping with Milt, the clamor starts up again. She turns around and blows her whistle full blast.

"Listen up, everybody!" she shouts. "We've got some *entertainment* for you today."

Groans fill the gym.

"Don't start with that. You do *not* wanna test me on a hot afternoon," she says, and then turns back to us and smiles warmly.

"We still have to change," says Milt. "Curtain technically isn't for another twenty minutes or so."

"That's fine," Miss Shirley says. "Bathrooms are to the left out the doors. They can wait till you all are ready."

The bathrooms are atrocious. Like the King, the stall walls are ripped out and the toilet is just sitting there, exposed and lidless. The boys are terrified to let their socks touch the grimy tiles. I can't imagine what Meghan's going through right now.

"This is gonna be bad," I say to Mar.

"You ain't the one with the fucking solo," he says.

We walk back into the gym in our sapien costumes and Milt steps out to introduce us. A few Players' parents in the front row clap, while a group of boys in the back row do the Arsenio whoop, fists helicoptering over their heads. Miss Shirley blows the whistle and glares at them.

"Hi, everybody, I'm Milt."

"Hi, *Milk*!" one kid shouts, and the rafters explode.

We're about to start when Mar's mother walks in. She takes a seat in the front and starts looking behind her suspiciously. The whitey next to her scoots over a little and then scratches his thigh, trying to play it off like the scoot was just a maneuver to create some scratch room. At least Mar's mom isn't wearing her high socks. She's got a decent pair of jeans on, a clean white shirt, and a jean jacket. Her hair's a little less messed than usual, but still kinda wolveriney. Aside from the chameleon eyes and the paranoid back-checks, she looks pretty normal today.

But then when the show starts, she starts fidgeting and rocking back and forth, arms around her knees. Some kid whispers, loud enough for me to hear onstage, "She *fiendin'*," and kids start snickering. Miss Shirley puts the whistle in her mouth and grills them. The noise fades fast.

When Milt starts up the first song, not even the whistle can stop the laughter. Mar's eyes are clenched closed and his cheeks are puffed, like he's been holding his breath for too long. He starts singing, all faint and wobbly. His voice still sounds dope, and for a second, everyone's quiet. Just as he's loosening up, beginning to move across the stage and really project, his mom starts up with some even weirder shit. She leans forward, pulls her jacket over her head, and grips it tightly, like she's hiding from a monster. Mar opens his eyes a crack and sees her crouching there. A white parent turns around and shushes the laughers, and one of the kids shouts, "You ain't my mother!" back at her. Miss Shirley finally gets right onstage, puffs her whistle, and shouts, "Shut your mouths and show some *respect*! These kids are here for you. They've got plenty better things to do with their time."

Milt starts up again on the keyboard, from the top of the song, but Mar won't sing. His mom's still in hiding, still holding her knees and rocking. The snickers start up again and Mar turns to Milt, says, "Fuck this," and storms off the stage. Milt starts to run after him, but then seems to realize he can't just leave all of us hanging, and he turns around.

"Dave," Milt says. "We need you to fill in."

"Can't we just cancel the show?" I say.

"I've never canceled a show in thirty-two years of theater. I believe in you, Dave. This is your must-go-on moment."

Milt walks back to the keyboard and starts up the song for the third time. He eyes me and nods and Meghan gives my hand a quick, strong squeeze. I step slowly to the center of the stage, open my mouth, and try to pump out the words, but my voice box is on lockdown. It's just like my pissing problem: The harder I push, the more mimed-out I get. I quit. No way I'm rocking my soprano act in front of this crowd. I decide to just speak the words in a monotone. Milt looks furious but keeps playing and I start saying the words in a sort of raplike tempo. One of the Players in the chorus starts clapping along and a smile spreads across Milt's corny mug and he puts the piano on a preset and starts clapping along himself. The chorus joins in and the crowd is rolling so hard at this point, I decide my best option is to try to get everyone in on the joke. I move closer to the stands, and start up with extra-wide, above-the-head claps.

Finally a kid near the back stands up and starts mocking me with an exaggerated goof-clap and a couple seconds later two girls sitting near him stand up and join in. Meghan beams at me. Little by little, everybody gets up, row by row, laughing and clown-clapping, but also seeming to have some straight-up fun. The louder they clap, the more I go ham. Mar's mom still looks lost, but even she's clapping now. I untuck my Torah pointer, pretend it's a mic, and stride back and forth across the stage. I launch into my finest Geto Boys for the final chorus—"There are way too many rats in this here town"—and point my mic to the crowd to complete the rhyme—"and we gotta get someone to bring the rats down!"

As the play goes on, the heckling fades and the kids start getting into the songs, even the ones I'm not rapping. Somehow we make it through the whole show, and when we bow, the kids give us a standing O. As we head backstage, I watch Mar's mom walk off, hunched under her jacket again.

"That was badass," says Meghan. "You should rap for us tonight."

"Only if you rap, too," I say.

"Maybe if I'm wicked buzzed," she says. "By the way— Marlon—what the hell?"

I keep my mouth shut.

"What he did was fucked," she says. "I hope he's not still planning on coming to my party."

"It's not like that. He was feeling nauseous before the show," I lie. "I think he was gonna get sick or something."

"Then he's definitely not invited. I don't want him puking all over my house."

"Nah, he's gotta come," I say. "We gotta have cast unity."

"I only invited eight people."

"Well, I don't know if I can make it if Mar's not there."

"Seriously?"

"He was dope on opening night and he should be a part of it."

"Whatever," she says.

"So, can you call him?" I say. "He's probably gonna need convincing."

"Why don't *you* call him?" she says.

"Feel like it'll mean more if it comes from you," I say.

I GO HOME to get ready. The phone rings as I'm doing push-ups. It's Mar.

"You had Meghan call me?" he says.

"She did that on her own," I say. "She really wants you to roll."

"I'm not trying to sleep over," he says. "I can only go for a little."

"That's cool," I say. "We can play it by ear when we get there."

"For real," he says. "Like a hour. How we getting there?"

"My parents are out with the Whale," I say. "We gotta troop it."

Before Mar gets to my crib, I go to the cabinet where all the wineglasses are and look for something to bring to Meghan's. I know my parents occasionally smoke chronic, but they barely ever get their drink on, and all I can find is a dusty bottle of slivovitz plum brandy that Cramps brought over ages ago. I take a whiff and it feels like nettles in my nostrils. I grab an empty seltzer bottle from the blue bin, fill it about halfway, and fill the rest of the slivovitz bottle with water to cover my tracks.

Mar arrives and we head to Meghan's. We curl around the Arbs, and as we enter Moss Hill the streets get wider and so do the houses. On my block, there are some big houses in the mix, but most of them are crumbly and crooked. Around here every house is huge, and they're all in mint condition. Some of them have pillars; some are made of bricks and look like they belong in Harvard Yard. Almost all of them are surrounded by whitewashed fences. We're about to turn onto Meghan's block when I notice a faint blue beam reflecting off a street sign. Five-o's creeping behind us. Mar sighs and slows his pace. I'm shook they're gonna chaperone us all the way to Meghan's house, but they eventually peel off.

I thought Kev was living large because his shit has three stories and a hooked-up basement. Now I realize his crib is a chumpstump. Meghan takes us for a tour: She's got a pool and a hot tub, a massive yard right up against the Arbs, a big bedroom with its own bathroom, a basement with a regulation pool table, and a kitchen the size of my entire first floor. The fridge is one of those titanium joints with double doors and a built-in bubbler. Meghan lets me sample the ice water and it's brain-freeze legit. I keep trying to meet Mar's eyes, get some backup on how bonked it is to be in an actual mansion, but he keeps looking down at his watch. I can't even get him to try the water.

"Let's go downstairs," she says. "I rented *The Princess Bride*. Everyone's waiting for us."

Meghan starts the movie, and all of the Players start reciting every line. It's a ten on the whitey Richter. I look over at Mar and smile, but he's in a sour mood and whispers that he wants to bounce.

"Look at all this pizza," I whisper back. No one is touching it, or the chips, or the onion dip. That's one thing I really don't get about fancy white people. They lay out mad grub at parties but don't eat it unless someone *else* goes first. I dive into the pie, not at all shook to be that someone.

"At least have a chip," I say to Mar. "This onion dip is banging."

"Not hungry," he says. "You ready to jet?"

We keep watching and Mar seems to be cheering up a little, especially when André the Giant cracks on the little baldy. And then, when Inigo Montoya gives his speech, everyone stands up and shouts, "My name is Inigo Montoya. You killed my father. Prepare to die!"—even Mar and me—and we all pull out our air swords. When the movie ends, Meghan goes upstairs and comes back a minute later.

"My mom's asleep. Now we can get this party started

for real," she says, pulling a bottle of Baileys Irish Cream out of her handbag.

"Yes!" says one of the girls. "Where'd you get that?"

"Paid that swearing bum on Centre Street."

"Jerry?" I say.

"We're not on, like, a first-name basis. I just gave him forty bucks, told him to get us some Baileys and keep the change."

This guy Chris whips out a bottle of Bacardi Limón that he swiped from his brother's dorm.

"That's it?" says Meghan. "You guys are *so* lame. This is enough for like three of us."

"I got something," I say, pulling the dented seltzer bottle out of my bag.

"Ew," says Meghan.

"Looks like you peed in the bottle," says another girl.

"It's slivovitz," I say. "Hundred-proof. Should be pretty good shit."

"I'm not touching that till you try it first," says Meghan.

Mar gives me a pastor glance.

I let one drop fall into the back of my throat and it tastes like a spicy poison hospital. I gag it onto my shirt and take a huge swig of Sunkist.

"There a bathroom down here?" I say. The four slices are circling like sharks in my stomach.

"Upstairs," says Meghan.

"I gotta go, too," Mar says.

I'm not about to stink up the nearest bathroom, so Mar and I go up another flight and find a bathroom inside

Meghan's dad's office. When I finish up, I take a look around. He's got his Harvard Law diploma mounted in a gold frame. There's a big glass desk with a leather swivel chair, plus a built-in bookshelf with a TV and a shelf for all his awards. Among the plaques, in a brick-sized, screw-tightened case, I see something that makes my blood hop: a 1981 Bird-Magic–Dr. J card. It's even minter than mine, wherever the hell it is.

"Maybe he's the one who yoinked it," I joke to Mar.

"We shouldn't be in here," says Mar. "I bet you he's got cameras all over this joint."

"It's fine. We're just looking around. You gonna go or what?"

"Don't have to."

"Then why'd you come up here with me?"

"I don't know. Feel weird around those heads."

"We've been chilling with those cornballs for months. Why are you acting shook all of a sudden?"

"They're drinking and stuff. I'm not feeling it. And I'm not trying to walk back home by myself, neither."

"You're starting to act like a bitch. It's just a party."

"Man, *fuck* you. I gotta get home."

"How come?"

"Why I always gotta spell shit out for you?"

"Why you always gotta make me guess?"

"My grandma's working tonight. I gotta check on my mom, aight? You fucking coming or what?"

"Yeah," I say.

"Good," he says.

Now I'm feeling mad guilty. Why *did* I make him spell it

out? Of course it had to do with his mom. Then again, if shit
at home was so urgent, why'd he come all the way out here
in the first place?

"Yo," I say at the foot of the stairs. "I'm ready to bounce
and everything, but, like, I *just* found out about Latin. We
never even got to celebrate together. Can't we just live a little? For like a half hour more?"

"You guys done making out?" Meghan calls up to us.
"Get down here. We're going to the Arbs."

Mar looks at me anxiously.

"Come on," I say. "We can take our bags. We'll dip
straight from the Arbs—it's in our direction anyway. Twenty
minutes. I promise."

We grab our stuff and follow along. Everyone tiptoes
across the backyard, and one by one we scale Meghan's
fence and hop into the Arbs. It's crazy dark and Meghan
guides us through the woods with the light from her pager.
Something crackles in the distance and Mar squeezes my
arm.

"What *was* that?" says one of the girls, Kathleen.
Meghan shines her pager in the direction of the noise, but all
we see is leaves.

"I heard there was a coyote in here once," says Meghan.
"It could be a coyote. Or a rabid raccoon."

"Where are you taking us?" asks Kathleen.

"You'll see," says Meghan. "Best spot in the whole
Arbs."

It takes me a second to realize we're on the same path
that goes to the cork tree, where Benno's box is buried.

"How perfect is this?" says Meghan. The cork tree is

standing tall on the bald hilltop and its leaves are shimmering in the moonlight.

"You know about this tree?" I say.

"Everybody who knows about the Arbs knows about this tree," she says. "It's the frigging cork tree."

Now I'm all ashamed in front of Mar because I acted like it was my secret tree. I honestly thought it was.

"Check it out," Meghan says, pointing skyward.

We're far enough away from any buildings that if you look hard enough, you can see stars.

"There's the Big Dipper," I say to Mar. "Looks kinda like a hoop, right?"

Mar doesn't answer. His head is tilted to the universe, but he looks more lonely than awed. Everyone else is smiling and pointing, and he's just standing there, squinting, biting his upper lip.

"There's the Little Dipper—the nasketball version," I say, trying to cheer him up.

Mar won't even crack a smile. We sit down in a circle and everyone but us starts swigging. Kathleen starts talking about the Shaw Center. I can tell she's already wasted.

"How awkward was that?" she says. "That was, like, way worse than the VA."

"It was cool," I say. "They liked it."

"It was a disaster," she says. "That place was, like, so ghetto."

Mar digs his sneaker into my toe.

"And what the fuck was up with that lady in the front row?" Kathleen says.

Mar digs harder and I tell Meghan we have to bounce.

But Meghan says, "Dude, we were just about to start spin the bottle."

"Let's *go*, Green," Mar whispers.

"One round," I whisper back.

Meghan locks her eyes on me and spins. The bottle lands on Kathleen and Meghan does a do-over. Her next spin points right at Mar. Everyone gets quiet and smiley.

"Can we play truth or dare instead?" Meghan says.

Mar draws a sharp breath through his nose and stares ahead defiantly. Meghan's the worst person I've ever met. Ninety-nine percent of me wants to get out of this sin-den, jet back to the boring purity of the crib, climb into Benno's tent, and watch C's tapes. But one percent of me, the worst digit in my body, is satanically hard.

"Fine," says Kathleen. "But you still have to go first."

"'Kay," says Meghan. "Dare, obvs."

"Okay. I dare *you* . . . to go into the dark part of the woods back there, for two whole minutes."

"That's way too scary," says Meghan.

"Dave can go with you," says Kathleen.

"It's not my turn," I say.

"Shut up and go with her," says Kathleen.

I look to Mar, but he's staring up at the sky and won't look back at me.

"We'll jet the second I get back," I whisper to him.

I walk behind Meghan, right over Benno's box and into the brambles. I let her get a little bit of a lead and then rip some silent breeze and flap my hand behind me to disperse the stank. We reach a clearing that's far enough away we can't hear anyone anymore.

"Here," she says, passing me the Baileys. "Stop being so gay."

I take a small sip. It tastes absurdly good, just like my go-to snack when I have no money at the bodega: free cream cups and sugar. I take a longer glug, and in a few seconds I get this tingly massage feeling that makes my muscles hang. Meghan softly pets my hand. I don't pull back. She loops her fingers into mine, leans close into my face, and whispers, "You know I like you, right?"

Meghan hovers before my lips. I think of every vile thing I can to put the wishbone in reverse. Even the Holocaust isn't helping. She leans even closer.

"Your breath smells good," I say.

"Why don't you kiss me?"

"I . . . want to," I say.

"So do it already."

"I want to."

"But?"

"Mar."

"So?"

"He likes you."

"But *I* like *you*. So kiss me, stupid."

"I can't."

"Seriously, are you gay? Do you not want to?"

"I just—lemme check on Mar for a sec. He's all stressed about the show. I just wanna make sure he's cool."

"You better fucking come back," she says.

I walk back toward the bald spot and pause in the bushes. Everyone's yapping and laughing except for Mar, who's standing off to the side, checking his Timex. What am I supposed to say to him? I decide on a simple plan: go back to Meghan, get my hug on, tell her I can't stay, grab Mar, and walk home. Once I'm in bed, I'll close my eyes, picture Meghan and her sweet cream breath, and tactic till I'm off to slumberland. It'll be close enough to the real thing.

When I get back to Meghan her jacket's around her waist. She's wearing a white tank and I can see some pink lace peeking out at her shoulder. I follow my plan, right up to the first hug, but Meghan holds on for longer, presses her chest right into me, and leaves it there. I'm telling myself, *I will not do this to Mar, I will not do this to Mar,* but Meghan leans into me again and the wood takes over from there. I was thinking lips only, but she goes full french. Tongues are way slimier than I'd imagined—in a good way. I let my tongue kick back and chill while Meghan slithers around my mouth. Then I try to copy her moves, but Meghan pulls back.

"You're putting it in way too far. Just a little, like this," she says, sticking out the tip and moving it in slow circles.

I try again, just dipping the tip, and now she's moving with me. I feel like we're dancing, and for the first time, I actually have moves. She pulls me to the ground and we lie on some damp moss and go at it for a long time. I'm so lost in the thrill of the kiss, I'm not even thinking about second until she grabs my hand and makes me cop cup. I'm too shook to go further, and tell her I just want to french for now. She calls me gay again and we dance for another long session. I'd keep going all night but that pizza bubble is growing in my gut again and I seriously need to get to a can. Once I pull back, I realize I've completely forgotten about Mar.

We walk back to the group and everyone oohs. Mar's gone.

"It's getting really cold," says Kathleen. "I think it's time for the hot tub."

I ask Kathleen where Mar went and she says he left a half an hour ago. Meghan lights up a cigarette—it's a Newport—takes a puff, and passes it to me. I take a pull and it feels like a Binaca bomb exploding in my chest. I start coughing and the mint spreads all over my brain and my body goes sauce. I suck in more and take another look at the sky. I'm feeling closer than ever to the stars. I got into Latin, I got with the hottest shorty in the Players, I touched a warm, 3-D tit—me, the sapien, the softest man alive. In a month I'll be done with the King. I'll never have to go to English. Anything is possible. Harvard is possible, mansions are possible, millions upon millions and maybe even billions are possible. The Dipper's right there. Tapping the Big Rim—even that feels possible.

Mar left a *half* hour ago. He probably got home before me and Meghan were even done. While I was sucking Meghan's gums, he was already in the PJs, probably force-feeding his mom pills. What if something fucked up happened before he got home?

No—not gonna taint one of the greatest moments of my life with guilt. Not gonna be like Cramps. Not gonna doggie-bag every opportunity. This is America. Meghan had her reasons for choosing me. I got into Latin because I'm smart, not because I copied a couple answers. Everybody cheats, even the president. I'll call Mar after the hot tub.

As we walk back to Meghan's, the guilt starts to swallow me. When we get there, everyone jumps in the Jacuzzi except me. I blame my stomach and head to the bathroom. I find some mouthwash, swish hard, and call Ma to come pick me up.

In the morning, I ring Mar over and over. No answer. On Monday he won't talk to me on the bus, and at lunch he moves his tray to another table when I sit down next to him. I follow him to the other table.

"Who said you could sit here?" he says.

"I just wanted to say, my bad."

"You lied to me."

"I know. It wasn't my fault, though. I told Meghan I wasn't down. I swear. She, like, forced me."

"It ain't even about that. You left me there. For mad long. With all those wack-ass white girls. I didn't have shit to say to them."

"Well, you better get used to it. There's gonna be a lot more of those girls at Latin. At Wilderwood, too."

"I ain't going to Wilderwood. I might not even go to fucking Latin."

"What are you talking about? You're acting bonk. You know Wilderwood's gonna be mad fun."

"You only want me there cuz you're shook to go to sleepover camp by yourself."

"That's some bull," I say, looking around. "And keep your voice down."

"You know that's the only reason you signed my ass up!" he says louder. Heads start turning our way.

"I signed you up because you're my best friend, you dick!"

Kaleem howls and palms the table repeatedly. "Best friend" is the most sapien thing I've said in public since "awesome." Mar stands up and starts carrying his tray to another table.

"If you're gonna walk away," I say under my breath, "at least tell me what you did with the Bird-Magic."

Mar turns back to me and says, *"What?"*

"You sell it?" I say. "Where's it at? Miami?"

"Fuck. You."

"I was gonna give it to you. You could've just *asked* me for it."

"I ain't asked for shit from you and I don't *want* shit from you, *white boy.*"

The crowd oohs. Jimmy says, "You gonna let him call you that?"

I stare at Mar, trembling.

"Did you just call me a white boy?"

"Fuck you gonna do about it?" he says.

"At least I'm not a—"

The force is screaming the unsayable inside of me.

"Not a what?" Mar screams.

My tongue touches the roof of my mouth and stays there.

"He just called you a fuckin' white boy!" says Jimmy.

"You're . . ."

"Say it!" says Jimmy.

"You're pyrite," I say.

Mar flings his lunch tray at me. Hot taco filling splatters on my chest and the Fresca flies over my shoulder, right into the lunch lady. The cafeteria goes crazy and Rawlins runs in, puts Mar's arm in a twist-hold, and drags him to the office.

I wipe my shirt with the plasticky caf napkins that absorb nothing and just spread the oil around. The loudspeaker blares: "David Greenfeld, please report to the office immediately."

I wait in a chair outside Dr. Jackson's office and I can hear him lecturing at Mar. After a few minutes, he comes out and says, "Your mother is on her way over here. So is Marlon's grandmother. I'm gonna need you and Marlon to explain to me *and* them what just happened here. With all the problems we've got here, the last thing in the world I need is issues with you two. You're supposed to be my good kids, my honors students. I don't need this."

I take out my notebook and doodle sharks until Ma and Alma arrive.

"Why don't you go ahead and explain to everyone why you messed up my perfectly good day by throwing your perfectly good lunch at Dave," Dr. Jackson says to Mar.

Mar keeps his head down.

"Marlon," Alma says. "You heard the man. What's wrong with you?"

Mar still won't answer, so I butt in.

"It's my fault. He didn't mean it. He wasn't even trying to throw it. It just kind of . . . slipped."

"Slipped?" says Dr. Jackson, unamused.

"It's seriously my fault," I say.

"Well, why don't you tell us *what* you said to him to set him off?" says Dr. Jackson.

I glance at Ma, who looks upset, chewing on the inside of her cheek.

"I can't remember. But it's definitely my fault. I don't"— I start choking back bitchwater—"I don't want him to have to go to the Barron Center."

"No one's going to the Barron Center," says Dr. Jackson, and for some reason the relief brings more water.

"What's going on here?" Dr. Jackson says. "What's the matter, son?"

"Nothing," I say. "I was just worried that this was gonna get Mar kicked out of Latin or something."

"Excuse me?" says Dr. Jackson.

"If you go to the Barron Center, you get an F in conduct, right? And if you get an F in conduct, you get, like, pre–kicked out of Latin. Right?"

Dr. Jackson slides his glasses down his nose and stares at Mar.

"Marlon," says Dr. Jackson. "We've got you registered in our system for seventh grade."

Mar's chin starts quivering.

"Were you telling people you got into Latin?" says Dr. Jackson.

Mar sniffs in short blasts of air.

"Answer the man!" Alma says to Mar. "You been lying to people?"

He stays silent. Tears are darkening his cheeks.

"Look at me," says Alma. "You tell Ms. Ansley that, too?"

He pulls his collar over his face, sniffles and heaves.

"All right, now," says Dr. Jackson. "I'm gonna step into the hall with your grandmother and Dave's mother. Why don't you two take a minute to work this out between yourselves. Nobody's getting suspended. I've got enough suspensions on my hands already. You're friends. Act like it."

I spend the longest seconds of my life sitting there next to Mar, whose head is on the desk, turned away from me.

"What happened?" I say. "With the test?"

"What you mean, what happened?" he says. "I didn't pass."

"Why, though? You were smoking those practice tests."

"I choked—that's why."

"But, like—"

"I don't know. I guess I just froze up."

"Yeah, but why?"

"What are you, Ms. Ansley? I ain't got a better answer."

"But, like—why'd you lie about it?"

Mar closes his eyes.

We sit there for a whole minute, and then quietly he says, "I didn't want people thinking I'm some kind of . . . Forget it."

"Some kind of what?"

"Some kind of ignorant-ass failure. *All right?*"

MA DRIVES US back to J.P. in the Whale. Alma sits shotgun and Mar sits with me in the back, his head leaning against the window. Alma asks Ma how she's feeling and they talk about the baby for a while. Then they start talking about the candlelight vigil planned for next week. Some kid in the PJs got shot and he's gonna be in a wheelchair for life. Alma says they got a permit to block off the street and they're doing a potluck. Ma offers to bring some sesame noodles.

"You know that kid?" I whisper to Mar. He gives me a little shrug, which I take to mean sorta.

"Was it the Hornets boys?" I ask.

Mar just keeps staring out the window as we drive past the Arbs.

We pull up to the PJs. Mar and Alma get out and me and Ma watch them walk up to the blue metal doors and disappear into the dark brick tower.

CHAPTER 11

Blood

Me and Mar are basically strangers again, not even dapping in the halls. Whenever I try to apologize, to explain myself, to invite him over, he recoils. Every time I take a step in his direction, he takes a step back. That crack between us—it busted all the way through. There's a gap now. We're separate shards.

The rest of school fades out like the bonus track of a wack album. I almost miss the drama of the early days. Now the King just feels like any old boring school. Angel's so shook of getting stomped again, he won't even come near the White Bitch Bench. Nobody, not even Kaleem, clowns my outfits. I don't even get called white boy anymore. I just get ignored. That's how I finish sixth grade: left alone but lonely as hell.

Mar keeps good on his vow to pull out of Wilderwood and I decide to sack up and go anyway. Once I get there, I discover that everyone's already friends and no one's interested in making new ones. Meghan apparently has a man, too—this CIT who's fifteen—and now she acts like we never even had history. On the first day, I sit around whittling sticks and write a long letter to Mar about the Celtics and how amped I am about the fact that Reggie's doctors cleared him to play again and how smart Mar was to ditch this camp and how P.S. I'm mad sorry and hope we hang when I get back.

That night I can't sleep and I've got a bladder full of Tang. Going to the boy's bathroom means leaving the bunk and walking through a wooded path. I get out of bed, creep to the door, and push it open. The trees are blocking out the stars, and the darkness is deeper than any I've ever been in. I pee through the slit in the door and end up getting half on my pajamas. In the morning, I call Ma and ask for a rescue. She arrives that night in the Whale and we beam our way through the narrow, unlit roads back to the highway. When we finally see the signs for Boston, I ask her if she can get off at the exit near Fenway so we can swing by the Citgo sign. I just want to make sure it's still on and it is, burning bright and red as it always has.

I END UP spending the summer the usual way, going to free city camps and kicking it with Benno in the late afternoons. I should be getting excited for Latin, but without Mar there I can already see what's ahead of me: an endless, friendless slog. I can tell Benno misses Mar, too, maybe as much as I do. He took the tent down a while ago, but he made a clay sculpture of the three of us under it, poking our heads out to watch the C's.

On the night of July 27, I get a call from Kev.

"You heard about Reggie?" he says.

"Don't tell me he got traded."

"Turn on the TV."

"If you're just joining us," says the anchor, "Celtics captain Reggie Lewis collapsed this afternoon during a light workout at Brandeis University. He was rushed to Beth Israel Hospital, where attempts to resuscitate him failed. He was twenty-seven years old."

This must be some kind of hoax. I change the channel.

"An emotional Celtics family mourns the death of Reggie Lewis," says another newscaster.

I grab my clock radio and turn on WEEI.

"First Len Bias. Now this?" says a caller. "We're cursed."

"What does God have against this city?" says another.

I call Mar but he doesn't pick up, so I run into the Arbs, right up to the cork tree, kick it as hard as I can, and then collapse under it, cradling my foot and crying from the pain.

The next day, in the *Globe,* one of the columnists wonders if Reggie's heart went bad from "self-abuse," and a couple days later another *Globe* writer says that the doctors who examined him are worried about drugs, too.

"What's goin' on here?" one caller says on WEEI. "Twenty-seven-year-old world-class athletes don't just die of heart attacks."

I keep thinking, *Holy shit. Curse of the Coke.*

I try calling Mar again.

"You were right," I say on his answering machine. "The Curse of the Coke. I can't believe it."

Still no reply, so I call him again the next day and leave another message: "Mar—it's Dave. I don't know if you got my letter from Wilderwood? Maybe I sent it to the wrong address. I don't know where you're at, I'm sure you heard by now, but Reggie died. Me and Benno are gonna go to the funeral if you wanna roll with us. Also, I heard the Aquarium's doing whale watches, right out of the Boston Harbor. My mom said she'd take me and Benno before the school year starts. Maybe you can come, too. Hit me back."

A FEW DAYS later Ma brings me and Benno to the memorial service for Reggie at Northeastern. It's our first funeral ever. When we get inside the stadium, I borrow the Handycam from Benno and pan across the crowd looking for Mar but can't spot him. We leave early so we can watch the hearse procession. Reggie's being buried in the Forest Hills Cemetery in J.P., and they'll be passing right by the corner of our street. We're stuck in mad traffic and I turn on WEEI. They're saying ten thousand people are still packed into the stadium—the biggest funeral in Boston history.

We make it back in time, and there are people lined up all along the street holding Celtics flags and RIP signs. As we pass by the Shaw Homes, Benno spots Mar. He's in a crowd of PJ kids. Some of them are still sporting Hornets gear, but Mar's wearing the C's jacket.

"Mar!" I holler out the window. "Hey, Mar—over here!"

"Mar!" one of the PJ kids mocks. "Over *here*!" he says, extra-white.

Benno gets it all on film. I can see from the flip-out screen that he's zooming in on Mar's face. Mar looks in our direction for a second, then turns and walks back into the crowd.

. . .

MY NEW LITTLE brother's gonna arrive any day now. I need something to get my mind off Reggie, so Benno and I decide to make a video for him. I want it to be an advice video, something he can peep when he's a little older, something that can help him avoid all my swiss moves and failures. The more I think about it, though, the more I realize that the key to coming up, for dudes at least, is the ability to ball. Me and Benno can't ball, and look how we ended up. Being the kind of dudes who make videos about how to ball.

I broke the nasketball hoop after one too many rim hangs and we still haven't gotten it fixed, so we head down to these brand-new courts, farther down Centre Street, that haven't had the nets stolen from them yet. I'm wearing a Reggie jersey Pops just copped for me. Benno films from his tripod while I go over the fundamentals: dribble drives, the Mikan drill, the proper way to box out. For the box-out scene, I ask Benno to step in front of the camera and stand a few feet away from the hoop. I shove my butt into him and crab-walk backward in the direction of the camera. We do a couple more takes, and as we're wrapping up the last one Kev and Simon roll up. This is where they come to blaze. I stop the action and stand there until they finish laughing.

"Keep going, yo!" says Simon. "You teaching little man how to box out? Lemme film it for you."

"We're all set," I say.

"Is that a Torah pointer around your neck?" says Simon.

"Looks like it's pointing to his dick, right?" says Kev.

"Look this way," Simon says in a circus emcee voice. "World's smallest dick!"

I tuck it inside and feel the cold metal finger tapping my bitch heart.

"Fuckin' fake Jew," says Simon.

"Chill," I say. "We're trying to make a video for our brother."

"The one who's on the way?" says Kev. "*Aw*. It's cool you're doing this for him. Keep going."

Simon grabs the camera and says, "Take two . . . Annnd action!"

I box Benno with all I've got.

Simon does a British nature show voice into the camera mic: "This is the mating ritual of faggots in the wild."

Kev cackles and I reach for the camera. Simon pulls back.

"He's just fucking with you," says Kev. "Keep doing the video. It's a good idea. I'm serious, yo. Swear to God. You know how I am when I say that shit."

Kev never goes back on a G-dash oath. That's his thing. So I go to the next drill: foul-shooting form.

"Okay," I say, making a decisive-looking chop motion into the camera. "The key to foul shooting is to bend your knees. That's the only way to create enough lift and momentum without jumping."

I bend slowly and Kev narrates, "This is how to get ready for some fudge-packing."

I grab the camera from him, and as we're walking off a kid rolls past us dribbling a ball. He's wearing purple and teal cutoff shorts and a matching sleeveless denim jacket. He's got lines shaved into the back of his head and he looks about Benno's age—nine or ten. I've never seen him before.

I wonder if he's from Moss Hill or is one of those gentrifying motherfuckers.

"Oh *shit,*" says Kev, squeezing Simon. "It's the Machine!"

The kid passes us nervously, eyes on his ball.

"Lemme see that camera," says Kev, snatching the Handycam and resetting it on the tripod.

"Yo, D," says Kev. "You need to take that shit back."

"Or at least steal on him for biting your steez," says Simon.

"For real," says Kev. "That's the fucking *Machine,* yo!"

It's not *the* Machine, but it's close. And a serious part of me wants to teach this little bitch a lesson. I mean, who the fuck does he think he is, wearing those colors around here? This little fronting fuck has *no* clue. Coming through here in those colors, right after Reggie died? Hell no.

"Where'd you get that suit?" I say to the kid.

"I don't know," the kid says. "My mom got it for me."

"You shouldn't be wearing those colors," I say.

"Tell 'em, D. Tell 'em!" cries Simon.

"You need to *steal* on this fool," says Kev.

I've never been in a fight in my life. I feel myself getting softer by the second. What if I hit him so hard he smacks his head on the concrete and dies? I'm not trying to smoke a nine-year-old. *Walk away,* I hear Pops and Dr. Jackson saying.

"He's rocking *your* shit, D," shouts Simon. "Steal on him!"

What's the point of stepping? Just walk. Then again, I've been walking my whole life. Where's it gotten me? Where

did all the walking get Martin Luther King? Jesus, Gandhi,
whales: Nothing soft stays alive.

"Why you hesitating?" says Simon.

I don't want to fuck him up. I want to be under the tent
with Mar watching Reggie play preseason games on channel
68. We match up in a million soft little ways—why can't we
just be boys again? It should be so simple. But the more I
think about it, the more I wonder if we were meant to be
shards from the start. Not just me and Mar—everyone.
Look around. Look at the Shaw Homes. Look at Moss Hill.
Everything Skip Taylor said was true. The force is everywhere, prying us apart.

"Fuck his ass up already!" says Kev.

I walk up to the kid and stare into bitch-blue eyes. Reggie's dead. Coke killed Len Bias and may have killed Reggie,
the captain, my favorite player of all time. Coke is killing all
kinds of people, all the time, cursing this whole damn country. Who the fuck does he think he is, wearing those coke-
boy colors?

I will be surrounded by dudes like this for the rest of my
life. White boys and white girls who grew up behind whitewashed fences, who grew up with *no idea,* for the rest of my
life. The force preordained it: Not only will I be surrounded
by them, I will become one of them, the thing I hate and
can't escape. Not a white boy or a whitey or a white bitch,
but a white *person.*

I walk up to the kid, cock my fist, and let loose—into his
stomach. The kid doubles forward and holds his belly. It
wasn't that hard of a punch, but he's gasping.

"Hit him in the *face,* you faggot," says Simon.

I wind up again and Benno grabs my sleeve. He's sobbing for me to stop.

"Tell your faggot-ass brother to shut up," Simon says.

"Fuck it," says Kev. He walks up to the kid and pops him in the nose. He shakes his fist and cackles, then sticks his face into the camera.

"You see that, little man? That's how you get it *done*. Don't grow up to be a soft-ass bitch like your big brothers!"

That's when I finally do it. I fly up to Kev and sling my fist into his jaw. It actually kind of hits the bottom part of his chin, more like his neck. But it's a blow, and it's on camera for my little brother to witness someday. The next thing I know, Simon is pounding my brain black and blue. I'm lying on the concrete and Kev is kicking me in the side with his Air Force 1s and Benno's screaming and pulling at them pointlessly. Some whitey passerby yells "Hey!" and the blows stop and I hear sneakers squeaking against the pavement in escape. The Machine kid scoops up his ball and staggers away. Benno crouches next to me and checks my pulse.

"Help me up," I say, reaching out my hand. I'm not hurt so bad. I could definitely get up on my own, but I've always wanted to limp off a battlefield held up by a brotherly crutch.

On our way up the hill, I curl up my tongue and let my nose blood pool into my mouth.

"You like the taste of your blood?" Benno says.

"Yeah," I say, acting like it's no thing. It's the first time I've heard him speak in over a year.

"Me too," he says.

. . .

IT'S NOT UNTIL we get home that I realize my jersey is ripped and ruined from the fight. I figure I'll buy another one. The stores are selling Reggie jerseys for seventy-five percent off now, the same way they do when someone gets traded to another team and they still have mad leftovers. Before I toss it, though, I scissor out this bloodstained spot and give it to Benno as a war souvenir. Benno's back to silence, but he motions to the Arbs from our attic and I can tell he wants to dig up his box and put the patch in there.

It's been months since we've visited the box, and when Benno opens it something new's inside. It's a thick rectangle, wrapped in notebook paper, bound by a rubber band.

"You came here without me?" I ask him.

He shakes his head.

I pick it up and I instantly know what's inside: the Bird-Magic.

The notebook paper has two words, all in caps, written across it.

NEVER SELL.

I CAN'T TELL if it's an opening or a closing. I decide to try Mar one more time. I know I can't just leave another message on his machine. I'm gonna have to get up the stones to roll into the Shaw Homes, knock on his door, and see him in person. The problem is, I'm still just as scared of the PJs, just as shook of the Hornets boys, as I've ever been.

I promise myself I'll do it before I set foot in Latin, and on the very last day of summer break I make my way down the hill, past Pops's garden and through the big blue doors.

The hallway is hot and dark and I can't find a directory. An old black man watches me walking back and forth from his doorway, comes out into the hall, and asks, "You looking for someone?"

"You know which unit Marlon Wellings lives in?"

He scratches his head.

"How about Alma Wellings?" I ask.

"Six D," he says. "Elevator's busted, so you gotta take the stairs."

I thank him and he says, "You one of them religious volunteers or something?"

"Just a friend," I say.

I head up the stairs and see a group of boys—one of them's wearing a Hornets hat—standing around a boom box in between the first and second floors. I turn right around and walk back to the main entrance, and the old man pops his head out again.

"Don't worry about those boys in the stairwell," he says. "You just mind your own and keep on walking."

I take a deep breath and head back up the stairs. I don't know why, but as I pass by the boys, instead of minding my own like the man instructed or staring at my feet and peeking over at them like I usually do, I just make eye contact and nod, and no one says, *Fuck you lookin' at?* or anything. One of them even nods back. I walk at a normal, nonracing pace up the rest of the flights and knock on Mar's door. Alma answers.

"David!" she says, squeezing me in a hug. "It's so nice to see you."

"Who's there?" yells a voice from the back. It's Mar's

mom. She sticks her head out the door, hair fraggled as usual, and inspects me.

"It's all right, baby. It's just Marlon's friend David. Go on back to your program. Everything's fine."

Alma turns back to me.

"Marlon's out right now."

Doing what? With who?

"You want me to pass him a message or something?" she says.

"Actually," I say, "maybe I could just write something and leave it for him?"

"Sure, sweetie," she says. "Come on in and let me get you some paper."

Mar's crib is small but tidy. The kitchen floor's made of linoleum sheets, but they're not peely like Jimmy's. There's some Bible-looking pictures on the wall, one that's definitely Jesus, walking with a lion and a lamb. There's a bookshelf full of novels—one level looks like it's all mysteries, another is mostly fantasy and science fiction.

"The mysteries are mine," Alma says. "All that Lord of the Rings stuff is Nina's."

Mar's mother's name is Nina.

Alma hands me a little spiral notebook and a pen.

"You want to go on into Marlon's room?" she says. "I'm sure he wouldn't mind."

I walk in. His closet door's open and I take a quick peek at his clothes—the church suit, the flannels, the C's jacket wrapped in plastic. There's a small shelf next to his desk lined with some library books and his C's tapes in chronological order. On top of the shelf there's an old Larry Bird

Wheaties box, and next to that a small framed photo of Mar when he was little, holding hands with his mom and dad. It's winter and they're all bundled up in big puffy coats, smiling.

Mar's bed is pressed up against the only window in the room. I sit on it carefully, because it's made tight, and look out at the view of Pops's garden. On the wall beside the window, next to a bunch of taped-up Celtics cutouts from the *Herald* sports section, is the big red flag from our canning triumph: HARVARD CLASS OF 1972.

I lie down for a second, close my eyes, and think about what I want to say to him. Then I sit up and start writing: *Dear Mar, Here goes. If you read this, I just hope you can feel me.*

Acknowledgments

Thank you to my teachers, especially Richard Ford, who freed me up to write *Green*. To Caitlin McKenna, for your belief in this book and your uncommon editorial brilliance. To the wise and ever-patient Elyse Cheney, who pushed me to do work I didn't think I was capable of. To the Edward Albee Foundation and the Blue Mountain Center, for giving me the space to write early drafts in spectacular settings. To Sam Freilich and my other very smart readers and commenters: Ben Mathis-Lilley, Caroline Zancan, Dan Gelbtuch, Eleanor Martin, Alberta Wright, Otilia Mirambeaux, James Jacoby, Daniel Stewart, Joshua Furst, Mike Harvkey, Angelica Baker, and Abe Kunin. To my friends who helped inspire the language of *Green*: Pete Nice, B-Bills, Witty Wiz, and Willy Styles. To my brothers, Joe and Jake Graham-Felsen. To the Grays.

And finally, to Sasha Weiss, who floodlights my world.

About the Author

SAM GRAHAM-FELSEN was born and raised in Boston. He has worked as chief blogger for Barack Obama's 2008 campaign, a journalist for *The Nation,* and a peanut vendor at Fenway Park. This is his first novel.

samgf.com

Facebook.com/samgf

Twitter: @samgf

About the Type

This book was set in Sabon, a typeface designed by the well-known German typographer Jan Tschichold (1902–74). Sabon's design is based upon the original letterforms of sixteenth-century French type designer Claude Garamond and was created specifically to be used for three sources: foundry type for hand composition, Linotype, and Monotype. Tschichold named his typeface for the famous Frankfurt typefounder Jacques Sabon (c. 1520–80).